Château des Corbeaux

A Bennett Sisters Mystery

featuring

Pascal d'Onscon

Lise McClendon

THALIA

The Bennett Sisters Mysteries

BY LISE MCCLENDON

Blackbird Fly

The Girl in the Empty Dress

Give Him the Ooh-la-la

The Things We Said Today

The Frenchman

Odette and the Great Fear

Blame it on Paris

A Bolt from the Blue

DEAD FLAT

1: Bottle of Lies

2: Outside the Bubble

3: Uncorked

Lost in Lavender

Birds of a Feather 1-2-3

Château des Corbeaux

plus

The Bennett Sisters French Cookbook

featuring recipes from the books

Château des Corbeaux

One

GIRONDE, NOUVELLE-AQUITAINE

His back throbbed after the long day of driving. Pascal twisted in his seat, behind the wheel of his old BMW sedan, as he slowed on the gravel road deep in the vineyards of the Bordeaux. He'd been on the road since early morning. It wasn't an awful distance home to Merle's cottage in the Dordogne but he'd taken more than a few detours, only some of which were official.

Neat rows of grapevines stretched up and over a low rise, neatly tended with a grassy strip down the center. At this time of year, spring turning to summer, the vines were growing rapidly. Some needed trimming as the tendrils bounced and spun in the wind. The pale green berries, the nascent grapes that would one day be plump and juicy, were still tiny and hard, their winemaking future uncertain.

He stopped the car, gazing out into the vineyard. This wasn't an area he frequented. He didn't know who owned this property— or any of the others nearby. He'd never had a reason to investigate this estate in his role as a wine fraud detective for the French Republic. There were thousands of vineyards, vast and quite small, especially here in southwest France where grape-growing was both a hobby and a religion. Not to mention an obsession.

Pascal pushed his sunglasses up into his black hair and rubbed his eyes. He leaned into the steering wheel to ease the pain in his back. In the west the sun was setting, turning the landscape a soft orange. He should get moving. Merle waited at home, probably with one of his favorite dinners on the stove.

All right, a moment to stretch. He opened the car door and leaned both hands against the hood of the car, feeling his back loosen. He frowned at the unsightly weathered patches on the once-pristine hood then looked up at the setting sun. Another vineyard lay on the other side of the road, nothing like the tidy property opposite. It was overgrown and unsightly, some vines brown and dead while others lay in heaps, last season's leaves weighing them down. Yellow grass and fresh new grass tangled between the rows, with dandelions and thistles and other weeds. The stakes holding the wires for the vines were tilted and askew, some lying flat on the ground. Although some vines had green leaves, they were overgrown and obviously untended.

In other words, the vineyard was a wreck.

Pascal stepped through the ditch and into the edge of the neglected vines. He shaded his eyes against the sun and could see signs of healthier, manicured vines far down the long rows. So someone cared for at least part of the vineyard. He wondered who it was, and why they had neglected this end of the not-insubstantial property. Over another rise he could see slate rooftops of several stone buildings, dotted with moss.

His investigator's curiosity burbled up. This was a waste of good terroir. Who owned this property and why were they so neglectful? Were they aging and losing interest in winemaking? Had they died and the heirs were failing? Were they absentee owners and their workers not up to the job? Were they inexperienced and over their heads? Did they run out of money, staff, time? So many possibilities.

He blinked into the last rays of the sun. Was this the one? The vineyard he'd been searching for? Visions of himself as a winemaking hero, swooping in to save the vintage, to refurbish the vineyard into all its glory, made him chuckle even as he felt light-headed with the idea.

He stood motionless at the edge of the mess of vines, listening to the wind rattle the brown leaves and the mice scurry in the grass. Lost in the fantasy that had been growing over the last few months, a dream of actually owning a vineyard and producing his own wine, he barely heard the car wheels on the gravel. A gleaming silver Mercedes sedan slowed and came to a stop behind his BMW.

A tall, slender man climbed out and rounded the front of the car, frowning at it. He was expensively dressed, in tailored slacks and leather loafers and a sports coat over a pressed white shirt open at the collar. His hair was dark with streaks of gray at the temples. His face tanned and gently lined, his age was about 50, Pascal guessed. His temperament? Not happy.

The man stopped, crossed his arms, and planted his feet. He glared at Pascal and asked, "Who are you?"

Two

PARIS

THREE WEEKS EARLIER

The meeting at the *Police Nationale* headquarters was the usual mix of camaraderie, boredom, and rage. Always someone grew angered about the lack of progress on an investigation or a perceived lack of respect. This particular conference had a rich mix of all of the above, plus a mediocre luncheon catered by the state, never a good prospect.

Pascal d'Onscon had, despite his reservations about the food, devoured it all and found it palatable. The carafe of wine shared with six colleagues gave them each a thimble-full. Maybe because it was a wine fraud investigation the selection of vintage was a bit better than the usual, definitely a Côtes-du-Rhône and at least *buvable*.

Since he had joined the upper echelons of the organization within the government that kept wine producers on the straight and narrow (a sub-agency of the *Direction Générale de la Concurrence, de la Consommation et de la Répression des Fraudes,* the DGCRF), he had attended many of these meetings. Most did not include food and wine. Was there some hidden message in that, even something as simple as—*please attend this meeting.* Pascal had grown to despise meetings.

The investigation involved a suspected smuggling ring off the Atlantic coast bringing in grapes from South America. So far he saw no great progress in the case. It was an old trick, nothing new there, but evidence and witnesses were hard to find.

As the sub-director in the Bordeaux region, this investigation should be his. Unfortunately it had attracted some sort of ministerial attention that was mucking things up. Now this lieutenant in the *Police Nationale,* a young officious type, was explaining why the attempt to intercept the last shipment had failed so dramatically, without a grape in sight.

Pascal sighed and picked up his knife, checking his reflection in the wide blade. He touched his forelock and checked his hairline for further regression. His temples were grayer. His boss, Étienne, looked as bored and old as Pascal felt today. Étienne's belly bumped the table edge, making his normally very proper, upright stance look ridiculous. He had bluish bags under his eyes. His hair color was an embarrassment, a sort of oxblood shoe polish shade. Pascal pledged to himself to grow old gracefully but it was often an inner struggle when one was, well, a bit vain.

Time ticked on, pride be damned. He replaced the knife on his empty plate. He pushed it away, toward the center of the table and scooted his notebook closer, as if that would make him look more attentive. The young field investigator next to him yawned, loudly.

In three months time, Pascal would turn fifty. It meant nothing to him. Really, it did not. He sighed, unable to fool himself. Fifty was the beginning of the slide to—what? Retirement, decrepitude, frailty, death. Of course, all that. But he was still vital and young, he also told himself. Again, not very convincingly.

He glanced around the table at his colleagues. The field investigator, as Pascal had been for many years, was fifteen years younger, at minimum. The boy— he barely had facial hair— had years of fun in the field ahead. The rest of them around the table were just plain old, either mentally or physically. Bureaucrats worn down by the system, clinging to whatever power they may have once possessed, blind to the ways others viewed them and the plodding trajectories of their careers. Even the young lieutenant had the dullness of a man much older.

They were all successful, prosperous even. They did good work for the people, for the Republic, for the business of grape-growing and wine-making. They had been promoted over other, less-worthy men. No women at this level. This was France. There were women investigators but it was a perilous job, usually solo without backup, often undercover, often in danger. Pascal himself had some narrow escapes where only his physical strength and quick thinking had helped him survive. He shuddered slightly, remembering the guillotine and the blinding thirst that almost killed him.

Still, this department was his life. He would not turn his back on it, on these people, ever. He smiled slightly at Étienne who raised his eyebrows in question. Pascal shrugged, noncommittal. They both turned their attentions back to the lieutenant who droned on and on.

Pascal felt the air go out of him for a moment, suddenly, like a loose balloon. A hollowness, a shriveled nothing. Soon he would be a husk of himself, dust. He would grow feeble and die. *Everyone dies, mon ami.*

Then, like clockwork, the man from Alsace exploded, angry about something, last year's harvest, his reimbursements for expenses, the many injustices he'd suffered, his stalled raise, and so on. A litany of complaints washed over them and they all closed their eyes in despair.

After the meeting finally adjourned Pascal and Étienne took themselves off to a wine bar on a barge on the Seine, the sort of tourist spot where they would never see their colleagues. The wine was decent, nothing special, but the two of them managed to quaff several glasses to wash the horrid monotony of bureaucracy out of their systems.

"Do you ever imagine," Pascal began, twisting his bar stool around so he could look out onto the brown water of the river and the golden bridge beyond, "this is all a dream?"

Etienne huffed a laugh. "Eh? A bad dream— a nightmare?"

"A meaningless Faustian puzzle, trapped like a rat in a maze, doomed to frustration? Or the sort you may wake up from someday."

Etienne drained his glass. "I am definitely waking up soon. Sunshine ahead. I retire in eight months and four days."

Pascal knew this but it still made him sad. The two of them had worked closely for years and thought alike on so many things. "But who's counting, eh?"

"Not getting any younger. I want to play with my grandchildren one of these days."

"You have grandchildren?"

"Not yet. But there is always hope." He slapped Pascal on the back. "It is not so bleak, my friend. Cheer up! Have some more wine. I will talk to you tomorrow. You head south tonight?"

Pascal looked at his watch. "Plenty of time to drown the nightmare on board."

An hour later the TGV, the speed train to Bordeaux, left the Montparnasse railway station, moved slowly through the suburbs then picked up speed in the countryside. Pascal sat in a window seat in first class, one of the perks of his job. He hadn't even spent the night in Paris. With the fast train service it seemed unnecessary. And his love, Merle, was waiting for him in Bordeaux, always a pleasant prospect.

Chin in hand he caught sight of his reflection in the glass. Who was that sour, despondent old man? Why did he hate this job, this department that was so good to him, that had nurtured and fed him all these years? A simple answer: he was turning fifty. It was hitting him hard.

Merle had turned fifty two years before— or was it three? Anyway she breezed right through it. She had reinvented herself at fifty, with a life in France. Upturned her whole world, for him supposedly but France had wooed her too. Was it easier for women? He doubted it. She had left her family, even her son Tristan, behind in the States. That can't have been easy.

He leaned back in the seat and shut his eyes. He was tired, maybe that's all it was. He wasn't going to the club car for more wine. No, he would just rest his weary head for a moment. Before he could drift off, the family across the aisle began to eat their supper, popping the cork on a bottle of wine and distributing baguette sandwiches of ham and cheese, oranges, and bags of chips. The man, presumably husband to the woman and father to the two children, looked rich and happy, a flush to his youthful cheeks. *He* wasn't as old as fifty. He looked content, smiling at his wife, joking with his children.

Pascal closed his eyes again. Maybe they would quiet down. He wasn't sure how much time passed before he felt the nudge on his elbow.

"*Monsieur? Pardon.*" The man had a plastic cup of wine in his hand, offering it across the aisle. He smiled at Pascal. "It is my own wine, my first vintage since taking over the winery from my father. Celebrate with us?"

Pascal smiled politely as he took the cup, holding it aloft in a salute to the vintner. "*Salut. Santé.*" Even the children raised their plastic cups of juice and smiled sweetly.

He sipped the dark red wine. It was silky and soft, tasting of berries and woodsmoke. He smiled appreciatively at the man and nodded his approval. "Can I see the bottle?"

The young vintner passed it over the aisle. When Pascal read the label a pang of envy hit him hard. It was uncharacteristic for him, this feeling. He had examined thousands upon thousands of bottles. He rubbed the classic-style Bordeaux label, the raised letters, the gold foil. He had seen this vineyard in his travels. It was in the Medoc, on sacred wine *terroir*. This man was lucky to have been born into this family.

Pascal passed the bottle back. "It's excellent, monsieur. *Merci. Félicitations.*"

The young man beamed. His little daughter was talking loudly about something she wanted for her birthday. Pascal looked back out the window. The silly fantasy that had flickered in and out of his mind the last few months rose up again. A winery of his own. Rows of perfectly tended vines, soil full of clay and rocks and the smell of old leaves. A southeastern exposure, as long as one is fantasizing. A stone tasting room. Modern vats and a large barrel *cave*, deep underground.

He shook his head, smiling at himself. He could never leave the department. Never. They would take him out feet first, no doubt. He sipped the delicious wine, savoring the last drops. No, he would keep vintners honest, making sure they carry on the grand traditions of French wine-making with all his legal authority.

That was all he could do.

Three

BORDEAUX

Merle Bennett checked the time on her watch, standing at the window, five floors up. The traffic on the street below had thinned out as evening fell, turning the sky violet. The streetlights were modern here, no fancy gaslight conversions in the suburbs. Across the street an identical building in drab 1960s yellow brick mirrored hers, complete with a solitary woman at a window. A single, scrawny tree at the end of the block had barely leafed out. It was pretty with white blossoms for a couple weeks in April but now barely qualified as landscaping.

Neither the utilitarian apartment building, nor the unit itself, were *bad*. She kept telling herself that. The apartment was clean. She scrubbed it endlessly because of some stink bugs that kept showing up. They'd bought a new bed and sofa and a small dining table for just the two of them. The kitchen was big enough for one person but no smaller than the one in her cottage in the Dordogne. For Bordeaux the size was adequate. Comfortable.

They'd had to give up the beautiful townhouse last summer. When the owner had been murdered and unceremoniously dumped into the garden, that lovely experience was over. His relatives sold the townhouse quickly and she and Pascal were out on the street again, searching for digs.

Where was Pascal? His train was due in from Paris a half hour ago. She turned back to the apartment and took the seven steps across the parlor to the kitchen. She poured herself a glass of rosé and stirred the *pot au feu* on the range. The roast was tender, falling apart now, and the carrots would be mush if he didn't come home soon. It wasn't her favorite dish to make but it was one of Pascal's grandmother's recipes that she tried to keep making for him. Basic and rich, easy really, and full of good smells. Add some *haricots verts* and a baguette and there was dinner.

Back by the window she eyed the watercolor on the easel with a critical eye. It was pretty bad. Awful actually, but she'd only started art classes two months before. She shouldn't have attempted a portrait of Pascal. Portraits were notoriously difficult, her instructor said, and she agreed. She'd taped the photograph of him on the easel above the paper. It was a pensive shot of him with the sun coming over his left shoulder, his sunglasses up in his dark hair as usual, eyes off to the right, slightly squinted. She'd taken the shot in the autumn when he'd taken her on a driving tour of wine country, a fraud discovery tour, he called it. Driving the back roads, looking for anything out of the ordinary during the harvest.

They'd stopped for a picnic lunch at a winery where he was friends with the vintner. She'd forgotten the name but it was an out-of-the-way place on a narrow farm road in the *Entre-deux-mers* region. Pascal bought a bottle of wine in the tasting room. Very expensive, she'd thought, but he said they gave him a friendly discount. Was that a bribe, she wondered, but kept it to herself once she tasted the amazing vintage. Bordeaux at its finest.

In the photograph, Pascal held a glass of the wine and gazed out into the vines pensively. What was he thinking about? What were they talking about that day? She'd forgotten that too. He wasn't the type to discuss every feeling with her. She didn't do that with him either. Yet they understood each other, maybe on a deeper level.

But now she moved closer to the photo. Was that a hint of sadness around his mouth? Or frustration? What were his eyes saying? She squinted, begging the photograph to spill its secrets, as Pascal came through the door.

"Ah, *chérie*, what are you cooking now?" He said, throwing his small briefcase on the floor. He looked tired, his voice gravelly.

"Just one of your favorites." They held each other for a moment. "We should eat before it all falls apart in the pot."

They sat in silence, eating companionably, smiling at each other. Merle was always happy when Pascal was home. But was he as happy? He glanced away from her gaze, looking around the parlor with its tiny blue sofa, straightback chair, and the small, dusty television that was rarely watched. It perched on a rickety end table across from the sofa. A small cocktail table Merle had found at a *brocante* was the only thing she really liked in the room. The marble top of the little table was worn and soft.

Pascal caught her eye and went back to his *pot au feu*. He set down his fork and wiped out the juices in the bowl with a torn piece of baguette. "Delicious, as usual. Mémé is looking down on us and smiling."

Merle sipped her wine. "I do try."

"And succeed. Not a small task with that kitchen."

She sighed. "It is tiny."

"At least we get a good stair climbing workout, yes? How many times do you go up and down today?"

She frowned, thinking of the rank smell of the stairwell, an enticing blend of rancid garlic and last week's curry. "Um, three times, I think, up and down."

"So six times. Good work." He raised his wine glass to her. After a sip he looked around the parlor again as if measuring the space. He wasn't very particular about their living quarters. His own cottage outside of Toulouse was small and barely furnished while he lived there. It was rented out now to the many tourists, young and old, who loved the French countryside. Merle enjoyed interacting with them from afar, over the internet, as they booked their enthusiastic vacations.

"So," he said as if starting a discussion.

She looked at him over her rosé. "What?"

He tipped his head. "You are happy here? In this little— apartment?"

She blinked. Had he been leading up to some other descriptive term? They had been renting this space for six or seven months and he had never asked her that. "I guess. Are you?"

He shrugged and drank more wine. "I think I am more a country man. *De la campagne, c'est moi.*"

She bit her lip. She loved the countryside too. It was where they met, where they had both lived for many years. She loved taking off on country roads, climbing hilltops, seeing what was blooming in the hedgerows, talking to sheep, the solitude and peacefulness.

"But your job is here in the city." His office was in the Cité du Vin, a glass-paneled and aluminum-clad modern building that was a wine museum as well as housing offices for the many agencies that dealt with wine, including his own wine fraud division.

"True." He poured himself another glass of wine from the Crus Artisans du Medoc, an association of small and medium-sized wineries. He had bought a case the last time he was in that region, north of Bordeaux. "This is good, isn't it? Maybe we should cellar some?"

"We can take it to Malcouziac," she said. They would have to— there was no *cave* here. "Do you want to look for a new place?"

"I don't know, blackbird. Perhaps." He sat back in his chair, arms crossed with the wine glass in one hand. "It is a lot of work though, yes?"

"It is." And she would be the one doing the legwork.

"Forget it. We will get by in this cracker box." He smiled. "That is right? Cracker box?"

She smiled. She loved his use of American slang, often not quite right. This time he was on the money. "This is definitely a cracker box."

"We will eat in bistros more. Walk outside this summer and eat on the sidewalks, under umbrellas, yes? Find one of those new places you like to discover. You don't need to cook so much, blackbird. No reason to be stuffed in this box, heating up the place all summer, eh?"

And just like that— her satisfaction, if it could be called that, evaporated. She no longer saw the apartment as cozy and comfortable but as cramped and tired. She thought of the tug of the bags on her arms and the burn in her thighs as she hauled groceries up five flights of stairs. The rattling of her heart as she drank a glass of water afterward. The tiny toilet room with the floor that never looked clean, no matter how much you scrubbed it. The bedroom where she had six inches on her side of the bed so she usually rolled out on Pascal's side. The stains on the ceiling, the warped floorboards.

It was horrible. She closed her eyes. Awful.

Pascal touched her hand. "It's fine, blackbird. We'll be *fine*."

She blinked at him and smiled weakly, trying not to widen her eyes in surprise. Who had said anything about 'us'? Was there a problem with 'us'? A knot was forming in her chest. He patted her hand then grasped it, a little desperately. "Do not worry about the living arrangements. Please, blackbird. They have a way of taking care of themselves, *n'est-ce pas?*"

She straightened, trying to look cheerful. "It's only an apartment after all."

Four

SAINTE-FOY AOC

Ernest Brooks pulled off his work gloves and slapped them on his thigh, sending dust flying in the evening air. There was no breeze, no sign of rain, only a violent torment of colors on the western horizon. He couldn't remember many dramatic sunsets back in England. His family lived in a valley, hills all around. He squinted at the dying sun glinting off the rows of grapevines that crept up the incline to the south, disappearing over the summit, and felt a deep contentment.

His own vineyard: it never ceased to amaze him. And Harris's of course. Harris had brought more money to the table but Ernest did most of the work on the land. Not that he was complaining. He loved mucking about with plants and dirt and sussing out the perfect blends of wine. His people were farmers back in Britain. Dirt was in his genes, not to mention his jeans, his fingernails, his nostrils, and his hair. Three years here and he was devoted to it. Obsessed with it. He loved everything about this place, the stone *mas,* the gentle hillside. All of it except what lay over the hill, that mess he preferred not to think about, the decaying, neglected hectares of vines.

At least they were out of sight. On this side—their side— of the vineyard, all was well. It was important to keep that firmly in mind. He needed parameters to his work, to his happiness, to his life. Boundaries. He knew that about himself. Given a blank canvas or unlimited possibilities, he would either balk in indecision or go into a wild frenzy of too many projects.

Probably the latter, he mused. He would work himself into the ground. He wasn't young anymore. He could still tear an old vine from the ground with his bare hands. That tightness he felt in his chest off and on was from hard work, he was sure. He rubbed a calloused palm over his bald pate and sighed. He would lick this, mend their problems, achieve their dreams. He would wrestle the problems to the ground, one way or another. There was never any doubt.

The hair on the back of his neck stood up suddenly. The wind? Or was someone there? He spun around. Here in the yard, next to the old barrel *cave* that sat empty and the mixing cellar that needed so much work, he seemed to be alone. He rubbed his forearms nervously then told himself he was being ridiculous. Harris was inside, working on the ledgers as he did every evening. No one was skulking about the vineyard.

A breeze blew up, high in the Italian cypress that lined the drive. He watched the pointy tips bend and swirl. Lately he'd had this feeling, that change was in the air, that something would suddenly arrive or appear and everything would be upended. It could be a good change, he told himself. It really could. Although he couldn't see how or why a good change could come, not with a foreboding like this. He shivered. He was not normally a pessimistic sort but it would more likely be a bad change, something drastic— a heat wave, a drought, shriveled grapes, thunderstorms, swarms of locusts, a thing out of his control. That was farming, whether it was wheat or lemons or grapes. Epic disaster was around every corner, waiting for you.

But this was different, a sort of existential threat. He couldn't put his finger on it. Maybe he was just getting batty. Best to keep his irrational drumbeats of doom to himself.

On a rational farmer's note, grapes did provide extra challenges, there was no doubt about that. So many rules and regulations from the government and the viticulture associations. Irrigation, only in exceptional situations and with permissions granted. That was fairly new. For many years, no watering at all, just whatever the heavens provided. No rain, tough luck. But even the old sods at the agencies had tipped to climate change. Unfortunately he and Harris didn't have the cashflow yet to put in drip irrigation. That was a few years off.

If they lasted that long. He shook his head. *No doom thoughts, Ernie.*

He hesitated to bring up all the myriad regulations about irrigation with Harris. A lecture would ensue. Sometimes Harris would frown at something he proposed and he would find out that it was not to be done. Harris wanted the vineyard to be biodynamic, putting an extra strain on everything. Farming by the seasons, by the changes in the calendar, was mostly a great adventure. But why did Harris have to be so soft-hearted toward insects, for instance? And rats? He coddled his flock of chickens, letting them take care of the vineyard insects. And that was why Ernest loved him, for his kind heart.

He turned to watch Harris through the small window. In a pool of light, at the kitchen table in his crisp white shirt and shock of brown hair over his forehead— a fine man, he was. The bookkeeping ledgers and stacks of bills piled in front of him, the checkbook at his right hand. Harris began filling in a check, a grim twist to his mouth. He tore it out of the checkbook, set it on a stack of envelopes, and sighed. His head lifted and he smiled as he saw Ernest peering inside.

"Come in," Harris called. "It's almost dark. Time for brandy."

He was gathering up his work as Ernest stepped in the door and kicked off his work boots. Harris stacked the financials on a side table and opened the bottle of brandy. It was nearly empty, Ernest noticed. Well, they had been sipping it every night as some kind of talisman for future success. God knew, they needed one.

He took a small snifter from Harris and they clinked glasses, smiling over them.

"To the weather," Ernest said cheerfully.

"To the grapes— and us," Harris replied, as he always did.

"You put the hens to bed?"

Harris nodded. "Sixteen eggs today. We can trade with the neighbors for cherries. I can make that clafoutis again."

Ernest let the fiery liquid glide down his throat, warming him.

When this bottle of brandy was gone, would the change come? Would they be able to afford another good bottle? Would it be good news or bad? Thunderbolts or biblical floods? Celebration or failure?

With a silent toast to Dionysus, god of the grape, Ernest admitted that he wasn't entirely sure he wanted to find out.

$$\mathit{Five}$$

ENTRE-DEUX-MERS AOC

The car paused at the top of a hill, and they got out of the car for a look. The Garonne Valley stretched below, in the heart of the *Entre-deux-mers* region, east of Bordeaux. "Between two seas" was not correct, Pascal explained in the car, driving at his usual breakneck speed on the Autoroute. It meant between two *"marées"* or tides, the two rivers, the Garonne and the Dordogne. It was a rolling, green land and from the bench where they sat, strategically placed on the rise, Merle and Pascal could see for miles. Vineyards, woodlands, rivers, and villages stretched out before them, like a delicious checkerboard banquet.

It had been two days since Pascal arrived back from his meetings in Paris. Two days since the glow dimmed on the Bordeaux apartment. Merle hadn't slept well that night, wondering if she should begin to look for a new place to live. Wondering if he was unhappy. Pascal had a couple long days at the Cité du Vin offices, paperwork and administrative work he loathed. But now, they had escaped the city as the temperatures began to rise and the humidity with it.

They had picked up lunch supplies in Libourne— olives, cheese, peaches, baguette, and sausages. Merle opened the box and handed

Pascal a napkin and a bottle of water. He was quiet now, contemplating the countryside, the sun on his face. He looked content.

"Nice, isn't it?"

He chewed the baguette. "Too many trees, not enough vines."

"Oh? Not enough work out there for you?" It was unlike him to be so negative.

He glanced at her quickly. "Can't have that, can we."

Merle sat back, popping an olive in her mouth. "What then?"

He shook his head. "Just an observation, *chérie*. Meaning nothing." He waved his arm across the landscape below. "You see the vineyards are mostly along the riverbanks. That's the best soil. It's surprising to see there are still forests in France."

Merle looked up at the large tree— a cedar?— sheltering them, keeping them shaded and cool. "They are protected now. By the state, right? The glorious Republic?"

They ate in silence. No more questions or answers. It was peaceful on this hill, a little breeze and shade from the sun. Then, suddenly, Pascal stood up. "Ready?"

Back in the BMW, Merle watched the scenery go by, content to just being out of the stupid apartment. Bordeaux itself was lovely, as she told everyone. Quaint, restored, some of the old medieval walls intact. The huge, majestic Place de la Bourse along the river, with the vast reflecting pools, was stunning. But the places they could afford were far from the old town, not picturesque at all. Pascal had to work in Bordeaux so they had to live somewhere, and somewhere they could afford.

In truth, *he* had to be able to afford it. She had bought the sofa and the new mattress but Pascal paid the rent. Merle had a little income from her legal work with Annie but it was sporadic and she tried to be frugal. She glanced at Pascal, fingers gripping the steering wheel, taking corners fast, leaning this way and that like a race car driver. Since he paid the rent, he called the shots on staying in the 'cracker box'— or moving on. He hadn't said another word about the apartment. But his mood, pensive, a little evasive, seemed to indicate something was up. Maybe she should start looking again.

Merle looked up when the car slowed to a stop on a narrow farm road. It was paved and well-maintained but the bushes in the hedgerows were thick and tangled. Impossible to see through or around them. She couldn't tell why he'd stopped.

Pascal pulled off on the grassy verge and put the car into park. "I'll just be a minute." He rolled his window down and got out. "Turn off the car, if you want. I'll be right back."

For a moment Merle wondered if he needed a bathroom break. The bushes would do. But he walked down the middle of the road about fifty paces and turned left, disappearing into the greenery. Was there a driveway there? A road? A footpath? She fidgeted and checked her watch. She turned the key to kill the engine. She checked her phone— no cell service.

After ten minutes, maybe fifteen, Pascal emerged onto the tarmac again, brushing off his pants and shirt. He flipped back his hair with a tip of his head and walked briskly back to car, smiling at her through the windshield.

He slipped behind the wheel. "Sorry. I had to check a vineyard from this side, far from the fancy gates and all that."

"See anything out of the ordinary?"

"Just grapevines. That is a big vineyard, at least twenty hectares."

"What's a hectare again— in acres?"

"A little less than twenty-five acres is ten hectares."

"So how many hectares does that vineyard have? The one you just sneaked around on?"

"Twenty. Fifty acres or so. Mostly in Merlot. A little Cabernet Franc. And a new plot of Sémillon."

"Can you tell a grape variety just by looking at it?"

He smiled. "It is my job."

"So you can tell if they're planting something that isn't allowed."

"Exactly."

"So what grape variety would you plant, if you were the *vigneron*?"

He glanced at her, eyebrows jumping. "I suppose whatever grows the best. It is all about the soil."

"What's the soil like around here?" Merle glanced out her side window, now that the heavy undergrowth had cleared. They were in a valley, a low one surrounded by hills, patch-worked with vineyards.

"All sorts, clay, limestone, *les graves* — gravel, it depends on the exact spot."

"That must make it difficult. I mean, to match the right grape variety with the exact soil type all over a vineyard."

"There are specialists. They test the soil, drill down. Make the core samples deep into the earth. Grapevines grow very deep. Fifteen, twenty feet sometimes."

"Do they drill core samples that far down?" she asked.

"Sometimes. To know what lies underneath the topsoil, to grow the right vines."

They stopped again about fifteen miles later, on the side of one of the nearby hills where a vineyard was terraced into lateral rows, undulating gracefully across the face of the hill. This time Pascal simply parked across from the winery's tasting room. No fancy gates here, just a dirt driveway lined with pink roses.

"Shall we try it?"

As they walked up the driveway she caught his hand and smiled. This was more like it, a country outing and a random wine tasting. "What's the name of this winery?"

Pascal looked around for a sign. "I forget. Let's just give it a chance, okay?"

The tasting room door was padlocked. Pascal cupped his eyes to peer in the dusty window. "Nobody." He walked around the low stone building, pausing to look into other outbuildings. The working parts of the winery, she figured, where the grapes were crushed, blended, and fermented. Possibly bottled as well, if it was a high quality operation. Merle knew enough about the basics of winemaking from her short stint as a tour guide at a winery near Malcouziac. Just barely enough.

She gestured toward the car to suggest a retreat, when Pascal stepped into the bright sunlight and hollered: "*Allo?* Anybody here?"

They listened for a door to open, an employee or the owner to appear. But nothing happened.

"Come on," Pascal said, walking fast in the gap between the buildings, toward the vineyard itself. "Let's see if they are close by."

To Merle's surprise he plunged into the terraced rows of grapevines. They were lush but only starting to grow grapes as it was still the month of May. Many tendrils reached out as she walked by them, as if trying to tell her something. The soil between the rows was grassy and hard, scattered with sharp rocks. She reached a gap in the row and paused, looking down the hill at the view of the valley where they'd been, trying to decipher where the road was, where they'd stopped, but it was lost in trees and fields. The view was gorgeous though.

"Merle?" His voice came from up the hill. She turned and saw Pascal waving over the vines. "I found him. Head back to the tasting room." He pointed in the direction they'd come, helpfully, as she was getting vertigo on these terraces.

By the time she returned to the tasting room the door was wide open, letting the musty odor waft out. Pascal perched on a stool while a flushed and anxious young man, wearing a blue coverall and straw hat and dripping with perspiration, listened to his new customer.

"You have a White Bordeaux? Seriously? A blend of what?" Pascal asked.

"Sémillon and Sauvignon Blanc, only the best."

"And the vintage?"

"2015. A good year."

"Is it cold? Yes? Let's have that." Pascal patted the other bar stool and Merle climbed up onto it. She squinted at Pascal. What was he up to?

The glasses needed washing, which took a few minutes. Then the young man, who introduced himself as the son of the owner, popped the cork on a fresh bottle of chilled white Bordeaux. The blend was simple, he explained, perfected over the years by his father and grandfather.

Pascal swirled and sniffed. "New oak?"

"Of course." He wrapped his hands around the bar towel nervously.

"Organic?"

"*Désolé, non.*" He winced.

They sipped the wine. Merle wondered if it was good. How can you tell if a wine is organic? He said this one wasn't. She had little experience with white Bordeaux. It was cold, she knew that, but what would you call that aftertaste? Chalky? Mineral? Sharp, acidic? She and the young proprietor watched Pascal. He was quiet, swishing it in his mouth, swallowing, taking another small sip.

"It's delicious," Merle said finally. "Bravo."

The young man gave her a pained smile then looked at Pascal again. Obviously the proprietor recognized him as a connoisseur. Pascal set down his wine glass finally and straightened his back. "Bravo is correct. Excellent, monsieur."

They came away with three bottles for their *cave*, stashing them in the box with the Crus Artisans they would cellar. As they drove away, waving merrily at the vigneron, Merle said, "What did you really think?"

"Well." He turned a sharp corner at the top of the hill and pointed the car down the other side, toward the Dordogne River.

"Not good?"

"Over-priced. It will pair well with some oily fish on a plate somewhere."

"What was wrong with it?"

"If that is Sémillon he's blending in there, I will eat my hat." He glanced at her and laughed. "And it will be even less tasty than his Bordeaux *blanc*."

Six

DORDOGNE

Malcouziac dozed in the early summer sunshine, the village still waking from the winter. The afternoon sun turned the stone walls of the bastide orange. The tourists had begun to arrive but slowly, a trickle adding to business at the restaurants and hotels. Merle had lived here long enough to spot them immediately, in their fancy clothes and inappropriate shoes. She didn't mind tourists, how could she? She still was nearly one herself, even after several years here. She doubted she would ever be completely accepted as a local.

Except for Father Albert, her neighbor across the alley. The retired priest, round and bald with bushy white eyebrows, came out to greet their return, knocking on the garden gate with a bouquet of white roses and a big grin. He followed Merle into the kitchen as she filled a vase with water for the flowers.

"The weather has been fine," he cried enthusiastically. "Just enough rain. Summer will be full of plums."

Pascal gave him a hug. "How have you been, old man?" They were old friends. Pascal's father had known Albert years before. Albert was responsible for Merle and Pascal getting together when he recommended Pascal as a roofer when Merle first moved into her cottage.

"*Pas mal,*" Albert said. "A bit of rheumatism, as usual."

"Join us for dinner," Pascal said. "We have some wine to open."

The men wandered out into the garden to sit in the afternoon sun and talk about whatever men talked about. Merle smiled, watching them, two of her favorite people. She put the groceries away, decided what to make for dinner, then her cell phone rang in the parlor.

"Francie, hi." Merle smiled at the sound of her sister's voice.

"Hey. I'm in Paris with Dylan."

"I didn't know you had a trip planned. Can you come down here? We're in the Dordogne at the moment."

Francie was calling to set up a visit for next week. She'd confirm the exact day later. Merle hung up, still smiling but curious. Francie wouldn't come to the Dordogne without some sort of agenda. She was a serious person despite her flirtatious youth. Did she want to discuss something serious? Merle hoped there was nothing wrong with little Phoebe, Dylan's daughter. Merle had a little auntie crush on that girl.

Maybe she and Dylan were thinking of getting married. Merle scolded herself. Why did her mind always go there? She and Pascal had decided to just live together. They both had been married, as had Francie and Dylan. Francie probably just wanted to see her semi-favorite sister, the countryside in the throes of springtime, the roses blooming, the wisteria in full purple, the lavender starting to show color in glorious clumps. Of course she did.

Merle paused, feeling the velvety petals of Albert's roses. There was something else. Francie had something to discuss with her, she was sure of it. But she'd have to wait until the visit to find out what it was.

THE NEXT MORNING Pascal was up at the crack of dawn. He made them coffee and brought Merle a cup then crawled back into bed. "I should go back to the city, blackbird."

"Today? No."

"Not today. I have to paint those door shutters you bought. You have the blue paint?"

Merle sipped the espresso. "I do. We have some chores to do at your place too, right?"

Pascal squinted at her. "I forgot. We have renters coming next week?"

"The yard needs cleaning up."

He sighed. "Such fun. Tomorrow?"

They agreed on a schedule although it was clear Pascal was itching to get back to work. Which really wasn't like him these days. His administrative job for the wine fraud division wasn't particularly compelling, it appeared. He could handle the paperwork, the forms, oversee the investigations, from anywhere, his office in Bordeaux, here in Malcouziac, or almost anywhere in the region. He disliked the paperwork, the reports, the regulations, but understood he had to comply with the bureaucracy. It was a French institution.

As he whistled, painting the shutters in the garden that afternoon, Merle wondered again if he was happy in Bordeaux. Despite his whistling he hadn't relaxed here. He kept that crease in his brow and a hunch in his shoulders. Whatever he was thinking at that winery with the white Bordeaux he'd kept close to his vest. She hoped he would open up to her. She was starting to think she might not be the woman for him. She hated moody silences.

No, stop that. Everyone had moody silences. She had been a bit out of sorts in Bordeaux over the tiny apartment. She'd been cranky about the search last fall, every day logging into rental sites, making lists, driving past dumps. Finding somewhere decent and affordable only to be too late to snatch it up— that irritated the hell out of her. She tried not to take it out on Pascal but he was the reason she was in Bordeaux. She'd wanted him to take this job, to be closer to Malcouziac, and now she regretted all that. No doubt she barked at him, or at least sighed a lot.

So she would be patient with him, let him tell her what was bothering him in due time. She had a feeling it was his job and there wasn't anything she could do about that. He was devoted to the wine fraud division of the DGCRF. But what had happened at that Paris meeting? Could the division be in chaos? People getting fired?

Pascal had pushed aside the heavy cupboard in the dining room and pulled up the trap door to the cellar. Merle grabbed three bottles from the case and stepped carefully down the old wooden steps. The basement had a dirt floor and a low ceiling but it had withstood the centuries intact. She unlocked the door to the *cave* with the big skeleton key and stepped over the threshold. Pascal's new motion-activated light blinked on, shining a blue glow over the wine racks. Merle placed the new bottles onto a rack and went back upstairs for more. Four trips and she was done.

After dinner they had a visitor, a colleague of Pascal's. Fabrice Vidal was about thirty, slender, with dark hair and intelligent brown eyes. He wore what looked like hiking clothes, pants with many pockets, hiking boots, and what Americans would call a fishing shirt. He smiled shyly at Merle and spoke to her in heavily accented English.

"Fabrice is going to help me in the field," Pascal explained. "Tomorrow we—" He slapped his forehead. "We were going to go to my place, weren't we? Can we change the day, *chérie*?"

"Of course." She smiled at the two of them, thick as thieves.

"*Merci*, blackbird." To Fabrice he spoke rapidly in French. "Tomorrow at six? We start early?" he added in English, apparently for her benefit.

Merle watched Fabrice walk down the street. "He could have stayed with us. He's your friend, right?"

"A colleague. He was in the area and offered to help me track down some wineries for potential fraud. He already had a hotel room."

"What's his specialty?"

"The vines, how they're grown, how they cut corners, all that."

They climbed the stairs. "But you know all that, don't you?" Merle asked.

He held up the covers so she could join him in bed. "You are right. I am a genius with wine. Most definitely a know-it-all." He laughed. "I don't know everything, blackbird. I am but a humble public servant."

"Hmmm. Very attractive but not humble at all."

Seven

MALCOUZIAC AND BEYOND

Pascal kissed Merle's forehead as he rose at five-thirty. The sky was barely gray as he dressed and left the cottage. The morning air was fresh and cool but the promise of summer warmth lingered. The streets at six o'clock were waking up— housewives throwing out cats, the rattle of pans on stoves, the scrape of a refuse can against the cobbles.

He slung his backpack over his shoulder and paused to retie one of his shoes. He'd dressed differently today, no leather boots, no bomber jacket, no denims. He had fetched hiking pants and a black t-shirt from the trunk of his car the previous afternoon in anticipation of Fabrice joining him today. Fabrice made him feel a bit old, perhaps even fifty, although there was no lack of pep in his stride as he made his way down Rue de Poitiers. A day in the vineyards was what he needed. He wound his way through the market square, past the fountain where birds were enjoying an early bathing session. There was Fabrice, waiting in front of the hotel. He raised a hand in greeting.

"*Bonjour, allons-y,*" Pascal said. As they left the village walls behind he began with an apology. "*Désolé.* I could not offer you a bed last night. My partner is not yet aware of my plans."

"Understood," said Fabrice with a nod. "Better not to get hopes up. This is a tough business, as we both know."

"And I am not even positive I will find anything suitable," Pascal continued. "My funds are not unlimited."

He drove north and west on narrow two-lane roads, over the provincial border, out of the Dordogne and into the large winemaking region of Bordeaux. Fabrice raised his eyebrows. "I had assumed something nearby Malcouziac."

"It is a possibility, of course. But the lure of Bordeaux is strong."

"Not to mention the pay-off," Fabrice said. "You have a list?"

Pascal reached into the back seat and pulled a folded sheet of legal paper from his backpack and handed it to Fabrice. The younger man read down the list of wineries for sale in Bordeaux slowly and carefully. He used his mobile to search for information. "We will look in this order?"

"Unless we get lost, run out of petrol, or die of hunger first."

"You have them on your GPS?"

"*Bien sûr.*"

Even with the satellite mapping Pascal made a few wrong turns to the first winery. It was too early for tastings or tours at Domaine Tranquilles but no matter. He wanted to see the land, the terrain, the nearness of the rivers, the vines themselves, how well they were tended. All this the two of them could do from a back road without announcing themselves.

The domaine was situated perfectly, facing southeast above the riverbanks of the Garonne, on a gradual slope that didn't need terracing. Fabrice got out of the car and stretched, eyeing the vines. "Merlot here," he said.

Pascal walked around the car, over the ditch, and into the edge of the vineyard. "They look healthy, yes?" How marvelous it would be to find the perfect vineyard on the first try.

Fabrice strode down the row, lifting leaves to peer at the berries, the nascent grapes, in tiny clusters. He bent close to the leaves, sniffing them, then repeated the procedure three times down the row. Pascal wondered if it was a chemical smell, or maybe just noble rot, the natural must, that Fabrice had noticed.

The œnologue returned to the end of row. "It is a good prospect. I am concerned about their use of pesticides however. There is a strong smell. They may be doing overhead spraying, not selectively, you know?" Fabrice lay a leaf in his hand. "The color of the leaves is pale, not a rich full green. Perhaps the soil is depleted. Or the variety is not well-matched to the soil."

Pascal wanted this to be the one and his spirits sank further when Fabrice commented again. "They want seven million Euros, my friend."

The next winery was equally expensive and not in as good a situation, high on a hillside where the soil was not as rich, and on the north face of the slope. Pascal had made his wish list without concern about price. The value of a winery, unless it was some storied Baron de Rothschild type, was always negotiable. Their wine may be selling for a very low price but they bottle mass quantities. You just never knew and thus he felt justified in putting these *très chèr* wineries on his list.

Number Two however was selling for nine million.

"Scratch it off," Pascal said after ten minutes there.

"Wait," Fabrice said, examining the list in the car. "Let's skip to something more moderately priced."

Pascal followed Fabrice's directions to a winery north of Saint-Émilion in small district called Montagne-Saint-Émillion. It was not quite as advertised, unless you called a small rise a 'mountain.' The village of Montagne however was picturesque and this particular winery for sale, Fabrice said, was small but well-regarded.

"What soils?" Pascal asked as they parked by the tasting room.

"Very consistent, clay and limestone. Good for red and white."

"How many hectares?"

"Fifty."

Pascal frowned. "Not so small." He hesitated to ask but they were about to enter the tasting room. "How much?"

"Three-and-a-half."

Pascal winced again. Still too much. The wine however was superb, a mineral-y white and a soft, fragrant red. He could do better, he thought, but knew he was deluding himself. He would never blend wine at an estate like this one.

. . .

By three o'clock the two connoisseurs had checked out seven wineries, eaten a leisurely *déjeuner* in a small village, and put three hundred kilometers on the car. Pascal was discouraged. They'd seen some nice wineries but nothing he could buy. Everything was so expensive. Fabrice tried to cheer him with saying they were only just beginning and could he possibly take out a bank loan.

"To the railway station?" Pascal said, turning the key on the BMW. He had been sure Fabrice's expertise as an œnologue would help him find a hidden gem, somewhere in Bordeaux. But perhaps he should look in the Lot. Wineries there were more reasonable. Small, not top quality and no Bordeaux *caché*, but decent. Even the Dordogne was getting too rich for his blood.

"Let's see," Fabrice said, staring at his mobile screen yet again. "What's the name of this village? Sainte-Foy-la-Longue. Nearest railway station is Caudrot."

Ten minutes later Pascal dropped his colleague in front of the *gare*. "Thank you so much for sharing your expertise, Fabrice. I will make it up to you someday."

"With some bottles of your own delicious wine?" He smiled in anticipation. "*À bientôt.*" He grabbed his duffle from the back seat and disappeared into possibly the smallest railway station in France.

Pascal sat in his car near the market square in Caudrot for a few minutes and tried to locate where in the Republic he was. He had driven far afield for many hours and his back was aching. He got out of the car to stretch. Leaning over the car roof he set his mobile on the hood and plotted his return trip to Malcouziac. These back roads were notoriously slow. He should go on the Autoroute. On second thought, he would scout out a few regions as he drove back.

He moved the map around with his thumb, remembering where he'd been and all the places he had yet to see in this vast winemaking region. But what was this? A small region that jutted out into the Dordogne, but was still AOC Bordeaux. It had almost the same name as the last village he and Fabrice had visited. Sainte-Foy. Foy meant faith. He smiled to himself. *Have a little faith.*

Eight

PARIS

Francie Bennett sat in her favorite little armchair in the apartment Dylan's law firm had rented for him. It was nice to be back here after the cramped hotel room last time in Paris. He didn't always get a comfortable flat, and sometimes had to house-sit one of the partners' apartments. But this time, thankfully, he— they— got lucky.

The view over the rooftops was classic, as was the black wrought iron balcony and dark orange geraniums in boxes across the street. There was something so satisfying, seeing all the French things you admired in one glance. The flat even smelled like it had been cleaned with lavender-scented soap. She leaned back in the chair and closed her eyes. It smelled heavenly but she was so very tired.

The fatigue began a couple months before, without warning. She lay in bed, unable to summon the will to get up. When was that? She was staying at Dylan's. It was a weekend. She was exhausted. That's all she could recall.

She had slept like a rock on the plane on the way over, nestled against Dylan's shoulder. There was no work for her at his law firm this time so she intended to do whatever she pleased in Paris. And it seemed sleeping was all she pleased. This was the third day she'd barely got dressed by ten a.m.

She considered calling her sister again. Merle needed to know when she was visiting. She loved that little village where Merle had inherited her stone cottage but the thought of packing, navigating a train station, fighting fellow travelers in the aisles— it overwhelmed her.

She was usually full of energy. Something must be wrong. Chronic fatigue? Guillaume-Barré? Cancer? Leukemia? Depression? Her mind spun out of control, the anxiety ratcheting up. She took a deep breath and calmed herself. She could be sick, that was true. But at the moment she only felt tired.

She had been working long hours for the last two months. Dylan had mostly been out of town so she took advantage of all that time to work twelve and sixteen hour days, many weekends, like she had when she first started out. As managing partner there was always a ton of paperwork. At least the assistant managing partner was organized and down-to-earth. He would be fine while she was away. Her new assistant, Claude, had a steep learning curve that he not fully embracing. She wondered, yet again, if he was cut out for the job. She should check her messages but the thought of it made her feel exhausted.

Somehow she managed to push up off her chair and pour herself a glass of orange juice in the tiny kitchen. It was freshly-squeezed and tasted amazing. It also perked her up a little, at least enough to call her sister.

"Hey, you. When are you coming south?"

"Um, I think it will be this weekend. Dylan is coming with me, he says. Is that okay?"

"Of course. I can't wait to see you two."

Francie played with the hem of her shirt. She wondered, in the long pause, if she should tell Merle about her exhaustion. But then Merle asked: "Are you okay? You sound funny. Is it Dylan?"

"I'm fine. He's fine." Francie bit her lip then sighed. "I have been really tired lately. Like dead tired. I hope it's not contagious. I don't know. I've been working a lot of overtime."

"Have you seen a doctor?"

"No. Is it hard to get in to see a French doctor?"

"Just ring up a clinic. The law firm probably knows somebody." Merle sounded concerned which made Francie's anxiety churn again. "Have you been eating and all that?"

"Yeah, no problem there. French food is hard to resist."

"True. So no other symptoms, just tired all the time?"

"That's about it."

"When did this start?"

"A couple months ago. I think around Easter."

"That's a long time to be tired. You should make an appointment. Do you want me to do it for you?"

"Dylan can handle the French if I need him. I'll call him."

"You can delay your trip, you know. If you're too tired."

"Okay." Francie closed her eyes again. Just having a conversation wore her out.

"You know," Merle said, "that's how I was when I was—" Long pause then Merle whispered, "You couldn't be, could you?"

"What—?"

"You know. Pregnant."

Francie recoiled in the chair. "Of course not. I'm almost forty-five for one thing, and Dylan always uses protection."

"Oh, okay. Well, they'll probably check at the clinic anyway. Forty-five isn't that old anymore."

"It sure feels like it. Hey, I'll call you later. I'm going to call Dylan."

Francie let her head drop back in the armchair, exhausted. This was getting ridiculous. When had felt like herself? She forced herself to punch in the number for Dylan's firm then waited for someone to answer. At eight rings she looked at her wristwatch and realized it was the lunch hour. Everyone would be gone. She hung up and closed her eyes again.

She should text Dylan. Yes, that would be simple. If she could only get the energy. *Come on, girl.* She swallowed hard.

'Call me when you can.'

Then Merle's words rebounded into her mind: "That's how I felt when I was—" Pregnant? No way. At forty-five? Impossible.

A picture came into her head, a memory. Some wild make-up sex, that night after Dylan had returned from Paris. They had been angry at each other over something, the distance, the time apart, working too much, his ex, something. She couldn't remember what. Maybe just an excuse for make-up sex. They'd made love three times that night, she did remember that because it was sort of a record. Twice, sure, that'd been done. But three was a never-before-achieved dream. Then they took a bubble bath together. Also sexy fun.

Wasn't there some issue with the condoms that night? She squeezed her eyes shut and tried to remember. She'd been too tired for sex for weeks. What about her period? It was not too regular at this stage in her life. She couldn't remember when she'd last had one. That didn't actually mean anything, did it?

Oh, shit. She lowered her head to her hands as her eyes welled. She had to see a doctor.

Nine

GIRONDE, NOUVELLE-AQUITAINE

"Who *are* you?" the man repeated.

On the gravel road, next to the tidy vineyard and the sad one opposite, the silver Mercedes shone like a bauble in the setting sun.

The tall man spoke in a gruff, challenging tone, eyebrows and mouth pulled down in a frown. He wore aviator sunglasses as if to proclaim he also flew his own plane.

Pascal had gotten out of his car to stretch then noticed the abandoned land to the right. He stood, solitary and probably looking out of his head, in the decrepit vineyard, staring at the dead vines and daydreaming. He walked up through the ditch to the road and introduced himself to the stranger. "Just out driving, admiring the vineyards," he explained. He really didn't want to get out his official identification. But this man looked like the type who might demand it so he was ready.

The tall man relaxed slightly, glancing out over the well-tended vines on the other side of the road. "They are worthy, are they not?" He gestured grandly across the road at the vineyard. "This is my land."

What a pompous toad. "Is that so? Very nice, Monsieur—?"

"Naudé." The tall man reached out a hand, jolted into his manners. "Luc Naudé. *Pardon.* I don't often see anyone on this road."

Pascal shrugged and smiled. Naudé didn't smile in return but took off his sunglasses as the sun was now behind the hills. His face looked strange without the glasses, his black eyes small and wary.

"What's the name of your domaine?" Pascal asked. "Just out of curiosity. It's a beautiful property. I'd like to try your wine."

Naudé squinted suspiciously. "I doubt you can afford it."

Pascal blinked pleasantly.

The man turned away, surveying his vines. "Domaine Champs-du-Puy. You have heard of it, I'm sure." He glanced at Pascal to check.

"*Bien sûr, monsieur.* A most noble wine." He had never heard of it but the man obviously was anxious about his label and needed a little stroke to his ego. A common ailment. Pascal straightened his back again and put his sunglasses in his shirt pocket. "Best of luck to you then."

"Wait," Naudé said suddenly. He stepped closer as if he suddenly meant business. His voice lowered to a growl. "I know what you're about. You must know that I will have that vineyard, that miserable piece of *terroir.*" He gestured toward the neglected vines. "You will not outbid me. I will have it." His tone was threatening, a tactic Pascal found comical. Also his breath was not particularly fresh. "Do not test me, monsieur. You will regret it."

Pascal raised his eyebrows in mock surprise. "This vineyard? Those sad, old vines? I have no interest in it, in *any* vineyard. I like to drink wine but I am but a simple policeman."

Naudé looked Pascal up and down, as if his hard gaze from his superior height was intimidating. His lip curled. "Then I will never see you again on this road, or in Sainte-Colette. That is *my* village. Go home. I will have that vineyard." He walked toward the door of his car, still open, and drove away.

Pascal slipped back behind the wheel of his car. The Mercedes shot gravel and veered around him, driving off in an angry cloud of dust. Pascal turned the key in the ignition and smiled to himself.

"We shall see, *monsieur.* We shall see."

HARRIS AUSTIN WATCHED the two men from the top of the rise. He was out walking before dinner, carrying binoculars to look for an owl he thought he'd heard a few days before. The vines on this side of the hill were crap, just crap, and he rarely ventured farther than the two cypress trees on top of the rise. Did owls nest in cypress? He had no idea but planned to look it up as soon as he got back to his computer.

He lowered the binoculars from his eyes. He'd glassed the two men standing by their vehicles for ten minutes. One he knew, only too well. The other man with the green sedan was someone new. From around here? He had no idea. Even after three years he could count on one hand the people he called friends. He knew shopkeepers and plumbers and the woman at the bank but they were just passing acquaintances. There were a few friendly ex-pats. He figured most of the French in the countryside had seen too many Brits come and go to invest the time into making a new friend.

And he understood that. His people were everywhere, buying up country houses and townhouses, renovating barns into lodgings, doing what he and Ernest had done— buying a small vineyard or leasehold to work the land, get some sun on those fair English cheeks, escape the Small Island for somewhere calmer, sunnier, prettier.

Land prices had increased, thanks to his countrymen and other immigrants. Everyone loved France. Strains on utilities, aquifers, community services, and transportation were common. Yet the French people accepted them, he and Ernest, more or less as they were. They spent their money locally, as was appreciated. If anyone disliked his and Ernest's lifestyle they were too polite to say so.

And yet there was always one. He supposed there is one abrasive person in every neighborhood. In their case it was their neighbor across the road, Luc Naudé. The dust from his Mercedes was still settling as he tore away, leaving the stranger to bat the air. He was such a— no, Harris told himself. He would not let Naudé get under his skin. He wondered what Naudé and that other man had talked about, if it was their vineyard. What did two men who met in such a clandestine manner talk about? Maybe the other man was someone Naudé had hired to look at the vines. An œnologue like the one they'd considered using when they first arrived. Or a property agent perhaps. Or a random criminal Naudé was hiring for more dirty work.

Naudé had been friendly at the start, when they'd first arrived, to a fault. Helpful and very welcoming. He sent his two young sons over to assist them with furniture and rugs, and his wife, Harmonie, baked them tarts now and then. It was everything Harris had dreamed of in a French country community, helping hands, trading vegetables and pies, waving to each other, offering advice when they could.

Ernest had helped them with their harvest the first year, delighting in a real French *vendange*, accepting nothing but a delicious dinner with the other neighbors in return. Harris himself had been ill. He often was, unfortunately, having a delicate disposition. Nothing fatal, he kept telling people, as you could see in their eyes the wonder. Just a summer cold. But it kept him from mixing with the neighbors that year. He wasn't much help in the farmhand department anyway. And as it turned out that was the end of the Friendly Times.

In the spring of the second year the little things began, tools stolen, vandalism in the form of spray paint across the old barn (which might never wash off and had yet to be painted over), the cold, brusque passings in town. The woman at the bank expressed surprise that they were still in the area. She was just going to call about closing their accounts, a comment that Harris thought he must have misinterpreted. But he heard it again, from the man who rented out the harvesting tractors. That they would soon be gone, he said. "You sell, *oui*?"

Harris set him straight, angrily. Who was spreading these rumors?

There was, of course, one suspect. Luc Naudé upped his game that summer. In late August he began the charm offensive, all fake smiles and invitations to tea. It was soon clear he wanted to buy their vineyard, to add on to his property. He had tried to buy it before they did, he explained, but the timing was wrong. Meaning, Harris guessed, he didn't have the cash on hand, or his offer had been rejected. Naudé wheedled the purchase price out of Ernest, making Harris furious. In many places what you pay for property isn't a state secret. Here perhaps, it was.

Harris told his partner to stay away from Naudé, to walk in the other direction or if confronted to simply tip his hat and move on. "Do not speak to him. Do not even look at him." There was something unnatural about the way Naudé coveted their property, as if without it he would wither and die. Which was ridiculous. The man owned five times as many hectares, across the road and another vineyard near the river. He was rich, far richer than Harris and Ernest would ever be.

Now, after three years here, there was a stalemate of sorts. No interaction with the Naudé clan had kept things under wraps over the winter. Harris held his breath, waiting for some new development, a sabotage of the vineyard, a suspicious fire, anything that might scare them off, or so Naudé would assume. He obviously wanted the land at a steep discount, a foreclosure or something terrible that would bring the price down. Maybe his tidy vineyard across the road wasn't as prosperous as it looked. Maybe he should spend more time on his own business and keep his nose out of theirs.

The man in the green car drove away, at a normal speed. He paused at their driveway, took note of the name inscribed in the wrought iron gate, and drove on. Maybe he too coveted their vineyard. Although why anyone would was beyond Harris's comprehension. If only these people could see his account books. A scary prospect, that.

He sighed. As he turned to walk back to the house he heard the flapping sound and froze. He craned his neck to look up at the sky and there she was, a magnificent *hibou,* a long-eared owl, her head adorned with huge feathery tufts like ears. She flapped her wings and soared over the barn, toward the fields and vineyards to the north, out of sight.

Harris felt a shiver down his spine, cool and enervating. In the distance the owl, or maybe its mate, hooted. Was the land trying to tell him something? That he was welcome here? That he belonged.

He shivered again and wrapped his arms around himself. He was home.

Ten

Luc Naudé pulled over and put his Mercedes into park, just before turning the last corner to his home. Although his vineyard backed up to that road where he'd been chatting so nicely with that *connard* of a Frenchman, his actual home was a mile away, on a beautifully treed lane with a view of the valley. His grandfather had built the small château as a country house after making his fortune in sardines in Bordeaux. His progeny were all businessmen like he was. They had just swapped tinned fish for bottled grape juice or souvenir shops or bistros, or in the case of Luc's father, a little bit of anything that lost money.

He pulled out his mobile and punched in the property agent's number. "Gaspard? What are you doing? Right now."

Gaspard Bain, a young and hungry type, gave an amused chuckle. "Walking home. And you?" He lived in Sarlat, over in the Dordogne, and while hungry for sales he seemed to spend an inordinate amount of time eating and drinking and walking around.

"Never mind that. What are you doing about the search on the property adjacent to mine, Château des Corbeaux?"

"It is on the agenda. For tomorrow, if you wish."

"You've done nothing?" Naudé growled.

"You didn't say it was a priority. Just that you were curious."

"I am more than curious, I am voraciously curious."

Gaspard could be heard speaking to someone on the street. "About what? Give me something to work on."

"Problems with the deed. Anything to prove the owners do not have full title."

"Ah. That will have been worked out when they acquired it, *non?*"

Naudé slammed his palm against the steering wheel. "Something must have been missed. Find it." He ended the call and threw his phone on the passenger seat. "*Imbecile.*"

Just thinking the word '*imbecile*' made his vision go dark. His own father had said that to him constantly, beating him down, telling him how stupid he was, how clueless. Well, he'd shown the old man. He was much more successful than that charlatan. Always trying some new trick on customers, some magical product, some *poudre de perlimpinpin.* Luc hadn't stooped to those depths although he wasn't far different from his father. He understood—and hated— that truth.

Still, his obsession with his neighbor's vineyard fell right in line with sticking it to the old man. His father would hate that ugly little vineyard, just as he did. But the old man could never afford to buy land. He knew old Boissieu, the former owner, and often called him a fool. But who was really the fool? His father had to rent out the family château his own parents had built. He was pathetic in his greed and incompetence, a blight and an embarrassment.

Showing up his father was always Luc's fallback position. If the future seemed cloudy, uncertain, or fraught with peril, there was always his hatred of his father. That was a constant, an ever-flowing river in his soul.

A rich vein he would milk for his purpose.

Eleven

PÂQUIERS

Pascal's little cottage looked forlorn. The grass was knee-high in the yard, the hinges on the shutters sagged, and the lawn chairs in the back, under the apple trees, had blown over and wedged themselves against the fence. Pascal took a hard look at his house and sighed. It needed care that he had not been providing.

The drive over from Malcouziac with Merle had been pleasant. He liked to drive, that was true, the faster the better. He steered through the winding turns, making her grasp the dashboard and laugh. They hadn't discussed much. He hadn't told her of his search the previous day, or the crazy feeling he got at the abandoned vineyard. He'd barely slept the night before, thinking about the possibilities there. A quick property search before bed had led him to the owners' names, two British nationals who had bought the property together three years before. That was all he knew but it filled him with an uneasy excitement. He tried not to pin his hopes on it but failed.

Merle gave him questioning looks in the morning. She had placed a hand on his shoulder as he rolled about the bed in the night, trying to calm him down. But she didn't ask him what was bothering him, making him restless. She must have made some guesses. He loved her for her forbearance. Many women would not tolerate a long period of anxious silence without explanation.

He attacked the tall grass with a machete while Merle swept the house and shook out the rugs. It was not particularly satisfying, doing a chore a medieval peasant could have done much better, like he was a character in a Van Gogh painting. But the income from the holiday rentals was necessary, especially now that Merle was looking for a new apartment in Bordeaux for them. All were too expensive, she said. Even with his promotion and the extra income it provided, living in the city was harder to afford than he had expected. His colleagues in the Cité du Vin building all had lived in Bordeaux for decades. They resided comfortably in the family townhouse, or commuted in from the farm or vineyard held by their relatives for centuries. If only Pascal had such relatives, he mused. Peasant, yes, he was.

After the picnic lunch Merle had packed for them was eaten, she walked the mile or so into the village to speak to the woman she had arranged to do the laundry and cleaning after each renter left the cottage. Pascal sat on the steps to his small porch and picked at the peeling paint. He really should give his cottage a little more care. But the thought didn't thrill him. Instead he went inside and stretched out on the bed for a nap.

The knocking woke him a half hour later. He blinked open his eyes, heard it again, and forced himself upright. It must be his neighbor, Irene, who raised goats and made cheese. Was there some emergency? In the living room he saw the doorknob was being rattled and went immediately on guard. Maybe Irene was in trouble.

He saw the small red Renault first. Then the two people on the porch came into focus against the backdrop of the sunny yard. A young couple, with backpacks. They startled and stepped away when he opened the door. The car turned around, the driver giving a wave. Pascal recognized the woman who ran the small produce stand in the village and wondered why she was delivering these people to his doorstep.

"Bonjour. Do you need help?" he asked in French.

The woman, blond and smudged with road grime, glanced at the man. Neither was more than twenty-five.

"Do you speak English," the young man said in English. He too looked road-worn, his curly brown hair dusty and wild, his pants filthy. Pascal nodded. "We— we rented this cottage for the week."

Pascal frowned. "This week?"

The man straightened. "Are you just leaving? We must be next in line."

"I am the owner. I'm not sure we have your arrangements." Pascal looked down the road for Merle. She was down the hill but close. "My partner makes the rentals. Wait here and she comes."

The woman leaned against the porch post and said something. The man asked, "Could she get a glass of water?"

"Of course," Pascal said. He fetched a glass of water from the kitchen and when he returned the couple were in the parlor, sitting in the armchairs, backpacks off, as if they were staying. He hadn't asked them to come inside. Plus they were quite filthy. Pascal handed the woman the water glass.

"Your names?" "Ivan and Lexi," the man said. His accent was difficult to place.

Merle waved as she skipped the last few yards up to the porch. Pascal stepped outside. "There is a couple here. They say they have rented this week."

Merle blinked, frowning. "This week? Our first booking is for next week."

"Well, come inside and we will work this out."

After introductions were made where neither Ivan nor Lexi rose from their chairs, apparently too tired from their journey, Merle asked, "When and where did you make the booking?" she asked.

Ivan said, "Online. Months ago."

"What is your full name, the one you booked under?"

This went on for ten or fifteen minutes. Merle asking for information, looking up the booking app, searching for 'Ivan Bristol,' and finding nothing. They had no credit card receipt or a printout. Nothing to prove they actually had paid. He paid in cash, he asserted. Then he changed his story to bitcoin.

"Where are you from, Ivan Bristol," Pascal asked pointedly.

"Norway. Way up north in the reindeer lands."

A reindeer farmer? That was a first. "How long have you been traveling?"

Ivan glanced at Lexi and spoke in Norwegian presumably. She replied and Ivan relayed the message: "For seven months. We spent the winter in North Africa. Morocco, Algiers, Egypt. Tramping around, loads of fun."

"Nice," Merle said. "I don't find any booking for you though. I'm sorry."

"We can stay though? We can even sleep here in these chairs."

"No," Pascal said sternly. "That is not possible."

Neither of the travelers got up to go. Ivan scratched his dirty hair. "We've been walking many miles. No baths, no water, as you can see. We will stay just one night."

"Where did you sleep last night?" Merle asked.

"In a cow shed about thirty miles from here. Then that nice woman gave us a ride from the village. Such a lovely kind woman. Gave us an apple too. All the people here are kind." He gave them a goofy smile.

"Because you told her you had rented my house?" Pascal asked. Ivan shrugged. He no longer pretended to be a paid renter which made Pascal even angrier. A blatant freeloader with no respect for property. "Who told you about this house?"

"My friend stayed here last summer. He said it was unlocked. I didn't believe him."

"So you were planning on breaking into my house? Staying here without a rental or any permission at all? Like a common criminal?"

Ivan jumped to his feet, fists ready. "What did you call me? You bourgeois—" Pascal stepped behind him, grabbing him in a bear hug as his feet kicked out. Pascal turned him sideways like a battering ram to avoid being kicked in the shins. Lexi grabbed her backpack.

Pascal walked through the door and dropped Ivan off the porch. Merle handed Pascal his backpack and escorted Lexi out of the house. Pascal threw the backpack to him.

"Don't come back, Ivan— or whatever your name is. I work for the *Police Nationale* and I can have you arrested for trespassing or worse."

"*Au revoir*, Lexi," Merle called as the girl broke into a run. Ivan scrambled to his feet. They watched the two of them scamper down the hill then Merle asked: "What the hell was that?"

He put an arm around her shoulders. "I think, blackbird, we must step up our security here."

LATE THAT AFTERNOON, after a trip to a hardware store on the outskirts of Toulouse to investigate home security, Merle and Pascal took a bottle of wine over to Irene Fayette, their neighbor. Merle had helped Irene when she was laid up after knee surgery, cuddling newborn kids in her goat sheds. It was a tough job but somebody had to do it, Merle always said when she recounted the story of her love affair with small goats.

Irene was not as agile as in her youth but still fiercely independent. Her hair was white but her dark eyes sparkled. She ran the goat farm with the occasional help from her daughter. Louise was now in graduate school, studying microbiology or germs or something, Irene didn't really know for sure. She was very proud of her though.

The man who lived there, Irene's cousin Jacques, was still tottering around the farm, keeping an eye on the helpers. The staff had grown to five. It was lovely to see both of them again, and looking so chipper. And a trip out to the pasture to see the frisky little kids was mandatory and heartwarming.

They shared the wine, sitting in wooden chairs on the lawn under the remains of the pink flowers of a cherry tree. They made small talk, in the French way, filling in the pieces of their lives.

"We had some visitors," Pascal said. "Backpackers, maybe from Norway. Have you seen anyone like that around?"

"Tramps," Irene spat. "If I am in a good mood, I let them sleep in the barn."

"Do you?" Pascal said. "These two seemed to be breaking in. They were surprised we were there."

"Did you run them off?" Jacques asked.

"Oh, yes. But they said someone told them the house was unlocked. So there may be more. Just a warning."

"*Mon dieu.*" Irene frowned and sipped her wine.

"Do you want me to check on the place?" Jacques asked. "The walk isn't far."

"Jacques, you are nearly eighty-five. Don't make promises," Irene scolded him.

"Yes," Pascal said, "remember your adventure in the cheese van."

"He almost died but for eating all the *fromage*."

Merle set down her glass on a rickety wooden table. "It wouldn't be often. We're booked through most of the summer. Anouk from the *boulangerie*? I hired her to clean and change linens between groups. It won't be empty more than three or four weeks."

Jacques wouldn't listen to a suggestion he wasn't fit enough for a few walks down the lane. It was decided that wouldn't be burdensome, and Irene could fill in if he was indisposed. She claimed her knee was as good as ever. "Also, we have the new van. We can take a little drive, or stop in on the way to the village."

"If you see anyone, see the lights on when it is meant to be empty, do not go inside," Pascal directed them. "I mean it. Call the *gendarmes*."

Jacques's eyebrows jumped. Merle promised to call Irene with the dates. Pascal explained about the new security cameras so if anyone broke in, or stole the television or whatever, they had a record of who it was. Irene claimed it wasn't necessary. They were nearby. Jacques reminded them he owned an old shotgun. Irene rolled her eyes. No confrontations, Pascal repeated sternly.

"Irene has herself a new machine," Jacques announced. "A computer. Louise set it up for her so they can write back and forth, and even talk like a video phone."

"FaceTime," Irene said, eyes wide. "Have you heard of it?"

Merle smiled. "I talk to my son in the States that way."

Irene, it appeared, also had email. She spelled out her address for Merle to put into her mobile phone then Merle and Pascal walked back to his cottage.

"What if," he said as they shut the door behind them, "we stay here tonight? Make sure the cameras are working. Get some dinner in that funny little café we passed. It's only a ten minute drive from here."

"For you?" Merle smiled. "Five minutes tops."

Twelve

PÂQUIERS

Everything seemed to be working properly in the morning, the cameras mounted above both front and back doors, the grass beaten into submission, the sheets changed. The sun was up early and the birds were celebrating. Summer had arrived. Merle gathered up the dirty sheets and put them in a laundry basket, stashing it in the back seat. Pascal locked all the doors and shutters.

In the village they stopped at the boulangerie for sustenance and a last word with Anouk. While Pascal was picking out quiche, Merle went to the back where Anouk was making bread. Even a small village went through a vast quantity of bread every day in France. Anouk wiped her damp forehead. "*Bonjour, madame.*"

"*Bonjour.* Where should I put these?" Merle asked, indicating the laundry basket.

"This way." Anouk opened a door to an enclosed porch with a washing machine. "Right there is fine."

Next to the washer were two more baskets of what appeared to be white sheets and towels, the sort used everywhere in rentals and hotels.

"Do you take in laundry for other people?" Merle asked. "I don't want to be a burden."

"It's not a problem. I do two other *gîtes* as well. Didn't I tell you?

49

They are right over there." Anouk pointed across the backyard to a side street where two identical cottages sat nestled together.

"Who owns those?"

"The old mayor's widow. She used to do everything herself, cleaning, dealing with renters, all of it. But she's nearly ninety. I think she will sell soon."

Merle opened the screen door and peered around it at the cottages. They were tiny but adorable, stone walls painted a pale pink with white trim, more in the English style than the French stucco and tile. Small flower beds in front were tidy, bursting with spring color. "Has she had any trouble with burglars, or guests arriving without a reservation?"

"I haven't heard about any," Anouk said.

"We had a pair of backpackers yesterday," Merle said as they walked back through the kitchen. "We put up security cameras, just in case. Out in the country, anything could happen."

Anouk promised to keep an eye out for tramps. Pascal was eating a small quiche at a tiny round table, cramming the last bites in his mouth. He handed her a pastry bag, warm and fragrant. Merle looked inside and saw an eclair and another small quiche.

"I couldn't wait, blackbird. It smells so good," he said, and laughed.

"Turn here. A little diversion," Merle said in the car as Pascal pulled out into the traffic lane. She had gobbled up her *petit déjeuner* as well. She pointed off the main street to a side alley to the right. "Something I want to look at."

He parked the car on a grassy verge. The side streets of the village weren't paved with asphalt, still dirt and gravel with encroaching weeds. "What is it?"

"Those two cottages." They reminded Merle of tiny houses in the US, impossibly small places, a hip and ecological if cramped way of life. In most villages in southwest of France, like Malcouziac, you would find medieval townhouses, stacked close together, each two or three stories, inside the old *bastide* walls. Here the low-slung buildings, some barns or sheds, were newer but still old. Up close the cottages looked very small, maybe just two rooms arranged front to back. Did they even have indoor plumbing? Or kitchen facilities?

There were no other vehicles on the street, no renters, no locals. The paint that appeared to be pale pink from afar she could see was peeling off the stone walls, showing an old rose color underneath a thin dash of white. It gave the places a sad, derelict look. The front porches were unpainted wood, maybe once white, barely wide enough for a chair. One of them sagged badly at the far corner. Merle got out, hesitating to go closer but wanting to peer inside. The shutters were latched across the two windows on each facade, and lace curtains covered the door windows.

"Do not go creeping around, my love," Pascal called. "It is not only Jacques who has a shotgun."

Merle sighed, defeated in getting a look inside. But she was not deterred. The cottages seemed to call to her, made her want to take care of them, spiff them up and show them off. How cute they could be, with pots of flowers on the porches, new paint, all the little touches that would bring them back to life. What a great thing for the village, reviving the little stone shacks.

Back inside the car she buckled her seatbelt again. "They're adorable, aren't they?"

"Eh?" Pascal smiled at her like she was slightly insane. "Like a puppy? Sure. And just as much trouble."

Pâquiers was a small medieval burg of less than a thousand inhabitants. She knew from the interest in renting Pascal's cottage that there was a solid tourist trade here. A tall bell tower stood near the church. You could hear the bells at Irene's goat farm. A pretty market square and a fountain in the middle, similar to Malcouziac. It didn't sit high on a hill but was surrounded by fields and pastures and vineyards. The bastide walls had either been taken down or never existed, letting the village grow naturally outward. It hadn't grown far.

She really didn't need a new project. She was busy with life in the Dordogne, in Bordeaux, with Pascal. But those little cottages. She sighed, and tried to forget them.

Thirteen

❧

MALCOUZIAC

When Merle and Pascal returned home, the market in the *place* was winding up. Merle ran off to buy some vegetables and maybe a chicken for dinner then spent the next two hours cooking dinner. She was very intent on her cuisine, Pascal noticed. Was that her normal manner? He looked in the kitchen from time to time and she was focused, a serious look on her face as she rubbed the chicken with lemon and herbs.

Pascal booted up his laptop on the small desk by the window. The view was bleak there, just a blank wall and dirt. He should plant something, he thought, wisteria or a rose bush. But he was no gardener and there was little sunshine on that side. He went back to his computer, catching up on email and reports until dinner.

Since the evening was mild with a fingernail moon high in the sky, they ate outside at the green metal table. The chicken was delicious. Pascal licked his fingers like a thug then laughed at himself. Merle seemed happy but quiet. Was it the apartment search that was getting her down? He had to ask.

"A little," she answered. "There are so few in the price range."

"Let me do it then. I will ask at the office," he said.

"Okay, that could help." She sipped her wine and smiled over the glass at him.

"Tomorrow." He set down his fork, wiped his mouth, and sat back in his chair. "Something else I should tell you."

She raised her eyebrows, concern in her eyes. "What?"

"It is not serious, *chérie*. Do not worry."

"Well, what is it?"

He wagged his head. "I have been thinking about something." Saying it out loud would make it real. His heart rate jumped. "About buying a vineyard." Her eyes widened. "Just a little one. Obviously, that's all I can afford."

She blinked. "But you always said you would hate to be a farmer."

"A small vineyard is manageable. I hope." He shrugged.

"But why? Are you unhappy at your new job?" She placed her hand over his. "I wondered. When you spoke about the apartment."

"I love the countryside, out where the action is. I am not a natural administrator."

"I could have told you that." She smiled at him. "You didn't get some negative feedback from Étienne, did you?"

"No, nothing like that. This is coming from here." He tapped his chest, over his heart. "I can't seem to stop thinking about it. Dreaming, really, like a schoolboy. Fabrice, remember him? He helped me scout out a few that are for sale."

"Did you find any promising ones?"

"Oh, plenty. But they are *coûteux*—too expensive. In the millions, most of them. Three, seven, or more."

"You'll find something."

"It meets with your approval? I will forget it, if I can, if you think it is a pipe dream."

She smiled. "Do you think it's a pipe dream?"

"I may be smoking something, that is true. But I am trying to be clearheaded about this. Not get in over my head, over my meager abilities. To afford something, to be able to manage the winemaking as well."

"Have you found anything?"

He stared at her, the abandoned vineyard swimming in his mind, morphing from dead branches and weeds to tidy rows with clusters of grapes in his mind's eye. "Maybe."

"Tell me about it." She leaned in, excited.

"No, no. It is too early for that. It is not even for sale. I will explain if it gets into the realm of possibility."

"Don't get your hopes up?"

"*Exactement.*"

MERLE WENT TO BED EARLY. Pascal sat at the laptop again, not working now but searching for vineyards for sale. Now that he had the tentative go-ahead from Merle he began in earnest, searching different areas in the Bordeaux AOC, then beyond, in the Dordogne and the Lot. He made notes on a few that were in his price range. One was on the far side of the Lot, to the east, a fair distance. Another, nearby, was at the high end of his range and small, unlikely to ever pay off.

After an hour it occurred to him that the only ones listed on these fancy property sites were ones with huge châteaux, built for the rich foreigner wanting to play at being a vintner. People with lots of money to burn. This was not his situation, at all. He wanted an arrangement where there was a possibility of a profit within a few years. Not right away, that was unrealistic, but not too far into the future. He couldn't sustain pouring money down the wine drain. It would all end in ruin that way.

He stared at a photograph of a turreted château with eight bedrooms, two guesthouses, and a swimming pool on a website. This was the wrong direction. He had to find another way to get into the vigneron trade, one that would work for him.

Would it be by buying a portion of a vineyard? By trading for services? By finding a bankrupt vineyard somewhere? The one in Sainte-Foy was back in his mind. How to find out more about their situation, their financial circumstances, the wine they produced? He made notes for the next day. He knew their names, Austin and Brooks. Tomorrow, he would investigate. With his access to winery records, it wouldn't be difficult.

· · ·

MERLE AND PASCAL said goodbye in the morning. She claimed to have some work to do in Malcouziac although he was sure she just liked it better there. He didn't blame her. Their little flat was depressing. He would try to work a miracle today and find a new place. A small place would do again, if it was on the ground floor and had a little garden for Merle. He thought that would make her happy.

He had suggested over coffee that she plant him something to look at out the side window, by the wall. "If anything will grow there, I'm sure you will find it," he said. The mission seemed to cheer her and they separated on happy terms.

At the spur of the moment, on the road to Bergerac, Pascal deviated from his usual route to drive by the Sainte-Foy vineyard. It was cheering to see it was at most a half hour's drive from Malcouziac on the back roads. Why had he never explored this region? Well, he was making up for lost time.

It was barely eight when he drove slowly down the side road that backed up to the abandoned vineyard. It looked sad in the slanted morning light, the vines twisted and broken. He parked, got out and took a few photos from different directions. He took one of that blowhard's vineyard as well, for comparison. He grabbed a handful of dirt from the edge of the derelict plot. It was dry but crumbly, not too rocky, not too rich. He smelled it, and caught a hint of limestone. He stashed the handful in his jacket pocket.

Back in the car he drove around the vineyard to the front gate. The house itself was not terribly grand but serviceable: two stories with rooms under the eaves on the third, a mansard roof that had pleasing curves, a patch of grass under a twisted olive tree, pots of herbs and lavender by the medieval door with wrought iron hinges. He clicked a few more photos, drove down the road to see what he could see of the working part of the vineyard.

As he got out to take a few more snaps on his phone, a man appeared from behind a barn. He was a large man, broad-shouldered, wearing a coverall and a straw hat. And headed straight for him.

"Hey. *Hé. Vous.* What are you doing?" The man had a menacing demeanor. Pascal thought he should just get in the car and leave. But instead he pocketed his phone and waved at the man.

"Bonjour, monsieur." He stepped up to the fence and put a casual boot on the lowest rail. The man spoke to him in French but badly accented. The owners were British, he remembered, so Pascal switched to English. And slipped out his wallet from his back pocket. "How are you this morning?"

"What do you want? Why are you taking pictures?" The man said in English.

Pascal held up his wallet with the police ID. "My name is Pascal d'Onscon. I am with the wine fraud division, attached to the *Police Nationale.*" He always left a beat there for this information to sink in. The man rearranged his arms to be a little less threatening. "And you are the owner here? At— what is the name— Château des Corbeaux?"

"That's right." The man relaxed a little more. "Ernest Brooks. Owner."

"I'm just doing a little scouting around." Pascal smiled. "That's what we do. Keep an eye out for fraud. For rule breaking."

Monsieur Brooks nodded warily. "We follow all the rules. No fraud here. My partner is a real stickler for regulations."

"I am glad to hear it. And you have heard of any of your neighbors who do not?"

Brooks shook his head. "We don't know many of the neighbors. We've only been here three years."

"So, not very friendly, are they?"

The Brit shrugged. "We're busy."

"I'm sure." Pascal wanted to probe about their harvest, their bottling, how they mixed, but knew he could get all that at the office. Still, he couldn't stop himself for asking about the abandoned plot. "Is that your land over the hill? The vines not being worked?"

"It is. We haven't had the cash to replant the vines but we're hoping to soon." He glanced away then back at Pascal. "That's not a crime, is it? To leave the vines to themselves, to go wild?"

"A bit sad but it happens." So they were a bit strapped for funds. This was promising. He pulled out a business card and held it out for the owner. "If you hear of any fraud, even a whiff of it, please call me. *Bonne journée.*"

Fourteen

BORDEAUX

Tourists were lined up at the museum side of Cité du Vin, the sculptural monstrosity in Bordeaux where Pascal had his office. The building was a modern marvel of aluminum, punctured and swirled to delight the eye. Pascal thought it was extravagant and even boastful but he wasn't a fan of modern architecture in general. Give him an old stone pile any day. But he had stopped registering his dislike of the building after a year working here.

He nodded to a clerk in the front office who clattered away on a computer, barely glancing up. None of the agents or administrators here had secretaries so the clerk, one lone young man, an efficient Algerian, was overworked with the minutiae of bureaucracy. Pascal knew better than to even speak to him when he was busy like this, which was his constant mode.

But he still had to make some inquiries about apartments. So he headed to the coffee room and made himself an espresso, the first step in any knotty problem. There was a message board there, littered with business cards, handwritten notes, and the occasional lost dog. He stood in front of it, sipping the steaming coffee, trying to find something recent about housing. Many postings were a year old.

While he lifted notes to read behind them one of his colleagues entered and started up the espresso machine. Pascal turned to see Michel Évrard who had started the office here in Bordeaux. He was well-known in the wine community, with a stellar reputation of integrity, not something to be sneezed at in the wine trade. Pascal and he didn't work in the same division but were friendly. Pascal told him good morning. "I was wondering, Michel. Do you have a recommendation for a property agent here in Bordeaux? I am having trouble finding a decent apartment for me and my partner."

Michel, a trim man of sixty with distinguished gray hair, sipped his coffee. "Where are you now? Not still in that hotel where they dump everyone, I hope."

"We found a flat last fall but it is not satisfactory. My partner doesn't like to join me in Bordeaux. Not good for relations."

"*Bien sûr.* Let me send you the name of my agent. See if she can find you something." He paused. "I will talk to her first. Tell her it is a priority."

Pascal downed his espresso. With that task on its way to completion, he returned to his office and began to search for information at Château des Corbeaux, the Castle of Ravens. Now that he translated the name in his mind excitement jolted him. *'Merle'* meant blackbird in French. A blackbird was very similar to a raven, yes?

It had to be a sign.

Fifteen minutes later the clerk, Josef, arrived at his doorway holding a sheaf of papers. Very thin with black hair and eyes so dark you could never see his pupils, Josef was indispensable around here. But Pascal hadn't dived too deep into the files about wineries in Sainte-Foy yet. "Yes?"

"These faxes came in for you from Paris. A few days ago." The clerk set the stack on the corner of his desk and backed away. Was he suggesting Pascal should come into the office more frequently? *Pfft.*

"*Télécopies?* Are we still using faxes?"

"Old habits, monsieur."

With a sigh Pascal pulled over the pile. The top sheet was from Étienne Cazal, his boss in Paris, to the entire wine fraud division.

About some rule change, some nuance of the law that had been decided in the courts and to which they must now pay attention. Pascal flipped it over.

Next was the actual proceedings of the court where the case was decided. As the sub-director for the Southwest France, Pascal knew he must review the decision and the changes implied. The case involved a well-known Burgundy vintner who was taken to court by the division, and the Police, for using illegal labor who then somehow were blamed for the poor quality of his wine. A full investigation determined he had secretly shipped in grapes from another vineyard and tried to blame the migrant workers. Even though it was a purchase inside the AOC and not a violation of those rules, there were other regulations that the vintner had circumvented. The business with the migrants complicated things.

Although Pascal had heard about the case, he hadn't read the particulars. He counted the sheets: forty or more. He sighed, leaned back in his office chair, and began to read.

When his phone rang an hour later he was relieved for the break. His eyes stung from reading the faint type on the slick fax paper. Old habits: ridiculous.

"*Bonjour, monsieur.* Carine Barrault, here. Michel Évrard, your colleague, I believe? He asked me to call you to see if I can help you with your needs."

Madame Barrault sounded competent to Pascal but his experience with property agents was limited. She had a Parisian accent. The one Merle used last summer had found them a sublet that turned into a crime scene. He didn't want to use her again. He told Carine— she was friendly for a Parisian, and they were soon on a first name basis— what he and Merle were looking for, their price range, and location. He wanted two bedrooms so he could work from home if he needed to. And somewhere close to the old town for Merle, and on a lower level. A garden would be ideal. He was sure she would say it was impossible, that what he wanted didn't exist. That he was mad, insane. But she paid close attention, asked a few questions and assured him all would work out to his satisfaction.

He hung up, wondering if Michel had bribed her. His requirements didn't seem out of line but he had doubts that Carine could simply snap her fingers and make the perfect flat appear.

Well, let her astonish him. He was ready for some housing magic.

HE WORKED LATE THAT NIGHT, finishing reading and making notes about the court decision and how it would affect field agents, drafting a memo to the agents, responding to email and other correspondence, talking to Paris. He had no companion for dinner so he ordered some takeaway at L'Exploit on the quai on the way back to the awful little apartment. Carine Barrault had not called him back.

In the morning though there was a message from her on the office telephone line. He had forgotten to give her his mobile number. He called her back when he had made himself the required espresso.

Her voice was smoky and warm. "I have three apartments that might work for you. Shall I send the information to you?" He gave her his email address, and his mobile number. "Call me and I will set up appointments."

Quickly scanning the listings she sent, none looked terrible. Can you tell without an actual visit? He didn't really want to slog around Bordeaux, poking his head into smelly apartments. He had work to do. So he forwarded the whole email to Merle and told her to check them out, see if anything looked promising. And of course asked how her day was going. She answered that everything was fine and she had found a flowering vine for his view. He sent her *bisous.*

Josef appeared in the doorway. He gave Pascal a level stare. "Your meeting, monsieur. Conference room two." He looked at his wristwatch. "Ten minutes ago."

Fifteen

MALCOUZIAC

Merle sighed and closed her laptop. All three apartments in the email from Pascal were expensive and two were out in the suburbs. The only one close in to the *vieux ville,* the old town, was twice what they were currently paying in rent. What would she tell Pascal? That the pricey one looked great? And make him pay that much? It seemed wrong. Was there any point in looking at any of these?

She pulled on her gardening gloves and picked up the clematis vine she'd bought for the area outside Pascal's window. A lovely purple flower, the Violet Star — *Étoile Violette*— she couldn't resist. She'd had a huge clematis back in the US and felt an immediate attachment to this straggly little vine.

The narrow space between her cottage and the wall that separated her garden from the neighbors' was gloomy and mossy but there was sun at the top of the seven-foot wall. Surely by midsummer it got a little sunshine. Gardening—hope in a spade.

In three days Francie and Dylan would be here. She was excited to see her sister again and get to know Dylan a little better. She stripped the upstairs beds and threw the sheets in the laundry. The sad little twin beds needed something to freshen them up. She grabbed her purse and headed out to see what sort of quilts she could find in the village.

More hope in a spade, or maybe a chamber pot. But you never knew what surprises this little town had in store.

DYLAN HARDY SAT in the elegant restaurant, one his favorites in Paris and usually reserved for client dinners, watching his girlfriend pick at her food. He'd splurged tonight because she seemed so depressed. Good food always cheered her up. But not tonight. This wasn't like Francie. She had a good appetite normally, and loved everything he cooked for her. Maybe this dish was a little too rich or something.

He set down his fork and sat back in the leather booth. "Something wrong with it?"

Francie startled, lost in her thoughts. "Ah. No, it's a lovely dish. I guess I'm not that hungry."

She'd called him a few days earlier about getting a doctor's appointment. She didn't explain really, just said she needed a check-up. But why not wait until she was back in the States? She insisted and he'd found her a doctor recommended by the law firm. He didn't like to pry into her affairs, her health, her feelings. He hated those kind of people. They weren't married, or even living together. But something was off.

"Did you make an appointment with that clinic?"

She nodded. "Next week."

"We'll be in the Dordogne next week, won't we?"

She rolled her eyes, annoyed. "I forgot."

"Call them back. Tell them you need to get in this week."

Francie promised. She leaned over her plate again as if making a concentrated effort to eat her dinner. The waiter came by and refilled Dylan's wine glass with the Bordeaux he'd ordered. The waiter hovered the bottle over Francie's glass. It was still full. Dylan shook his head at the waiter who scurried away.

"Did you get the train tickets?" he asked.

She nodded, eyes still on her plate.

"Is Merle going to pick us up in Bergerac like before?" Another nod.

"What would you like to do in the Dordogne? Do they have any plans for us?"

Francie smiled then. "Do you want to go sightseeing?"

He chuckled. "Not particularly. But what's that fancy town near Malcouziac that everybody talks about? The one built into the cliff. Famous for its goat cheese."

"Um. Rocamodour?"

"That one. Let's check it out. Plan a day of it. Go full *turista*."

Francie blinked at him. "Okay. Sounds fun."

Her voice betrayed her. Where was her usual enthusiasm? Her get-up-and-go?

"And maybe those châteaus on the river? I looked them up. Wait." He pulled out his mobile phone. "Beynac and Castlenaud-du-Chapelle. They're close together. You love old castles, don't you?" He waited for her response then said, "A different day, of course. We need to pace ourselves."

"So you do want to go sightseeing," she said, her eyes flashing with a little of her usual spark. "Do I know you?"

Dylan reached out his hand and took hers, feeling a sudden rush of emotion. This was Francie, who had come back to him after so many lonely years. Beautiful, vivacious Francie who could have had any man in law school, student or faculty. Who had been jerked around by that asshole pilot she married. Who had rejected legions of admirers over the years, to find her way back into him.

He squeezed her hand. It was cold and almost brittle. His heart clenched. What was wrong? "Yes, my love. You do."

Sixteen

BORDEAUX

It was nearly six when Pascal called Carine Barrault. None of the three apartments were suitable. Two were far into the suburbs, and the third was wildly over their budget. He reiterated what he could pay, what he requested in size and location, again.

"I will look again," Carine purred, unfazed by the rejection of her first round of choices.

"There must be something for us."

"I will dig deeper."

"And find a gem, I hope," Pascal replied, letting a touch of a threat into his voice. He didn't like to threaten people but some simply didn't perform unless the possibility of going elsewhere hung in the air. "Michel says you're the best, Carine." He paused. "Perhaps you can also help with another property search. I am on the hunt for a vineyard property. Again, it must be a low price for I am—" as he kept saying— "a simple public servant." Well, it was true. He took no money under the table to look the other way, like some of his colleagues.

"How exciting," Carine said brightly.

"Well, not really. I have been looking for almost a month and can't find anything in the Bordeaux AOC that is not in the millions."

"It is the most prized region, is it not?"

"Also very large and diverse. I am sure there is something I can afford, somewhere. If not in Bordeaux then perhaps the Lot. Or the Dordogne."

A clacking of computer keys over the phone, then Carine replied, "I am not really that sort of a property agent. But I have a colleague. I will send you his information."

"Thank you, madame. And please, find me a decent apartment. For my mental health."

"And your relationship, *non? À bientôt.*"

And my relationship, oui. He called Merle back to tell her not to worry, that the agent is back on the hunt. She didn't answer so he left her a message. Carine would probably have helped him find a winery if he'd said he could pay top dollar, if he was a baron of industry or royalty.

He checked his email. She'd sent the name and address of a property agent who specialized in vineyards and was located in Sarlat. Thankfully not some pretentious person from Bordeaux or Toulouse who he would have to tolerate as they crisscrossed the region together. Sarlat, near Malcouziac, was much more civilized.

Pascal added the new agent's information to his phone contacts and shut down his office for the evening. He needed to get outside, take a walk, something. The *bureau* was suffocating sometimes. That meeting in the morning that lasted for hours, for instance. It was enough to make a Frenchman turn to drink.

By no coincidence he found himself along the quai again, across the bridge at a tapas bar, with a wine glass in hand and pizza ordered. The sun was setting over the city, turning the water of the wide Garonne orange. He sat away from the crowd, with the sun in his face, sunglasses shading his eyes. The sun was warm, nurturing, stripping away all the hours spent uselessly inside, battling the culture of paperwork and endless meetings. The light made him remember the sunset by the abandoned vineyard that day, the way the rays played down the rows of broken stakes and tangled wires.

He would call this new agent tomorrow and ask about the vineyard. Château des Corbeaux. It was a beautiful name. But could he make a beautiful deal for it?

He had no idea.

THE NEXT DAY was another horror show of bureaucracy. Pascal grit his teeth and went from meeting to meeting, email to email, report to report. He didn't hear from Carine Barrault. He had a notion to ask Michel about her. But give her a few days, he told himself. *Patience.*

He was back in the smelly little flat about eight o'clock, scrolling through his phone, when he remembered the agent in Sarlat. Was it too late to call?

The vineyard agent didn't answer. Probably sitting down to dinner. Pascal had good memories of Sarlat. Why didn't he and Merle go there more often? Because he was stuck here in Bordeaux. He left Gaspard Bain a message, explained who he was and who had recommended him.

Pascal forced himself to use the moldy shower stall. He was saving water, he told himself, taking the shortest possible bathing time. He hadn't told Merle how much he despised this *salle de bain.* With any luck they'd be out of here by the end of the month. Then he realized that was only ten days away. Not much chance of a quick departure.

Toweled and changed, he checked his phone. Gaspard Bain had called back. Pascal quickly returned the call.

"Ah, Monsieur d'Onscon. I am so pleased that you have entrusted me with your search for a wine property." Gaspard sounded young but had a deep, confident voice. Pascal decided to like him.

"I am pleased that you are in Sarlat. I live in Malcouziac, not far away."

"Ah, such a sweet village. Still some renovation opportunities there for the right buyer?"

"I'm sure. But I am interested in a vineyard. A small one, with potential. You have any such properties in your listings?"

"In what area? That is the key item," Gaspard said.

"Bordeaux, for now. In particular the Sainte-Foy AOC."

Gaspard hummed. "Not many properties for sale, I'm afraid. Let me check."

Pascal waited while he clicked on his computer, sipped something liquid, and gave a sigh. "It's scarce there at the moment. One massive vineyard, some two-hundred hectares with a château. Seven million?"

"I need to be under one million."

"Ah, any other areas?"

Pascal had already done his homework on Sainte-Foy. He knew that wineries were usually inherited by family members. "I saw a property in my travels. You know I am with the wine fraud division?"

"So you said."

"I drive the backroads as part of my job. I saw an abandoned vineyard. Part of a small winery called Château des Corbeaux. It is near the village of Sainte-Colette."

Gaspard made no comment. Pascal waited, thinking he was using his computer again but there was silence on the line. Finally he prompted: "Monsieur?"

"Oh, *pardon*. I know the vineyard. I'm afraid it is not for sale."

"You have made inquiries there?"

"Last year for another buyer." Gaspard lowered his voice to a rough whisper. "It is not for sale, monsieur. I assure you. The owners are quite dug in."

Pascal remembered the conversation with the neighboring vintner, Naudé. He'd done a little background work on his label, Domaine Champs-du-Puy. They had low output for such a large property, perhaps they were doing something wrong over there. The tidy rows could be deceiving. The wine he produced was not highly rated. But he must be the other buyer looking at Corbeaux. He said as much.

"I see. Is there an offer outstanding for it? From a neighboring vintner perhaps?"

Gaspard gathered himself, put a smile back in his voice. "Can we widen the search, monsieur? Entre-deux-Mers or a southern region like Saint-Macaire?"

"Of course," Pascal replied, mimicking the agent's sunny temperament although certain now that this man was working for Naudé. "Why don't you do some research and send me a list? Can I give you my email address?"

Pascal doubted he'd hear from Gaspard Bain again. What luck, getting the same vineyard agent that Naudé used. But there weren't a huge number of experts in the field. It was like the market in private islands.

He poured himself a half glass of the Crus Artisan he loved. He was trying to ration it, it was so good. Then he called Merle. She was already in bed. He checked the time and saw it was after ten.

"Pardon, *chérie*. I am calling so late."

"I wasn't asleep. What are you doing?"

"Getting over my office job." He sipped wine. "The best way I know. A little wine."

"I wish you were here. I could help you unwind."

Pascal groaned. "Don't even start. I am so lonely." He looked around the tiny apartment. "And this cracker box is even more depressing when you are not here."

"Did you get any more prospects from Carine?"

"Radio silence. We will have to find a different agent, or do it ourselves."

Merle sighed. "Give her a chance. It's only been one day."

"Blackbird, I have to say, I do not want to live in the city. Unless she comes up with something out of this world, I am ready to chuck Bordeaux. That is the word— chuck?"

She laughed. "Yup, that's the word."

"So, I should tell you about that vineyard I had my eye on."

"Yes, please," she said.

"Well, it is in the Sainte-Foy AOC. Very close to us. Called Château des Corbeaux. That means ravens."

"Oh, lovely. And you've seen it."

"I have. But I just heard it is definitely not for sale. In fact it is set to be acquired by a neighbor who lives across the road."

"That's disappointing."

Pascal rubbed his forehead, feeling the finality of the quest. It was hard to let it go, but he must. "*Dommage*. But let's discuss it no more. It is fruitless."

"Oh, Pascal. Something else will turn up. Hey, speaking of real estate, those two little cottages in Pâquiers got listed today."

"*Quoi?*"

"Remember those two little houses, side by side?"

"You are serious?"

"I'm not serious about buying them. Not yet. But guess what they're asking. Twenty-thousand Euros for both of them."

"*Pfft*. How bad must they be?"

"No indoor plumbing? No heat? I'm hoping Francie will go see them with me. You never know until you go inside, right? Are you coming back for the weekend? Dylan will be here too."

He promised her he would return. It was good of her to try to change the subject, distract him from his disappointment. The vision of the wrecked vineyard, waiting for rejuvenation, sprang into his mind but he wiped it away with a silent '*non*.' It was not for sale. He must try and forget it.

Thankfully he had the wonderful Merle. She would distract him with her kindness and affection. He should focus on the good things, right? She had given him so much. He rubbed his forehead again and sighed.

So many gifts. Including somewhere to live besides this stinking cracker box.

Seventeen

DORDOGNE

At noon on Friday Merle stood at the railway station in Bergerac, as the train from Bordeaux pulled to a stop. She spied Dylan first, his tall frame was hard to miss. How random that they had run into him, Francie's old flame from law school, in Paris two years before. It was one of those 'what ifs' that could have gone completely differently. He carried two large suitcases that he dropped on the pavement. Then he guided Francie down the steps.

Merle held out her arms. "*Bonjour! Bienvenus.*" She gave them each hugs and grabbed the handle on a suitcase. "This way. Oh, but you know." She glanced at her sister who had been quiet so far, barely saying 'hello.' Francie wore her red trench coat, rumpled and drooping from her slumped shoulders. Her hair was messy but she had all her makeup on at least. "How was your trip?"

Francie didn't reply, walking purposefully as she concentrated on her footing. Dylan straightened and said, "Can't beat French trains."

The drive back to Malcouziac was strange. Francie, usually so talkative, was silent. But maybe she was just tired. Merle reached over the seat and patted her hand where she sat in the back. "So good to have you here."

"Lovely to be here, Merle. As always," Francie said.

"Thanks so much for having us," Dylan added.

"Is there anything you'd like to do while you're here?" Merle asked.

"Dylan wants to go sightseeing," Francie said, a familiar edge to her voice. "He's wild to go to Rocamodour."

"That would be fun," Merle said, thinking she'd just let them have the car. She'd been there before. "Or a cave maybe?"

"A prehistoric cave? With cave paintings? That would great," Dylan said, glancing at Francie. She was now reclining sideways on her tote bag, eyes closed. He turned to Merle, his face somber and worried. "But maybe a little strenuous. It's been a busy spring."

At the house in Malcouziac, the cottage Merle had named *Maison Chanceuse*, the Lucky House, as it had been the giver of so many good things, Francie went upstairs to take a nap. Dylan hauled the bags upstairs and unpacked their things into the armoire.

Merle made herself a little lunch. Neither of her visitors was interested in food, they said, having snacked on the train. She took her goat cheese salad into the garden and sat in the sunshine. And began to seriously worry.

Francie looked terrible. She was pale, almost ghostly white. Dylan looked fine, he always looked fine, but seemed nervous, flitting around her, trying to make her comfortable. What was going on? Merle would have to wait until Francie had rested.

After Pascal arrived, around six, while Merle was cooking a special welcome dinner of lamb chops and white asparagus, things settled down for a minute.

"Why don't you take Dylan for a walk around the village?" Merle suggested to Pascal, sticking her head out the back door. They were talking, drinking wine in the garden. Francie was helping Merle in the tiny kitchen.

Pascal frowned at her but she nodded enthusiastically. He got the message. "Stretch the legs, Dylan?" He stood up. "Maybe the sunset will be happening," he added.

Dylan shrugged, set down his wine glass, and they left through the garden gate. Merle went back to tending the dinner. She picked up her glass of rosé. "Glass of wine?" she asked her sister.

Francie shook her head. "Makes me even more tired."

Merle turned off the burners on the stove and turned to face her sister. "Let's go outside." She pulled Francie out the door and pushed her into a green chair. "Now. What's going on?"

Francie sighed dramatically and pushed her hair behind her ears. "Well. I saw the doctor."

"And?"

"You were right." Francie looked her with round, blue eyes. "Pregnant."

Merle sprang up with a cry and hugged her. "Oh my god, that's amazing." She sat down again, put off by her sister not hugging back. "Or is it?"

"I'm also anemic. I started iron pills and vitamins today. No magic recovery yet."

"But— how far along are you?"

"Two and half months, maybe three." Francie shrugged, staring at the blue sky. "Is this the way you're supposed to feel? Dead tired, no enthusiasm for anything?"

"At least you don't have morning sickness. Or do you?"

"Spared that one."

Merle leaned closer and took both her hands. "It will be all right. The pills will start to work and you'll feel better." Francie's eyes welled up with tears. She bit her trembling lip. "It's okay, honey," Merle whispered. "We'll all be there for you."

Francie cried for a minute then wiped her face. "I cry a lot."

"Hormones are a bitch," Merle said. She couldn't believe her wildly successful, independent sister was going to be a mother. It would change everything for Francie, her career, her life, her— "What does Dylan say?"

"He doesn't know yet."

Merle sat back. "You just found out?"

"Yesterday. A quick visit at a walk-in clinic. Long enough to pee in a cup, get prodded and poked, and get the results." Francie frowned. "I'll tell him. Soon."

"Does he know about the tired thing?"

Francie nodded. "I think he's worried I've got a terminal illness. I should tell him, shouldn't I?"

"Ah, yes. He is the father, right?"

"No question."

Merle sighed, relieved at least that was certain. "Are you worried about his reaction?"

"We never talked about kids, Merle. Ever. Except his daughter, Phoebe. Not a kid of our own. We never even talked about getting married. Or really anything future-wise."

"You don't have to get married."

"I realize that. But having a baby puts everything back on the table." Francie's eyebrows pinched together. "We were just bopping along through life, happy as clams to see each other once in a while. Happy to jet off to Paris. What if he doesn't want another kid? I'll be a single mom. I'm no spring chicken. I don't know if I—" She started to sob.

Merle went inside for tissues. Francie mopped her face, her streaming mascara. Merle squatted next to Francie and hugged her again. "We'll figure it out. Be strong, honey. You aren't alone."

Later, in the kitchen, Francie whispered to Merle that she might tell Dylan at dinner. Merle told her that wasn't fair to Dylan. "Tell him in private, Francie. It's between the two of you."

Dinner went as well as could be expected under the strained circumstances. When Pascal and Merle went to bed, Pascal whispered, "What's going on with them?"

Merle pulled him under the covers. "She's pregnant," she whispered. "And she hasn't told him yet."

"Oh." Pascal rolled onto his back and stared at the ceiling. "Is that all."

"She doesn't know how he'll react. She's worried."

"Because she is so old?"

"That's not as big a deal as it used to be."

"She is so white. Like a ghost. Is she always so *blanche*?"

"She's anemic— you know, not enough red blood cells. She's taking iron. She'll get her color back."

They were quiet then, listening through the door as Francie and Dylan talked softly in the loft bedroom. There was little privacy in the loft but at least there were no other guests. Merle had pushed the twin beds together for them. It was all she could do.

There were no squeals of delight, no sobs of despair, from the other room. A sigh, a squeak of bedsprings, that was it. Whatever they were discussing, or doing, was their own business. Pascal flicked off the bedside light and rolled toward Merle.

"Are we happy for her?"

"Oh, yes, Pascal," Merle whispered. "We are very, very happy."

Eighteen

MALCOUZIAC

On Saturday Pascal proposed a trip to Sarlat the next day, all four of them. Merle was surprised but pleased. She loved Pascal's little jaunts, with fast driving and good food. Francie and Dylan agreed, putting off their Rocamodour trip for another day. They had dinner at home again. Pascal and Dylan were in charge this time.

"How are you feeling?" Merle whispered to her sister as they did the dishes. Pascal had taken Dylan somewhere for a nightcap. "Better?"

"A little. I think the pills are helping. And all that delicious beef for dinner can't have hurt. I ate a lot of it, didn't I?"

Merle glanced at Francie. "You didn't—"

"No. He was so sweet last night, I didn't want to spoil the mood." She shrugged at Merle's frown. "There's no rush, is there? You didn't tell Annie or Elise or Stasia, did you?"

"Just Pascal. He won't say anything." She dried her hands. "You're really worried he won't like it, aren't you?"

Francie sighed. "Terrified. He is crazy busy between Paris and New York. Plus he spends most of his free time with Phoebe and his ex already. How will this affect them?"

"I imagine Phoebe will be over the moon. The ex, not so much."

"I think Phoebe likes being the only child. She gets all Daddy's attention now."

Merle held her sister's shoulders. "These things have a way of working themselves out. Don't worry about something that might never be a problem."

Francie sighed and leaned her forehead on Merle's shoulder. "I hardly slept last night. I'm going to bed."

AFTER A LEISURELY BREAKFAST the next morning they headed to Sarlat for lunch and a bit of shopping and walking around. The old city was much like Malcouziac, pedestrian only, but much bigger and fancier. It was not a long drive the way Pascal drove and they were settled at a bistro table in the May sunshine by 11:30, a ghastly early time to a Frenchman but fine for everyone else.

The medieval village of Sarlat-la-Canéda, shortened to Sarlat, was full of tourists. Pascal remarked about the lineup of tour busses in the city parking lot. But as the summer had not quite begun and the day was not terribly warm, there were no crowds to battle. They visited the cathedral, the garden behind it, a medieval mansion made into a museum, and shopped for tablecloths, soaps, *foie gras*, and scarves. By four o'clock Merle declared herself done. She could have kept going but Francie looked wiped out.

"Shall we hit that grand estate outside of town?" Pascal asked, as they piled back in the BMW. "What's it called, Merle?"

She thumbed through her guidebook. "Château du Puymartin?" Francie had her eyes closed, leaning her head back on the seat. "Maybe just a drive by. Thank you for taking us to Sarlat, Pascal."

Dylan also thanked him then glanced at Francie and Merle in the back seat. He bit his lip. Then, ominously, his mobile phone rang. He spoke rapidly in French to someone on the other end then replaced the phone to a pocket.

"Sorry. That was the firm in Paris."

Pascal glanced at him. "Emergency?"

Merle leaned forward. "What is it?"

"One of the older partners took a fall at his country house. You know how they all go somewhere on a Sunday, back to the family home? Well, this fellow was supposed to be in a settlement meeting tomorrow. There aren't very many lawsuits in France but we have a big one going on."

Francie opened her eyes. "What's happening?"

"Paris. Dylan," Merle whispered.

Dylan turned in the seat. "Shouldn't take too long, a few days. I'm sorry, Francie. This always seems to happen. Something spoiling our vacations."

Francie blinked. "I'm sorry too."

"When must you go?" Pascal asked.

"Tonight, I'm afraid. I'll have to get up to speed on the case."

"Drive to Bordeaux with me then," Pascal said, clapping Dylan on the shoulder. "It'll be nice to have some company."

They stopped for an early supper at a country inn near Belvès. Nothing fancy but good onion soup, lovely bread, and an excellent cheese selection. Merle thought a cheese tray would cheer Francie but she turned a little green. No one noticed she barely ate. Except her sister.

By seven-thirty they were back in Malcouziac. The men packed in a flash, said their reluctant goodbyes, hugged, and disappeared down the highway. Merle locked the shutters, then the front door.

"Go to bed," Merle told her sister. "You look exhausted."

Francie slumped toward the stairs. With her hand on the rail, she squinted her eyes in anger. "Do you think he plans these things? Has someone call him? So he doesn't have to go on vacation? He never takes a proper holiday with me. Something always pops up. It's always work-work-work."

Francie stomped up the stairs. She rarely took a decent vacation either, Merle noted silently. Both she and Dylan were dedicated to their law careers. How would that change? Something would have to give.

SAINTE-FOY WAS close by and the sun had not yet set, as they were nearing the solstice. The light held in the sky for at least another hour.

Pascal turned off the main road. He glanced at Dylan. "Just a short side trip. A detour."

"Sure," Dylan said, checking his wristwatch. "My train is the last one, at ten-thirty."

"Plenty of time." Pascal took another turn, a little too fast as he hit the gravel. He did a movie-style spin-out, the back end of the car swerving, laughing as he steered the car back into control. "Whoa. Fun, eh?"

Dylan didn't answer, his hand tight on the dashboard, bracing himself. Pascal made himself slow down. He thought about apologizing but, really, no one was hurt.

"I have my eye on a vineyard over here," he explained to the American. "Nothing special. May not get a chance at it. But it sticks here." He pounded his chest. "In my craw. That is correct? The craw?"

"Sure," Dylan said again, absentmindedly agreeable. "Why won't you get it? Money?"

"Or lack of it. I am hoping for some financing from the seller but it is unlikely. Plus there is another suitor."

"Suitor? Oh, someone else wants it?"

"Someone rich. And determined."

Dylan looked out the side window at the lines of grapevines. "That's a bad combination."

In minutes they were on the dirt road behind the Naudé vineyard, next to the abandoned field. There was no one about that Pascal could see. He stopped the car and gazed at the ruined vineyard.

"Isn't it lovely?" Even his voice was dreamy. He was out of his mind.

"What?" Dylan asked. "Where?"

"Oh. The mess is obvious." Pascal pointed to the empty rows. "A few vines struggle on. But it could be something, right?"

Dylan squinted out the side window. "I guess."

Pascal swatted him playfully. "Use your imagination, man."

"This is the one you want to buy so badly?" Dylan looked incredulous.

"I can't afford some fancy place," Pascal said, pointing to the Naudé vines, "like that."

"Someone's coming," Dylan whispered.

Pascal looked down the dirt road. A man walked toward them, right down the middle. It wasn't Naudé, too short. Nor the Brit he'd spoken to, he was built like a bricklayer. This man was slender. He walked with a slight limp and wore a wide-brimmed straw hat.

"Let's take off. I don't really have time for a confrontation," Dylan urged.

"Why do you think it will be a confrontation? This is public property."

Pascal watched the man get closer then he got out of the car, leaving the door ajar. Dylan got out on the other side. The man paused as he took in both of them then veered toward Pascal.

"Just a little chat," Pascal told Dylan quietly.

"*Bonsoir*," the man called as he got closer.

"*Bonsoir, monsieur*," Pascal said, smiling. The man smiled back. He was forty or so, with freckled skin, bright roses in his cheeks. Thick glasses over pale gray eyes. He pulled the hat off his light brown hair.

In French the man said, "Can I help you? Are you having car trouble?"

"Oh, no. We're fine. Just out for a drive." Pascal paused. "Are you English?" he asked in the native language.

The man's eyes widened. "My accent is terrible, I know it." Pascal shook his extended hand. "Harris Austin, pleased to meet you. Do you live around here?"

"No. My name is Pascal d'Onscon. I have been by here a time or two in my travels."

Austin nodded warily. "I thought I recognized your car. You don't see many green ones."

Pascal patted his BMW. "She's a beauty, eh. A little road weary. This is Dylan Hardy. He's American. I'm taking him to the TGV in Bordeaux."

"Hello." Dylan raised a hand. "We should get going, Pascal. I can't miss the train."

"A moment, Dylan." Pascal turned back to Austin. "I'll be straight with you, Harris. May I call you Harris?" The man nodded, wary again. "I am looking for a vineyard property. I saw this sad side of your vineyard and thought it might be something I could help you rejuvenate.

Rebuild." He sighed dramatically. "But then I hear you are selling to Luc Naudé. Is that true?"

Austin pulled back his chin indignantly. "Absolutely not. We are not selling to anyone."

"But especially not to *them*?" Pascal gestured across the road. Harris said nothing, his lips clamped together in anger. "Are you contemplating selling any part of the property?"

"I told you: no."

"I understand. If you change your mind, could you call me?" Pascal fished a business card out of his wallet and scribbled his mobile number on the back. "I have a feeling we could do great things together. *Bonne soirée.*"

Pascal turned the car around and headed away from Château des Corbeaux. He wanted to go by the front again, review the outbuildings, the vines, the acreage, but held himself in check. The obsession was gripping him.

As they hit the highway again Dylan said, "You really want that property, don't you?"

"Sadly, yes. It is a bit irrational but I see such potential there. I am doomed for disappointment."

"You never know," Dylan said, surprisingly upbeat. "They may have money troubles. Or just want to unload that abandoned section that's obviously making them nothing."

"Or both," Pascal said, grinning. "I am holding out for both."

Nineteen

SAINTE-FOY AOC

Harris chased his hens back into their enclosure for the evening. It wasn't much of a task, they always complied, running like crazy except for a reddish one he called Rosie. She always wanted to beg first. This evening he gave her a little shove with his shoe and she squawked like he'd injured her.

This constant rumor that they were selling was really getting under his skin. He felt jumpy, angry, annoyed with each person who brought it up. Maybe because it appeared everyone thought they were failures. Was it such a widespread opinion? He hated that.

Who was this man in the green BMW anyway? His card was mostly blank, just his name and phone number. He didn't look like a fancy con man but you never could tell. They wear disguises, don't they.

Harris finished filling the feed trays for his girls and locked the gate. "Go to bed now," he called as he always did. He turned back to the house, the annoyance of the meeting on the road still with him. Maybe Ernest had bought more brandy. He needed a nip tonight.

In the kitchen he glanced at the sideboard. No brandy. They'd finished off the bottle two days ago and neither of them had been into the village to restock. He sighed. He didn't need to drink alcohol anyway. It wasn't good for you, was it? Yet the French seemed to think of it as medicinal.

Was there wine left from dinner? He poured a splash into a tumbler and settled himself to the books. He used to love the habit of entering figures, making them balance, getting a clean, true picture of their affairs at the vineyard. But the last year had made the chore less pleasant. He frowned as he added up the figures, subtracted them from their accounts. They had sold most of last year's wine already, underpricing it because they needed the cash flow. It would be months, nearly a year, before they would have more wine to sell. What would they live on? He checked the savings account, the money he'd brought over four years before. It was down to a few hundred Euros.

He stared out the window. The sun was setting, lighting the edges of everything with gold. It was an apt metaphor. The sun appeared to be setting on this crazy enterprise, this vineyard dream. Why had he thought they could make it work? They had so little expertise, a dysfunctional mixing shed, no barrels, too much overhead, things they had to hire out, things they couldn't do themselves.

Could they live on eggs and vegetables for a year? Not without paying the light bill. Or the harvesting help. And so many other expenses.

When Ernest came in the door, Harris had his head in his hands. He didn't look up, just listened to Ernest throw off his boots and scrape the chair on the floorboards. A quiet settled. Still Harris clutched his hair in silence.

"Is there a problem?" Ernest said with concern. "Are you ill?"

Harris took a deep breath and looked at him. "I've been looking at the accounts. It's pretty sickening."

Ernest rolled his eyes. "Oh, don't be so dramatic."

"The savings are almost gone. Last year's wine is down to four cases." He stared at his partner. "What will we live on?"

"Let me take a look," Ernest said, holding out a hand. Harris turned the account book so he could read it. "Where is the bottom line?"

Harris pointed across the table. "There. Bills outstanding: 36,400 Euros. Savings: 237 Euros. Unpaid invoices: 2,000 Euros."

Ernest frowned. "What's this— 'bills outstanding'?"

"That's what we owe people."

"*We* owe *them*?"

"That's how much we're in the hole."

"From what?"

"Mostly last year's harvest— the bottling, labels, co-op fees, distributors. If we did it all here on the property we wouldn't have all those costs. And we could sell the wine for more as *'mis en bouteille au château'* and use those Bordeaux corks you fancy. But we aren't going to start bottling any time soon."

"We've been through this," Ernest said. "The process we've set up is the most cost-effective."

"But it's gone tits up." Harris sighed and turned the accounts back around. "We're about to starve, Ernie. And that's the truth."

Ernest poured himself a little wine. He sat down again and pulled something from his pocket.

"This guy came by a few days ago, taking pictures. He said he was with the wine fraud division, looking for cheats, but I wonder. Maybe he's a property agent." Ernest set the card down on the table facing Harris.

"So what if he is? We aren't selling." Harris squinted at it. "Hold on." He plucked Pascal's card from his shirt pocket. "Same bloke. I just spoke to him out on the road. He wants to buy the back side, the ruined vineyard."

Ernest sat back. "That's interesting."

"I told him no, of course. He said he'd heard Luc Naudé was buying the whole property."

"That old canard. Always floating around, that rumor. That blowhard is more skint than he lets on. He'll never make us a proper offer. But selling just that back half is an idea."

"I don't like it. We should keep the property together. The old abbey, the history of the Benedictines— that's history, it's precious. It shouldn't be split up. And I don't want to ever sell to Naudé, after all he's done to us." Harris looked at Ernest.

"Are we selling to anyone? Are we done here? Are we going home with our tails between our legs? We need to discuss this, Harry."

Harris melted a bit at the sound of his childhood name. He held out his hand for Ernest, who squeezed it in his meaty grip. "We'll figure it out. Won't we?"

Twenty

MALCOUZIAC

Francie rose early on Monday morning, after her solid twelve hours of sleep. Merle still hated Mondays, after so many years in an office. She hid her head under the pillow until she was wide awake. She heard noises in the kitchen, pots and pans clanking. She got up quickly and ran downstairs.

Francie had made coffee in the American coffeemaker and was sitting in the garden in the sunshine in her flowered robe and flip flops, strawberry hair piled up on her head. Merle stood in the doorway, amazed. She grabbed a cup of coffee and joined her sister.

"You look better." Merle smiled over her mug. Francie's cheeks were pink and her lips were no longer a dull gray. Even her ears were rosy. "Much better."

"Must be those iron pills. Or maybe that steak the other day. Plus I slept like a rock." She tipped her face to the sunshine. "Can you get iron from the sun?"

"Vitamin D. Also good for you. Hey, let's go to the store and buy some liver today. Make a paté. I read that's the best source of iron."

"Sounds delightful," Francie said, snark back in her voice. "Sorry about last night. I was so tired, and then Dylan just flits off like it's no big deal."

"If you'd told him you were pregnant, maybe he wouldn't have gone."

"He thinks I've got some serious illness and he went anyway." Francie opened her eyes. "Actually I told him I was anemic and taking iron pills. And that it was nothing to worry about."

"There you go. You can't keep secrets from people and expect them to understand."

"What? I thought you were a mind-reader."

"I am, of course. But most men are not."

Francie drained her coffee cup. "What shall we do today? I feel like we need to do something. I have done almost nothing since I've been in France. Except Sarlat."

Merle smiled. "I do have a little project for us. Do you want to take a drive?"

AFTER SOME MARKETING, and making a calf's liver paté with onions and herbs and molding it into a terrine, the sisters packed a picnic lunch and headed south in Merle's beat-up Peugeot. Francie acted as if she'd never seen the car, remarking on its many dents and paint chips.

"It runs great. That's all I care about," Merle said.

"You're sure." Francie examined a hole in the upholstery. "So tell me about this adventure. Are you thinking of buying another house?"

"Two, in fact. As *gîtes*— tourist rentals. They're very close to Pascal's house. They're tiny and adorable, Francie. Wait until you see them. But first, check the map for Castelsarrasin. I think it's about halfway. We can have lunch there."

Francie unfolded the map in the guidebook. "I see it. Near Montauban."

After lunch in a grassy park along the Canal du Midi that cut through the picturesque town, followed by gaping at the ornate, gilded clock on the town hall and a short spurt of shopping because they *were* women, and they *were* in France, they kept driving south. By two they arrived in Pâquiers. Right on time for their appointment with the property agent.

Merle parked in the same spot as before, directly across the street from the two cottages. "Here we are."

Francie peered across at them, frowning. "Are you serious?"

"That's what Pascal said," Merle said, laughing. "You have to use your imagination."

"Whatever you say," Francie said, exiting the car. "But I may pass on going inside."

Merle looked at her phone for a message from the agent, who had not arrived yet. But fifteen minutes late was 'on time' in the countryside. Maybe even thirty.

Ten minutes later a very small, lime green Smart car rounded the corner from the main street and parked behind Merle. A hand came from the window, waving madly, followed by a sixtyish woman dressed in a tight pink skirt, an equally tight black blouse, and shiny black stiletto heels. Her silver hair was cut geometrically and she wore fuchsia lipstick and matching glasses. She skipped up to Francie, shaking her hand, then to Merle. "I am Thérèse Levett, your property agent. I speak English, do not concern yourself." She laughed merrily. "Which of you is Madame Bennett?"

Merle said, "I am Merle Bennett. This is my sister, Francie."

"So," Thérèse said, sobering, "What do you think of these little houses?"

"I'm not sure," Merle said. "I am intrigued though."

"I have not even been inside, or in the back garden," Thérèse admitted. She got out her phone. "I need to take some photos. Come, we explore together."

Francie remained by the hood of the car. Merle turned back: "Are you coming?"

"Give me a report."

Merle followed the agent through the overgrown grass on a narrow brick path to the cottage on the left. This one had the sagging porch and the wooden step also looked rotten. Thérèse paused, hitched up her skirt, and took a delicate step up to the porch itself. Merle followed her lead, stepping uncertainly on the weathered boards.

The agent found the right key. With some effort it turned in the lock and she pushed open the old door.

A rush of fetid air swept past them. The agent stepped back, hand over her nose. "*Mon dieu,*" she muttered, blinking hard. It took Merle another second to get the odor, but she got it. The smell of dead mice and rotten food.

Thérèse looked over her shoulder at Merle. "Wait? Or just move on?"

Merle stepped to the side of the door, allowing the smells to dissipate. "I can wait. Tell me about the houses."

Thérèse joined her by the window and read off her phone. "Two houses, as you see, sold together. Each has one bedroom and one bathroom."

"So there is plumbing? And it works?"

Thérèse frowned. "*Peut-etre.* It says from the 1950s. No condition given."

"And a kitchen?"

"A sink. That is *typique.* Most homes do not have a fitted kitchen unless they are very new."

Merle craned her neck to look inside, inured to the dissipating odor. She could see wood floors, plaster walls. A sitting area. The walls and ceiling looked solid but dirty. She moved to the other side of the front door and nudged it wider with her foot. A dining nook. Behind that was the mostly bare kitchen, also with wood floors. She wondered if they would clean up well.

"I guess I don't want to go inside," Merle said. "Maybe the other house is a little cleaner?"

They trooped over to the second cottage, a mirror image of the one on the left. This time when the door opened there was the smell of talcum powder and dusty roses. Much nicer. They stepped into the front room and found peeling chintz wallpaper on the walls. Someone had left two hardback chairs, lined up against the side wall. In the dining area a drop-leaf table was covered with dust.

"Ah, some treasures remain," Thérèse said. "Not mentioned by the owner."

"Did she live here?" Merle asked.

"I don't think so. Maybe her sister? I heard something like that."

The kitchen was stripped of everything but a sink on legs. Behind it a door led to the bath. An old claw foot tub sat by the back window. It was rusted but might be salvageable. The toilet, mirror, and sink were beyond repair.

Another door from the kitchen led to a room which must have been used as a bedroom. It was tiny. It reminded Merle of the bedroom in their awful flat in Bordeaux: cramped, dark, and gloomy. The small window was so filthy little light came in.

"Well." Merle rolled her eyes at Thérèse.

The agent pursed her lips. "Small, yes. But it is just a room for sleeping. Maybe two beds on top, how do you say?"

"Bunk beds?" Merle frowned.

Back on the street the agent and Merle chatted politely, shook hands, and promised to be in touch. In the Peugeot Francie raised her eyebrows in question. "What's the verdict?"

"Oh, you know," Merle said. "Tiny, nasty, and full of potential."

Francie nodded. "I looked at the backyard while you were inside. I think somebody's been camping back there."

Merle frowned. "Are they still there?"

"The tent is."

Merle turned off the car. "Come on." She got out and waited for Francie to follow. They walked through the tall grass on the south side. Garbage had escaped a tipped-over refuse can. They gave the area a wide berth and rounded a small, weathered outbuilding.

The grass in the back garden had been flattened or cut recently, making a clearing where a green tent was anchored. Next to it were two backpacks, leaning against each other. A fire ring contained blackened wood and ashes.

"Just backpackers, I bet," Francie said.

"Maybe those two Pascal scared off. But annoying. I'm going to tell the agent."

"Should we check on his house, since we're here?"

They drove out into the countryside to Pascal's place. The grass in the yard where he'd cut it down looked dry and sad, but the house appeared fine, the front door open and two young people sitting on the front steps near a late model car.

No reason for concern. All was calm and lovely and oh so French.

On the drive back Francie was quiet, staring out the side window. Merle tried to engage her in conversation but she didn't want to talk, that was evident. Finally, as they made the turn off the main road onto the narrow one that led to Malcouziac, Francie turned to her sister.

"I don't know how well things are going with Dylan, to be honest. He's not around much, always traveling. Dotes on his daughter and even his ex-wife. He's constantly doing little handyman jobs for her. And this thing where the firm says jump and he says 'how high?' It's really getting to me." She sighed. "I don't know if it's going to work out with him, Merle, I really don't. And if we have a baby, what does that mean?"

"It means you'll have a child, Francie. Your baby, your child. You can't predict what might happen. There is no point in worrying. There is no crystal ball."

"Obviously or I wouldn't be in this predicament. But—" Francie bit her lip. "Is that really what I want? To have a child. To be a mother. I've never really thought that much about it. I never imagined it would happen."

"You *do* want it— the baby?"

Francie sighed dramatically. "I do now. Yes. But everything feels so — unsettled. Can you just change your priorities overnight, in the blink of an eye? Your life, your career, the core of your being? It seems like I would have to change everything about myself. And then would I still be me?"

"Women do it everyday. You'll still be yourself. Having a child makes you a better person, honey, less selfish, less me-oriented. It's not necessary, of course, to be fulfilled or happy. Look at Annie. She's happy as a clam. But children give you perspective. Someone to live for. A reason to hope."

Francie didn't answer. Merle pulled into the parking lot outside the city walls and turned off the car. Francie unhooked her seat belt and stared out the windshield. Tears streamed down her cheeks.

Merle grasped her hand. "You can do this," she whispered.

Francie's eyes welled over. "I'm so scared, Merle. So, so scared."

Twenty-One

BORDEAUX

Pascal wasn't expecting to hear from the two Brits any time soon, so the call two days later on his mobile surprised him. He almost didn't answer. He was in another conference, his phone on vibrate. The number had no name attached.

His supervisor, Étienne Cazal, had come down from Paris to address the field agents and other bureaucrats. He droned on in a boring fashion, repeating items off the memo that Pascal had already sent round to everyone about the new procedures.

Pascal pulled his mobile up and stood. "*Pardon.*" He waved his phone in front of the group and spun to exit the room. "Pascal d'Onscon." He stood in the hallway near a map of the wine regions of France.

There was a pause, breathing. "Ah, monsieur. This is Harris Austin."

Pascal blinked. "Yes. *Bonjour.* Hello."

Harris began to haltingly tell him that he and his partner, Ernest, wanted to discuss his proposal. No promises, just discussion. They agreed to meet in neutral ground, the café near the market *place* in Sainte-Colette, on Friday afternoon. Pascal kept his voice even, trying not to show his excitement, but as he ended the call he punched the air with a fist. He was excited to tell Merle about this new twist. It just might happen.

The next two days of meetings and emails and office politics dragged on but finally Friday came. He left the office for lunch and sent a text to Josef that he could be reached by phone over the weekend if needed. As an administrator it was a rare event.

As he drove east out of Bordeaux, he ruminated on the fact that he was so often unnecessary to the running of his office. Yes, he had to write up memos for the agents, interpret laws and regulations, and settle disagreements. But he wasn't made for any of that. Étienne had cooked up this job for him, as a favor for helping him out of a jam last year. This vineyard opportunity, if it turned into an actual one, might soften the reality that he was not needed much any more.

Sainte-Colette fit somewhere between a provincial village and a market town. The café was a large one, the only one directly on the *place,* with a red awning and many round tables extending out onto the cobblestones. Harris Austin said they would meet at three but Pascal had skipped lunch, eager to leave Bordeaux, and was now early for the appointment. Conveniently, as a café, food was served here.

The day was warm and the tourist season was ramping up. Almost June now, he mused, wondering where the spring had gone. Down some office rat hole apparently, never to be recovered.

His empty plate whisked away and sipping his wine, Pascal saw the two men crossing the market square. They were an odd couple, one thin and short, the other burly and slightly taller. The farmer had the rolling gait of a brawler, his bald head whipping this way and that, as if looking for an enemy. He wore denims and a tropical shirt covered with palms and sunsets, like a tourist. Harris wore khakis and a short-sleeved white shirt, bland as if offsetting his partner's colorful attire.

Pascal rose as they saw him inside the café ropes and each raised a hand in greeting. At the table they shook hands and sat.

"Pardon, I had some lunch," Pascal said, flicking crumbs off the table.

"Was it good?" Harris asked. He had nicked himself shaving and had a scab on his chin.

"Perfectly." Pascal smiled and sat back. He could see they were nervous. He would let them set the agenda.

"*Verre du blanc?*" Harris asked his partner.

"Why not." Ernest looked like he could use a relaxer.

Soon they had their wine. They took a few sips then set the wine-glass away, toward the center of the table. Harris took a deep breath.

"What can you tell us about yourself, monsieur?" Ernest asked Pascal.

"Anything you'd like." He paused but they waited for more. "As I said, I work for the Republic, in wine fraud. For many years I was in the field, checking vineyards and vintners for irregularities, investigating them. Now I am in an office in Bordeaux. I live there and also with my partner in Malcouziac. Not far from here in the Dordogne."

"I've been there," Harris said, smiling. "A pretty village."

Ernest eyed Pascal. "So you are not a property agent?"

"No, monsieur. A simple public servant." Pascal leaned forward, forearms on the table. "I am eager to work on the land. As you do."

"Why?" Ernest again, sharp. "Were you a farmer once?"

"No but I love grapes, monsieur. On the vine, in the vats, in the mixer or the bottle. I have spent my life in the vineyards of France and I can't imagine another way to live."

"Where did you grow up?"

"Partly in Paris and some in the southwest. My father worked in Toulouse for some time but we had a little cottage in the Dordogne."

"Do you consider yourself a copper?" He sounded like he didn't like police.

"In the field, sure. I worked closely with the *Police Nationale* and the *gendarmerie.*"

"Ever get into trouble yourself?" Ernest continued as if he were doing a background check. He grimaced and rubbed his arm as if it pained him.

"Speeding. It is my downfall. I drive too fast." Pascal grinned, unrepentant.

"You wouldn't be alone in that," Ernest muttered.

Harris perked up. "What sort of arrangement did you have in mind? I know you're interested in the back section, the abandoned half."

"What happened there? Was it like that when you bought it?"

Ernest nodded. "Nothing there for years."

"And the rumor you are selling to Naudé? Just an ugly rumor?"

Ernest blinked at him. "Nothing to it."

Pascal folded his arms across his chest. "Perhaps you can tell me about your operation. How it works for you."

Harris and Ernest relaxed then, sharing anecdotes of their nearly three years on the vineyard, the outbuildings and their state of disrepair, the ruin of the abbey on the property. The chickens, the barn, the empty *cave*. They admitted they didn't have cash enough to blend and bottle themselves, using the local *cave coopérative*.

The facilities were there, it appeared to Pascal. There were at least three large outbuildings. The men simply didn't have the cash or know-how to set them up properly. He gently explained his experience in winemaking, mostly theoretical but he had deep knowledge of the inner workings of small and large holdings by vintners, all over southern France. He had traveled to hundreds of vineyards, walked their rows. He had seen the *caves* and barrel rooms of nearly 300 wineries.

"That doesn't make me an expert," Pascal smiled. "But it's the groundwork. The basics. A deep understanding of the *terroir*."

"But you would just be growing grapes for a few seasons," Ernest reminded him.

"I could help you set up your own operation. If that's what you want." Pascal looked between them. "Until my grapes are mature."

Harris shook his head. "We don't have the funds for that."

Ernest blinked at Harris. "He would be making an investment in the land. And maybe part of the outbuildings?"

"Of course." Harris smiled at Pascal, making him look about sixteen except for the hairline.

One in the bag, Pascal thought. But what about the brawler? It depended on the money, he reckoned.

"I know people in the business," Pascal said. "Many people. Œnologues, you know these people? Experts in the soils, the vines, the blends?"

"And who would pay for that?" Ernest demanded.

Pascal shrugged. "Everyone?" He paused. "Have you had an œnologue out to the vineyard to consult with you?"

Harris shook his head. "We've done some courses."

They needed help, that was clear. Finally they got down to the money. It seemed to Pascal as if they weren't committed to selling half their vineyard— not yet. But maybe, if the money was right, they would be soon. He asked them for a figure and they demurred, almost embarrassed to be discussing such crass matters as finances. He proposed his own figure. They stared at each other then at him. It didn't go badly, he guessed from their expressions. But they would need time to think.

And they all stood and shook hands again, friendlier this time. Pascal sat down again and finished his wine. The other two hadn't touched most of theirs. How could you be a vintner and leave wine on the table?

He looked across the *place* in the direction they'd gone. The two were talking as they walked, gesturing wildly. Were they angry? Shouting? Disagreeing? Maybe just excited about the prospect of working the vineyard with a Frenchman, a true man of the grape. Something anybody would jump at.

He smiled. Well, the right Frenchman of course.

Twenty-Two

SAINTE-COLETTE

The boy was eating an ice cream cone on the sidewalk outside the patisserie on Sainte- Colette's market square, watching people go into shops, walk dogs, hold hands with their children. He threw his overgrown brown hair back to keep it out of the ice cream which was seriously good. Cold and creamy. He loved ice cream.

His father had some banking to do in town while Rémy got his treat. School was over for the week. The half-day on Saturday had been cancelled again and Rémy Naudé was glad. He wasn't that interested in his studies. His father didn't seem to care. He never asked Rémy about tests or homework. That was his mother's job. When his father had offered to pick him up after school, Rémy jumped at the idea. He knew his father would give him some money for a treat while he finished his business.

The sun was warm, beating down on the cobblestones. Rémy, who had just turned twelve but everyone said was big for his age, moved across the *place* to find some shade. He planted himself on a curb near the old market arches and concentrated on finishing his ice cream before it all melted.

He was stuffing the remainder of the cone into his mouth when he saw them. The two neighbors, the British guys his father disliked, walked right by him. They were speaking English so he didn't know what they were saying. Rémy liked the big one named Ernest. He helped out at harvest a couple times. He spoke terrible French but he was nice.

Rémy stood up, watching the two men walk around the fountain and down the other side of the square. They hadn't seen him. They seemed excited about something, Ernest especially, waving his hands in the other guy's face. Rémy's father called them bad names at home, the kind of names that get you in trouble at school. It was curious, how angry his father seemed at them. Rémy's brother Jean-Luc and his friends laughed so hard at them, making awful jokes. To Rémy they seemed like any other men, just, you know, friendlier.

Rémy walked back to the patisserie just as his father turned into the square from a side street. He had his head down, hands in his pockets. Serious, as if something had happened at the bank. His father almost ran right into him. "Ah, there you are. Did you get a treat?"

Rémy nodded, wiping his sticky chin. "*La glace.* Chocolate."

His father frowned. "You've made a mess. Go back inside and clean up."

Before Rémy turned to go inside, he said, "I saw those neighbors. Ernest and the other one. They were here a minute ago."

His father waved him on. "Go on. Wash your face." Rémy disappeared back inside the shop.

Luc Naudé pulled out his mobile phone and checked for messages. Nothing. He leaned against the wall of the small shop, enjoying a moment's quiet in the sun. Across the *place* the collector who had inherited his father's art gallery waved at him. There was something a little sleazy about him. Luc didn't return the gesture. He turned away and immediately saw the man.

He recognized the stranger immediately, the same black jacket and curly hair, same Gallic nose, sunglasses, and athletic build. He rose from a table in the café, spoke to the server, put a bill on the tray and secured it with a rock. He hitched up his denims, pushed back his hair, and moved through the tables to the exit. When the sun hit him he paused, like a cat enjoying the warmth. Same scufffed moto boots. *Le bouffon—* such a loser— took a few steps across the cobblestones then caught Luc's eye.

Naudé didn't wait for him to approach. His blood boiled. What the hell was going on? Rémy had just told him that the two neighbors had been here. And now here is *le mec*, the guy he met on the road, examining the abandoned half of their vineyard. Luc knew they couldn't be discussing anything else.

"You." Luc put an arm out but the other man had already stopped, seeing him walk toward him. "What are you doing here?"

"Do I—" The man frowned, tipping his head. "Have we met?"

"You know perfectly well who I am. Luc Naudé. Domaine Champs-du-Puy."

"Ah, yes. We met on the road behind your vineyard."

Luc moved closer and lowered his voice in a menacing whisper. "I told you never to show your face in town."

The man twitched, his eyes darting. Still he looked calm, unfazed by Luc's temper. "This is the village you were referring to?"

"Of course, you imbecile. What have you been doing?" Luc turned in the direction Rémy pointed, where the two neighbors had disappeared. "Were you talking to them?"

"I don't know who or what you refer to, monsieur," the stranger said dismissively. "Now, if you will excuse me—"

Luc grabbed the man's arm at the bicep. It was more muscular than he expected. "I will not excuse you. You will tell me what you were doing with my neighbors. The owners of Château des Corbeaux."

The man very slowly pulled Luc's fingers one by one off his arm. His nostrils flared. He did not look pleased with the contact. But Naudé had several inches on him, if it came to that. Something inside Luc made him wish for that— the fight, the fists, the beating. He could feel the fire, *un taquet*, inside, ready to explode.

"*My* business, monsieur, is not your business." The man squared off, palms up, ready for whatever Luc had planned, as if he could read his mind, feel his fury. "It was so pleasant talking to you on this fine afternoon. *Bonne journée*."

The man, whose name Luc never got, took a step to his left and continued walking carefully backwards until he reached the fountain. Rémy stood on the opposite side of the crusty old thing, staring at his father and then at the stranger. He looked afraid. Luc shook himself then, taking a breath, and trying to calm the rage inside him. He was glad he hadn't made a scene in front of his son. But, *merde*. The nerve of that *con*. This was his town.

And that was *his* vineyard, or soon would be.

As soon as he got in the Mercedes, Naudé called the property agent in Sarlat again. He hadn't heard from Gaspard Bain for two weeks. What had the lazy *flaneur* been doing? He was supposed to find something on those two Brits, on their deal, the deed, the taxes, something. Anything to put their ownership in jeopardy. Luc started the auto and pulled out into traffic.

"*Ah, allo, Luc. Comment ça va?*" Gaspard was outside again.

"You have a report for me, I'm sure," Luc growled.

"A report?"

"I ask you for help, Gaspard. Are you not going to help me? Why do I pay you?" Rémy looked up in question from the passenger seat. Luc's wife didn't know he was paying Gaspard Bain for services not related to actually buying a vineyard. But Luc would subtract it from his fee, eventually, when he acquired Corbeaux. He shook his head at his son as if to say: *It's nothing.* Rémy turned back to his phone.

"Gaspard. You must find something for me. Today I saw the two owners talking to that *mec louche*, the one I found wandering around their vineyard. I know he's interested in it. I can smell it."

"This is Corbeaux you speak of?"

"You know it is." Luc rolled his eyes.

"Funny thing. I had another inquiry about that vineyard."

Luc felt a charge of fear. "From him? What was his name?"

"I remember it—Pascal d'Onscon. I have an excellent memory for names."

"What did he look like?" Luc demanded.

"We only spoke on the phone. He was in Bordeaux, I believe. One of my colleagues referred him. But I told him the vineyard was not for sale. So nothing to worry about. I will find him something else." Gaspard chuckled. "Although he did seem very keen on that vineyard."

Luc cursed under his breath. "Where does he work, did he tell you that?"

"For the government. Some agency that deals with wine."

Luc gulped another curse. He had cut more than a few corners at the vineyard and still it was barely making a profit. The last thing he needed was some wine detective snooping around. And right across the road? Disaster.

"Find out everything you can on him, will you? This is important, Gaspard. Call me tomorrow." He clicked his phone off.

Rémy stirred. "Everything okay?"

Luc strained to smile and clap his son on the knee. "All is well. Nothing to worry about. Nothing at all."

Twenty-Three

Pascal watched Naudé and his son climb into the silver Mercedes. They hadn't noticed, apparently, that Pascal was parked just four spaces to the south. Naudé was a loose cannon, a hot head. Pascal could still feel the tight grip on his arm. Naudé would have swung at him if his son hadn't appeared, Pascal was convinced.

Out of habit he got out his small notebook and wrote down a record of the encounter. Something told him it might be useful in the future.

The ebullient mood from the meeting with Ernest and Harris had evaporated. But as he headed toward Malcouziac, he put his mind back there. He imagined the barrel room, cleaned and restocked with wine in oak. He saw himself planting grapevines and pulling wire between stakes. He took a deep breath and tried to rein in his impatience. He wanted to start, to plan, to plant.

He found Merle and her sister sitting in the garden, wearing sundresses and drinking wine. At least Merle had rosé in her glass. Francie may have been drinking something orange and fruity. Orangina at her age? He remembered then the pregnancy thing. It must be true. He gave both women a hug and two cheek kisses. Then one on the mouth for his *copine.* She looked delicious in the low-cut red dress, the sun on her shoulders.

Merle dashed inside to pour him a glass of Pinot Noir. While she was gone he sat down at the metal table and smiled at Francie. She did glow a bit. "How was your week?"

"Relaxing. Fun. Slept a lot." She squinted at him. "Merle will tell you about her new project."

"Ah. Not another one."

Merle returned with the wine glass and set it in front of him. "You didn't tell him, did you?"

Francie shook her head. "Tell him about the invitation first."

Merle gave her secret smile. "We have been invited to a party."

Pascal sipped the wine. "It's about time, *n'est-pas?* The people in this village have finally wised up to our charms."

"It's not in the village," Merle said. "It's in Sainte-Foy-Bordeaux. Wait— is that where you—?" She raised her eyebrows.

"Possibly. Who is this invitation from?"

Merle sat forward. "Remember that woman, the ambassador who visited us last winter?"

"The friend of the sketchy French caterer. Very—what did you call her?"

"Hoity-toity. She said she would invite us to her summer soirée, and she did. She remembered, Pascal. I couldn't believe it."

Merle retrieved the engraved invitation from the cottage, running her hand over the lettering then handing it to him with reverence. "It's next week."

Pascal looked at her eager face, knowing they would have to attend this society event whether he liked it or not. He read the invitation.

You are cordially invited to attend
the annual summer soirée
and petit fête du vin
at Château Vianden
Gironde
the home of Mme Éloise Hugo, the honorable ambassador for France to
Great Britain, and the late M Guillaume Chauve
near Rabouchet

Summer formal attire

"'Summer formal attire.' What is that?" He threw the invitation on the table. A memory of a different rich woman in a château in Provence last summer flashed into his mind. Her smooth oiliness, her deceptions. He wanted to go to a fancy dress party to swan around with a bunch of snobs like he wanted another hole in his head.

"Linen suits. Flowery dresses," Francie said, obviously guessing.

"*Mon dieu.* You have been to summer parties in châteaux?"

"Well, no. But you must have something in the back of your closet, Pascal. What do you wear when you visit your boss in Paris?"

Pascal ran his hand down the front of his shirt. "Nothing more."

Merle said, "We could rent something. Or, you know, actually buy something."

"Rent a tux?" Francie asked. "Too formal. That's winter formal attire."

Merle sat back. "You don't want to go anyway, do you?" She looked at Pascal, the disappointment darkening her face.

He chastised himself, reached out, and squeezed her hand. "You want to go? Of course. So we go. But I am not buying—or renting— a linen suit."

Merle sprang up and hugged his neck. "Thank you," she whispered in his ear.

Francie said grandly, "It will no doubt be the party of the summer. The height of sophistication. Written up in gossip columns. Champagne will flow."

Merle laughed. "*Très chic.* That's us." She sat down again. "I wish you and Dylan could go with us. Do you think we can bring guests?"

"Ach," Pascal said. "You would have to call and ask and I am not doing that. The woman is frightening."

"You should have seen her, Francie," Merle said. "Standing here in the garden, with two burly bodyguards, in the dark, wearing a huge fur coat, high heeled suede boots, and fluffy fur hat— she looked like a bear."

"And her manner," Pascal said. "You know that phrase—She Who Must Be Obeyed?"

"Oh, yes," Francie muttered. "They call me that at the law firm sometimes."

They sipped drinks. Was Francie going back to work then? Pascal wondered how long she would stay in France. Merle told Pascal, "Dylan is coming tomorrow. For the weekend."

He glanced at Francie. "No big holiday then?"

She winced. "Nope."

"He's needed on the lawsuit," Merle said. "Broken leg?"

"Ah, yes. That old canard. The old man probably was sick of the law and ready for *les grandes vacances.*"

"I know I am," Francie grumbled.

"At least we'll see him for, what? Thirty-six hours?" Merle asked.

"Whoopee," Francie replied sourly. "Merle told you, right? About my— delicate condition?"

Pascal nodded. "Congratulations." He clinked his wine glass to her orange soda.

"Thanks." Francie grimaced. "I guess."

Merle looked sympathetic then told Pascal: "She hasn't told him yet."

"No? But Dylan is the papa?" Pascal asked. He would be thrilled to be a father. But Dylan? He didn't know the man well enough to say.

"He is." Francie sighed again. "I just don't know if it'll make him jump for joy."

"Because he already has Phoebe? But that doesn't mean he can't welcome another child." Pascal glanced at Francie. "And you? Do you jump for joy?"

"I don't know, Pascal," Francie said. "I can't make up my mind if I am serenely happy or scared out of my mind. Or just hormonal."

Pascal patted her hand. "That seems normal to me. But what do I know? Only that I am happy for you."

THE THREE OF them took off for Bergerac early the next morning to get some marketing done before they met Dylan's train. It arrived on time and soon they were headed back to Malcouziac, chatting madly in the car.

Not a word was said of Francie's situation but the prospect of the fancy dress soirée made up for it, an endless round of fashion talk, shoes, wraps, linen versus cotton, and so on. Pascal tried to tune it out but there was no way to have a second conversation in the car. They walked back from the city lot, carrying sacks of produce and pulling suitcases.

The weather smiled on them. Sunny, mild, with a shimmering blue sky and blushing roses opening on bushes, it was decided by all that this was the first day of summer.

"It has really arrived, with sunshine and everything warm and merry!" Merle laughed like a crazy woman as they skipped up the cobbles on Rue de Poitiers. In moments they were in the cottage, Merle and Pascal putting away groceries and Francie getting Dylan settled upstairs.

Pascal helped rinse the lettuce for salad. "They seem fine, eh?" he whispered, looking toward the ceiling.

"They do," Merle agreed.

"But you're worried?"

"A little. I don't know him that well."

In a few minutes Francie and Dylan came downstairs, holding hands. "We're going to take a walk around the village."

Merle smiled. "What a great idea. Get some lunch somewhere. There's that café—"

"I know it," Francie said, giving Pascal a wink. "Be back later."

Merle watched them go through to the front door and pass the window. "I wish I could, oh, I don't know—eavesdrop."

Pascal took her shoulders from behind. "It will be fine, blackbird.

She is a smart, beautiful woman who is having a man's child. No man is stupid enough to turn that away."

"Some men are incredibly stupid," Merle muttered.

"But not all, *chérie*?" He was kissing her neck.

She laughed her soft, tender chuckle. "Not all."

"What about the ones who take afternoon siestas with their lady friends?"

Merle nibbled his earlobe. "Geniuses."

Twenty-Four

BORDEAUX

On Sunday night Pascal drove back to Bordeaux, delivering Dylan to the TGV station again for his return to Paris. The weekend had been calm enough, no big distractions or emotional blow-ups, but Dylan wasn't saying very much. Francie, together with Dylan, had on Saturday night announced the pregnancy with some fanfare. They were to pretend ignorance— to save Dylan's feelings, Pascal assumed.

In the end it wasn't difficult to feign surprise and joy. Whether Dylan bought it or not, they didn't know. He was quiet the rest of the weekend, moody even. Not a great prospect for family life. Francie kept up a good front but it was obvious she was still concerned about their future together. Too many things to discuss to make any quick decisions, and too little time together.

Dylan surprised Pascal, somewhere near Saint-Émilion, by asking about the vineyard. "Did you make a deal?"

"We'll see. I had a serious meeting with the owners."

"How much does a vineyard like that cost? If you don't mind me asking."

"Good question. I would be buying just half the acreage, the bad half. And some use of the working buildings, the blending *cave*, the barrel room, and all that. But that side of the vineyard itself is fairly worthless at the moment, just dirt. It has no income and none expected for a few years at least. So—" He shrugged. "It's a guess."

"You have a figure though."

"*Oui.* I told them one."

"And can you pay it all, in cash?"

Another shrug. "We'll see." He glanced at Dylan. "You want to know the number? For ten hectares?" He told Dylan the figure he'd given Harris and Ernest.

Dylan's eyebrows jumped. "Not a small figure." He blew air out dramatically. "What if— what if I threw some money in?"

Pascal took his foot off the gas pedal for a moment. "Seriously?"

Dylan nodded. "I've been thinking about it all week. It's become like a shiny object just out of reach but one that would make me happy." He laughed. "Okay, that sounds weird."

"Not at all. That's the way the vineyard is to me. I am so attached to the idea it is crazy." Pascal hit the gas again. "You have cash lying around, itching to go to work?"

"Some. But it would be an investment. I can cash in some stocks."

Ah, Dylan owned stocks and bonds. He was ahead of Pascal then, who was simply socking his money away in safe places. He still had most of his inheritance from when his mother passed away. He'd been keeping that nest egg safe and dry. Ahead the Bordeaux skyline emerged from the purple twilight. "How much were you thinking?"

"Thirty percent of your investment maybe. I could go forty. I don't want to encroach on your management or anything. So definitely less than half. Very silent partner. But a little grape harvesting or something would be amazing. And of course just the shiny object will keep me going, knowing I own a piece of France." Dylan gave his shoulder a jab. "Just think about it. It's your thing. I won't be insulted if you don't want some New York lawyer as your partner."

Pascal grinned. "I am fond of New York lawyers."

Back in Bordeaux Pascal didn't hear from Harris and Ernest. He checked his phone relentlessly then wore himself out with nerves. The week dragged on, more meetings and emails. He went out into the field with a young agent, to introduce him to some of the vintners in the Medoc. They rarely had any problems with these elite wineries but it was good to have them on your side. They stopped in at a distributor for an impromptu inspection, just to let them know someone was watching. Then back to the city, the offices, and boredom.

On Thursday Merle sent him a text while he was in a meeting. It contained a link to a news article. He assumed it was something about the search for a new apartment, something he felt guilty about. Carine had apparently abandoned them to their moldy fate.

He waited until he was back in his office, then clicked on the link.

UNKNOWN PERSON FOUND DECEASED
IN BORDEAUX VINEYARD

His heart lurched. Not Harris or Ernest, please. But they wouldn't be 'unknown.' They were owners. He read on.

The Police Nationale announced today that the deceased person found in a Sainte-Foy vineyard was believed to be the victim of foul play. La Crim', the murder squad, has been called in from Paris to coordinate the investigation, according to spokesman Ignace Chasseur. The local gendarmerie will be helping to secure the area and taking tips from the citizenry.

The body of a man was found by the owner of the property near Sainte-Colette. Harris Austin of Château des Corbeaux was walking the property in the evening on Tuesday when he discovered the remains. No word was provided on how long the body may have rested there. No other details were released.

M. Austin did not speak to the press.

PASCAL CALLED Merle as soon as he'd read it three times. "What is this? Did you just hear?"

"Albert read it in the Bergerac newspaper." Merle sighed. "That is the vineyard you're interested in, isn't it?"

"Yes. I know this Harris Austin. He is one of the Englishmen, the owners."

"You should call him. See if he's all right," Merle said. "What a shock."

Harris probably went white as a sheet. It would be Ernest who called the police. Pascal pictured the two of them, standing in the dark in the vineyard, over a corpse. Was it on the thriving side, close to their home, or the abandoned side? Would this make his deal with them go bad? He scolded himself for being selfish, thinking of himself. But he couldn't think of any reason off-hand that it would slow down their negotiations.

"I will call. Thanks for sending the article."

"Pascal? That party is Saturday. Did you find something to wear? You might have to go shopping in Bordeaux."

Quel joie. Not only a party but shopping as well. He sighed. "Something for summer? Maybe just a colorful shirt or a light jacket with regular trousers? Is that what you said?"

Merle agreed. The sisters had gone to Sarlat again and found a party dress for her. Francie was headed back to Paris tomorrow.

"Is our little mother doing okay?"

"She seems fine. Quiet. Still working on her fatigue but it's getting better. I've been feeding her all sorts of healthy things." Merle sighed. "She and Dylan have been having long phone conversations every evening."

"That's good news. I didn't tell you about Dylan's offer, did I?" He filled in Merle on the proposal Dylan had made in the car.

"How nice of him."

Pascal agreed. "It means I could spend more, invest more in the vineyard." He wanted his hands in the dirt, planting vines, as soon as he could. This summer, for sure. He had a stab of doubt. What about this death?

"Maybe don't bring it up when you call them," Merle said.

"Just condolences." They said goodbye after he promised to go shopping then drive back to Malcouziac the next day.

Standing at his window looking out over the river Pascal punched in the number for Harris Austin, saved from his call the week before. It went to voicemail. Pascal almost hung up. He hated to leave voicemails. Maybe he would just text. Was that too impersonal? But the phone clicked through before he could decide.

"Harris? This is Pascal d'Onscon. I just heard about your terrible discovery in the vineyard. I hope you are all right and you and Ernest are fine. So— just checking in on you. *À bientôt.*"

He hung up, grimacing. It was a dull, ridiculous message but he supposed it didn't really matter. It wasn't as if someone Harris knew had died. But Pascal knew from experience that viewing any dead body, no matter how they die or how close you are to them, is upsetting.

Who was this person? A transient or a visitor to the area? Foul play was suspected but what? How gruesome was it? A knifing, a bullet, a strangulation? He didn't really want to know yet it did matter.

He would have to pull a few strings with *Brigade criminelle.* He knew a few *la Crim'* detectives. And at least one owed him a favor.

Twenty-Five

DORDOGNE AND SAINTE-FOY

Sending Francie back to Paris was harder than Merle expected. They'd had two lovely weeks together. And Francie had so many good ideas for the tiny cottages, ways to fix them up, make them inviting. Mostly decorating ideas. She had no idea how to modernize the bathrooms, find plumbers or carpenters, hoist up the corner of the porch, or dislodge the campers in the backyard.

Not that Merle had decided to buy the houses. It was still a fantasy. She was still working the numbers, figuring out how much it would cost to make them rentable. She hadn't told Pascal yet that the security camera on his own house had caught someone sneaking through the yard, trying to open doors and windows. What could he do? And besides, there was no harm done. The guests had slept through it all.

The consequence of that was that it made Merle think twice about becoming a landlord. All this washing, cleaning, yard work, electric bills, taxes, internet transactions: it was a lot to deal with. But she didn't have a job, she reminded herself. What else was she going to do with her time while Pascal worked in Bordeaux? Paint sad watercolors?

She looked at her bank statements. She had enough money to buy the two cottages but were they going to be money pits? Her own cottage, free as she'd inherited it from her late husband, incurred significant modernization costs. Running water, for instance, was a wonderful thing but pricey. The saving grace of the two tiny houses was that they weren't as ancient as this place. The water, sewer, and electricity was already installed.

Who was living in the tent in the back? Could it be a homeless person?

Merle worked in Legal Aid, in the housing section, back in New York. She knew the struggles of many people to keep a roof over their heads. She'd also learned that the French weren't immune from social problems. Maison Chanceuse had been used by a squatter while it was semi-abandoned. Was there some way she could help the person in Pâquiers and reclaim the backyard at the same time?

She opened her laptop and began searching for housing agencies in France. Maybe charities who worked with the homeless. Anyone specifically in Pâquiers, or the Tarn-et-Garonne region. She made one of her famous lists. She would work down it next week. She added the name of the agent, Thérèse Levett. She needed a lot more information to make a knowledgable decision.

Pascal blew in early, before six, making her happy. He was quite pleased with his shopping adventure. He had bought himself a patterned, orange long-sleeved shirt and a flaxen-colored jacket of manmade linen. Close enough, he said, and no wrinkles. When he put them on, with his jeans, he looked suitably summery.

Merle put a hand over her mouth to stifle a laugh. He spun, showing off his outfit in the parlor. "Very gay, *non?* The essence of summertime."

"Perfect, really." She sobered then. "We don't say gay anymore, meaning 'fun' or 'high spirits.' Just, you know, it means homosexual. In English anyway."

Pascal straightened his new jacket. "*Pardon.* I knew that. The Englishmen, the owners at Corbeaux, they are gay."

"Are they?" She wasn't surprised. "Did they tell you?"

"No. But, I know." He pulled off his jacket and hung it on the back of a chair. "I called Harris and left a message of condolence about the body in the vineyard. But no answer."

"I hope they're not traumatized. Dealing with police can really shake you up."

"The voice of experience," Pascal said, taking her hand. "You did not get shook up. Even when a gendarme chained you to the stairs."

She smiled. "That was traumatic. But I've had so many interactions. Even back in New York, I dealt with cops all the time on evictions and court and all that."

"I forget sometimes you had a life in New York that I knew nothing about."

She pulled him close. "A lifetime ago."

Saturday dawned clear and sunny, the perfect day for a garden party. Château Vianden dominated a section of the wine region of Sainte-Foy, not far from Malcouziac as the crow flies. Its vineyards marched up and down the hillsides and the castle itself was enormous. They spied the many turrets in the style of Viollet-le-Duc, with slate tiles and pointed tips with tiny pennants, before the entire expansive château came into view. The sight was breathtaking in the soft afternoon light, the golden sun glancing off the metal flashing and the hundreds of glass panes.

Slightly intimidating, it was, like the hostess. But Madame Hugo was just a woman after all, a professional woman like Merle. A rich one, sure, but no one to be afraid of. And yet, Merle hadn't been to any fancy parties in years, let alone with French vintners. She began to obsessively count the turrets to calm herself and reached eleven before Pascal turned the BMW into the large grass area set aside for parking.

She smoothed the front of her dress, still unsure if it was too fancy or not fancy enough. Madame was an ambassador. She must have a closet full of Chanel and Givenchy. Couples walked carefully over the field, arm in arm. Some of the women wore full-length gowns; others were in dresses similar to hers, below the knees and fancy but more like a daytime wedding outfit. There was one woman in lavender, just like hers. She took a breath; she would be fine.

Pascal was examining her face. "Second thoughts?"

He looked so good in that orange shirt, the collar popped around his ears. She smoothed it down and smiled at him. "Nope. You?"

He chuckled. "Same as my first thoughts. You have the invitation? Let's get announced like royalty."

The crunching of fine gravel under many feet melted away as the crowd converged on the magnificent front entrance. Heavily carved doors stood open, inviting them in. On the stoop stood a serious man in a dark suit, wearing white gloves. He glanced at each invitation as guests went by. But, sadly, there was no trumpeting or announcing of Lord and Lady Humpbottom. All he did was mumble: "Straight through to the garden."

As Merle stepped down the marble stairs leading to the large walled garden, she paused. The sight was stunning. Three huge tents covered most of the grassy area, leaving the blossoms of the vast flowerbeds to frame the edges. Round tables filled the space, covered in white table-cloths with bunches of pink and red roses in vases. On the left was a busy bar, champagne corks popping and wine flowing. On the right trays of hors d'oeuvres were being brought out from a kitchen some-where, one after another.

Pascal paused too, waiting for her to continue. He tugged on her arm. "Come on. It's not that incredible."

"Isn't it?" Merle stepped down beside him.

"The rich have money to burn, *chérie*. We may as well enjoy it."

And they tried. The champagne in particular was icy and smooth, from one the best vintners in France. The rest of the wine on a long table across the back showcased wineries from the Sainte-Foy depart-ment, big and small. Winemakers stood behind the tables, pouring samples and talking discreetly about their methods.

"Many of these guests are winemakers themselves," Pascal whispered to Merle over a glass of Pinot.

"Have you met them before?"

"They are wearing name tags, blackbird. Only the little people like us are anonymous."

"All the better," Merle said. "We can drink them all."

IT WAS AN HOUR, a glass of champagne, two glasses of wine plus several thimblefuls of samples, and a plate of hors d'oeuvres later that a person Pascal did know appeared. Luc Naudé was speaking to someone behind the wine tables, maybe one of his employees at Domaine Champs-du-Puy. The man nodded tightly, agreeing with everything then turned his gaze to a female customer holding out her wineglass. Naudé stepped away. When he spun around to survey the guests, Pascal turned his back, trying to melt into the crowd.

No such luck.

They were standing at the edge of the flowerbeds, near the tent poles. Merle frowned at Pascal who seemed to have a sudden interest in geraniums. She sipped her second glass of champagne, thinking she should eat more to soak it up, when she saw the man glaring at them, his eyebrows pinched. He moved toward them. Merle nudged Pascal. "Someone's coming over," she whispered.

Pascal glanced at her, then over his shoulder, turning slowly to face the crowd. Naudé was flushed, by heat or wine or something else. Whatever, it was a bad combination, playing into his hot temper. As he got closer Pascal said to Merle: "A good time for you to head over for more asparagus and shrimps. Fill me a plate, will you, *chérie?*"

Merle slipped through the crowd toward the hors d'oeuvres. As she walked away she heard the stranger say, *"Qui t'a laissé entrer?" Who let you in?*

She moved down the exotic offerings, pausing to pop an olive into her mouth. Whatever business Pascal had with that man it didn't concern her. That was what he seemed to be saying. He would spare her the dirty details of their disagreement.

Was the stranger wearing a name tag? She thought he was. By the look of him, tall with sharp patrician features and a condescending expression, an owner. Could this be who Pascal was trying to buy land from? But he spoke French. Perhaps an old enemy from his days in the field.

Pascal hadn't said much about his meeting with the two Englishmen. He seemed excited about the prospects but holding back a little. He'd said little about the news of the dead body in their vineyard. Was he concerned about his deal?

She turned to peek through the mingling crowd. Where was Madame Hugo? The hostess hadn't been seen yet, at least by Merle. Would she make a grand appearance? How long did these things last?

But there was no one to ask. She was alone. Pascal was deep in conversation with that stranger and she knew no one else. She stood awkwardly, absentmindedly munching on melon and prosciutto, shrimp and roe. It was a magnificent spread, she had to admit. And she was hungry.

A red pepper draped over some kind of aioli sauce went into her mouth. And also down the front of her dress. She gasped, set her plate down with a clunk, and looked around for a napkin. Where were the flipping napkins? She craned her neck, feeling the sauce dribble down her cleavage.

Oh god.

"Madame? Pour vous."

She spun at the charming voice. Éloise Hugo stood behind her, a polite smile on her face, her eyes dipping to the saucy spot, offering a white cloth napkin at the end of her pink-varnished fingertips. Her turquoise gown featured drop shoulders and a wide flowing skirt that skimmed her shins. She wore diamonds at her throat, decidedly evening wear but she pulled it off like the lady she was.

She twitched the napkin. *"S'il vous plaît, madame."*

Merle took the proffered *serviette* gratefully and began to dab her chest. She said in English, "Thank you, Madame Hugo."

The hostess had begun to turn her attention to the many other guests crowded around her but stopped. "You are the American?"

"Y-Yes," Merle stammered. "Um, sorry. We met last winter, at my house in Malcouziac. Merle Bennett. Thank you so much for inviting us to your soirée. It's so— so—"

"Give me the napkin," Madame demanded, hand outstretched. Merle returned it, chastened. What had she done wrong, she wondered, besides make a fool out of herself by spilling sauce down her bosom?

"You will need water," Madame Hugo said bluntly. She rattled off a demand to the man in a black suit beside her. He went behind the table, found a water pitcher, and poured some into a glass. He handed it to his boss.

She dipped a corner of the cloth napkin in the water glass. Turning to Merle she motioned her closer. "Now, my dear, I would not do this to a man, nor would I let a man do it to me. But you need help. And I am a lady."

Madame Hugo delicately wiped Merle's bare chest above the bodice then tipped her head sideways. "You must do the— the other part yourself." She motioned down, inside Merle's dress. Merle blushed as she turned away and stuck her hand inside the napkin down between her breasts, wiggling it to wipe off the sauce. "Sticky, isn't it?" Madame chuckled. "I will remember to tell the caterer next time: no drippy sauces. Now give it back."

Merle handed over the napkin again. Madame eyed the wet spot on the bodice of Merle's lavender dress. "This won't make it much better. You must get it cleaned immediately." She proceeded to wet another corner of the napkin and poke delicately at the stain. "It has mostly soaked in, I'm afraid."

"It's fine, really." Merle glanced around. People were staring at them. "It's just so embarrassing to walk around with a big splotch on your chest."

"Put your scarf on," Madame suggested.

Before Merle could reply that she didn't bring a scarf—*sacré bleu*— shouts rose above the din of chatter. Merle's heart sunk. She recognized that voice. Surely Pascal wasn't making a scene here at the party. Even if he disliked that man, whoever he was, he wouldn't do that.

Madame Hugo straightened her shoulders with a determined look. "*Excusez-moi, madame.*" With her bodyguard in tow she stalked toward the commotion. The guests stepped back, parting like the Red Sea, and a hush went through the tents.

At the other end of the opening stood Pascal— and that man.

Twenty-Six

SAINTE-FOY

Pascal lost his temper.

It wasn't something that happened often. He rarely let his occasional rage erupt, mostly just a flare of the nostrils or a steely squint. This was usually enough to make adversaries think twice about engaging him in serious disagreement, whether physical or merely shouting.

But not today.

Luc Naudé had a way of pushing his buttons, Pascal was aware. That elitist sneer on his face was almost enough by itself. Pascal had a strong desire to smash his nose in. But combined with his annoying and very effective way of twisting his opponent's words to suit his own point of view, the dice were thrown. This was no polite meeting of equals.

This was war, French-style.

Pascal had just sworn at him, calling Naudé a filthy snob. "*Vas-y mollo, connard,*" or 'chill out, stupid,' which may be what really set off the vintner who told him to '*Casse-toi alors,*' one of Sarkozy's favorite lines, meaning basically, f— off. That set Pascal off for a second time and he was on the brink of saying, "*Ta gueule, enfoiré,*" 'shut your mouth, idiot,' when they were thankfully interrupted.

Éloise Hugo stopped at the end of the path widened by guests backing away, her hands on her hips. She was a tall woman with a lot of hair piled on her head. Now, draped in diamonds and turquoise silk, she pulled herself up to her full, frightening height. She glared at both the men but settled on Luc Naudé. Pascal swallowed hard, trying to slow the pounding of his heartbeat.

Madame's other bodyguard appeared next to her, a burly sort, stretching the seams of his black suit, ready to intervene if things got nasty. Luc Naudé hands were fisted at his sides, his face crimson. Madame cleared her throat. "Monsieur Naudé. Luc. Can you explain this to me? Why are you wasting time during this lovely gathering of your neighbors to make such a *tapage*? Why would you embarrass yourself, and your hostess, with this rudeness?"

Pascal took a breath. Soon Madame would have him in her sights and he would have to explain his breach of polite society. Footsteps on the wooden platform sounded and Merle skirted Madame and the bodyguard to stand beside him. "Okay?" she whispered. "No injuries?"

"I am— sorry, blackbird," he whispered back. "Things got—" He was at a loss. How embarrassing.

"Too much champagne?"

"Presumably."

Luc Naudé was attempting to mollify his hostess. He babbled incoherently, attempting to explain his extreme distress at the unfortunate volume of his conversation with Monsieur d'Onscon. On hearing Pascal's name, Madame Hugo turned her fierce blue eyes on him. She saw Merle standing there holding Pascal's arm, then glanced at the splotch on Merle's dress then at Pascal's colorful shirt. Something about them or their outfits made her frown.

Pascal didn't try to explain. "*Pardon*, madame. Please excuse my rudeness."

Éloise Hugo looked him over in an appraising way. "D'Onscon. You are the one who helped clear up that business in Wales last winter, *n'est pas?*" Pascal nodded solemnly. She stepped closer. "Have you heard what happened to the caterer, my so-called *friend*, Louis Bordeaux?"

"No, madame," Pascal said in a low, courteous voice.

"It was kept quiet by the British, for some reason. He was suspected of helping some Frenchmen launder money and evade taxes. Perhaps he did, I don't know. But then there were the girls." She rolled her eyes. "Well, he was deported back to France. Now we must deal with him here."

"I will keep an ear to the ground for Louis," Pascal said.

Madame smiled. "I'm sure you will. He could be anywhere in France by now. Or overseas, basking on an island. I have washed my hands of him."

Pascal simply nodded. "Thank you for the invitation to your soirée, madame. Merle and I feel privileged to visit your magnificent château and the lovely grounds. And the pleasure of your company."

Madame's face lit up for a moment as her eyes rose to the turrets above. "Have a wonderful time." She dismissed them with a flip of her hand. She turned to Naudé, who for some stupid reason remained standing frozen in the circle, still hunched with mortification. She switched to French to berate him a second time. "What are you thinking, Luc? These are your neighbors, your friends, are they not? Have some pride, monsieur."

Pascal almost let a chuckle escape. A lack of pride was not a problem.

Naudé hung his head like a scolded schoolboy then raised it to show he was not ashamed, not without pride of who he was, who he stood for in this community. His countenance hardened. "You are correct, madame. I am a leader in the region, well-known and respected. My wines are unparalleled. The acts of minor players—" his eyes flicked to Pascal— "are meaningless."

His phone pinged then, loud in the silence of the crowd. He pulled it from his jacket pocket. His eyes scanned the message while the crowd stared, transfixed.

Finally he raised his voice: "Good news, madame. They have made an arrest for the death of the man found in the vineyard next to mine. You remember it? Château des Corbeaux?" He straightened, glancing again at Pascal with a flicker of satisfaction.

"Of course. Oscar was a good friend, a fine gentleman. I still miss him, dear man. But who has been arrested?" the Ambassador asked.

"One of the new owners. An Englishman named Ernest Brooks."

· · ·

A FEW MINUTES later Pascal and Merle huddled in a corner of the tent as he searched on his phone for details of the arrest. The commotion of the argument and subsequent reproach from Madame Hugo had ended with Naudé's announcement of the arrest. Whispers and gasps ran over the crowd in waves. The English winemakers must be well-known. Naudé looked pleased with the effect and strode away, head high.

Merle could see Madame Hugo working the crowd. She had moved on from the argument, putting on her beatific hostess face. Surely a mask, Merle thought, but the party must go on. Had the two Englishmen been invited? This appeared to be a party to celebrate local wines and winemakers but maybe that didn't extend to the non-French ones. The locals could sometimes be so— local.

Pascal gazed out at the crowd, his hand with his phone dropped to his side. Merle whispered: "Is it true?"

"I'm afraid so."

"But who was it that was killed? Have they identified him yet?"

Pascal nodded. "Let's get another glass of wine."

At the winery table they fortified themselves with a local red blend, a fruity Côtes du Bordeaux. Pascal encouraged the server to pour a little more and he obliged. Perhaps he'd also had his moments with the man Pascal told her was the owner of the winery next to the one he was interested in buying. No one could forget an encounter with that man.

They stepped back into the crowd. Guests glanced at them and whispered in small groups. Merle straightened and sipped the wine. No one was going to scare them off. Especially not the friends of Luc Naudé. The vintners were no doubt all comrades.

"Well?" she said impatiently to Pascal. "Who was he? Who was killed?"

"A man in the village. Not a gypsy, but more or less. He worked the fields and grape harvest. Everyone knew him as he'd asked them for spare change and leftover food."

"Homeless? Poor thing. What was the reaction in the village?"

Pascal raised his eyebrows. "Surprising. Outrage. One of their own struck down. A Frenchman killed by an Englishman. As if that had never happened for a thousand years. As if they'd ever really cared for the man."

Merle flinched. "You think Ernest killed him?"

Pascal shrugged and took a slug of wine. "I don't know. Only that they have arrested him for it." He looked at his feet then back at Merle. "His name, the victim, was Roméo. But everyone in the village called him Chicken Man."

"Did he have a pet chicken?"

"He liked to steal them and eat them. He had been arrested several times in various hen houses."

Merle looked up. "Ernest and the other guy— they have chickens?"

"I'm afraid they do."

The crowd began to thin. Merle and Pascal ducked into a throng going up the stairs into the château. When they exited into the court-yard with other couples exhaling in relief, giddy to be released from the rigors of drinking in the afternoon, the evening light was soft. Shadows from the tall roof spread across the gravel. Merle grabbed Pascal's arm and they trudged back to the car.

Cars were backed up in a long line to leave the property. Pascal tapped his fingers against the steering wheel. Merle registered his annoyance. He hadn't wanted to go this party at all and now it had turned out so badly. She'd never seen him quite like that— angry, cursing, red in the face, ready to hit the tall man. But she knew he disliked those types, the fancy, landed people, the elites who continued to dominate French life despite a very well-publicized revolution. They didn't have the power they once had, but they still had some of it, or thought they should.

"So. Straight home?" she asked. It was barely six o'clock and the sun had a few more hours of daylight for them.

Pascal blinked, his mind elsewhere. "What a mess, eh? I'm sorry, blackbird."

She took his hand, prying his fingers off the steering wheel as he eased the car forward. "I'm sorry I made you take me to the party. I guess I— well, I had no idea what it would be like."

"Not your usual crowd?"

She chuckled. "Hardly. And I spilled sauce on myself." She pointed to the dark spot on her bodice. "Did you see Madame cleaning me up? She wiped my décolletage with a wet napkin."

"Madame Hugo?" He rolled his eyes. "*Mon dieu*. She is a frightening aspect. I can't imagine her that close."

Merle squeezed his arm. "You're not still afraid of that lovely woman."

"*Un peu*. But the wine was delightful."

"So what do we do about Ernest?" she asked. "Should we go over there?"

"To see Harris? Oh, I don't know. What would I say?"

"But you know him. Both of them. You were about to do business together, right?"

"Possibly." He glanced at her. "You don't mind? The vineyard is close. I don't know what help I can be—"

Merle leaned in to kiss his cheek. "Your presence, Pascal. It makes everyone feel better."

"Ha. Not everyone, *chérie*."

Twenty-Seven

NEAR SAINTE-COLETTE

Château des Corbeaux looked sad and abandoned, the wrought iron gates closed, the shades pulled down on all visible windows. Pascal drove into the driveway and turned off the BMW. He sat stoically, staring at the padlock.

"What now?" Merle asked.

Pascal craned his neck to look at the stately building, nothing so grand as the Ambassador's but tall enough and well-preserved. He hoped for motion in a window, some sort of sign that they'd been spotted.

"We wait, I suppose. Maybe he will see us?" He glanced at Merle. "How long do you want to wait, that's the question."

She shrugged. "Do we have any snacks?"

Pascal opened his door and got out. Time to stretch the back again. Merle followed suit and leaned against the car, her back toward him. She had taken her hair down and it swung across her neck in the breeze. This was probably a bad idea, just showing up at someone's place after they have experienced a trauma like an arrest. Obviously they didn't want visitors, with this locked gate.

Still, he found he did want to see Harris. He would be feeling alone, and vulnerable, in need of a friend. Pascal wanted to know what evidence the police had on Ernest. He hadn't contacted his colleague in the *Brigade criminelle* yet. Was it too late? They'd already decided who was guilty.

What was to become of his deal— if there was a deal— with the two Englishmen? He peered down the fence line at the vines, still in their bright spring green. Could Harris keep the vineyard going by himself? Ernest was the actual farmer between them. How would Harris manage?

And was it crass of him to think he could help by buying in now? Pascal pondered the morality of it, the descent on the carcass, so to speak. It seemed wrong and wildly inappropriate. No, if they helped Harris today it would be strictly as a friend, to offer support. Nothing more. He tried to disengage his hopes.

Fifteen minutes later Merle cleared her throat. "A car is coming."

Pascal turned. Beyond the drive, from the south, a vehicle approached, dust kicking up behind it. He didn't recognize it. That was good because he knew what Luc Naudé's Mercedes looked like. He rounded the BMW and stood next to Merle, turning her toward him. "Don't stare, blackbird. It could be anyone."

She smiled and put her arms around his neck. "Shall we kiss?" She puckered her lips and he smiled.

A quick peck on the lips, his hands around her waist, and he whispered, "I feel like someone should clean your décolletage, madame. My tongue awaits your command."

She chuckled. Before he could say, or do, more, the car slowed beside the drive. It was a dusty, ancient British Morris Mini, a sardine can of a vehicle, mint green and at least fifty years old. The steering wheel was on the right. And behind the wheel was Harris Austin.

He leaned in to stare at them. Pascal smiled and raised a hand in greeting. "It's Harris," he whispered to Merle.

"Who's the woman?"

Pascal hadn't noticed the passenger, sitting back in the shadows. "I don't know." He could barely see her, but she appeared youngish, with fair features and light brown hair.

Harris pulled the emergency brake and got out of the car. He paused, unsure of his next move, and crossed his arms. He frowned at Pascal.

"You're blocking my drive," he said in English.

Pascal took a step closer. "Harris, it's me, Pascal d'Onscon." He glanced at Merle. "And my companion, Merle Bennett. Pardon, we were in the area."

The woman got out of the car. She was slight, and very pale in the English way.

"What is it, Harris? Do we need to call the police?" the woman said in a very posh accent. She held up her mobile phone as if ready to strike.

Merle raised both hands as if in surrender. Pascal touched her arm to reassure her. Harris stirred finally, blinking.

"Oh, right. It's you. It's all right, Jane. I know him."

Jane lowered her phone hand. "Do you?"

"Yes, it's fine. But you are blocking my gate," Harris said. He walked around the BMW and pulled out a set of keys. He unlocked the padlock and pushed back the gates. "You may as well come in."

Pascal and Merle got back in the car. Merle whispered, "I don't think this was a good idea after all. Let's just turn around and go."

Pascal started the engine. They pulled into the gravel park by a twisted olive tree and he turned off the car again. "I'll talk to him. Just for a moment."

Merle began to protest. But he exited the car and closed the door, cutting her off. He would just apologize to Harris, offer his help, and be on his way. The Mini pulled in next to the house. Harris and whoever Jane was emerged, she pulling a black duffle bag from the back seat. Pascal walked slowly over to them.

Harris looked shellshocked. Dark circles ringed his eyes and his clothes were wrinkled and unkempt. He wore a plaid shirt and tan pants but they were both a mess. His shoes were untied. He rubbed his unshaven chin as Pascal approached.

"I'm sorry to intrude," Pascal said softly. "I just wanted to offer my support, my help, in whatever way I can."

Harris blinked rapidly. "I appreciate that. I don't think there's anything though, not really, unless you know who killed that man."

"That I do not know. I'm sorry for that too." He paused then asked, "Why do the police think Ernest is the guilty party?"

Harris took a deep, frustrated breath and exhaled. "They say they have something but I don't know what it is."

"A weapon?" Pascal was fishing. He had no idea what killed the man.

"I don't know." Harris scratched his head. "It's all unbelievable. One day we are planning the summer work, talking to you about, well, you know. Then—" Harris began to tear up. Pascal gulped, unsure how to comfort him.

Jane came to the rescue. She set down her duffle bag and gave Harris a long hug. He was sobbing now. Pascal stepped backwards, giving them space.

"Buck up now, Harry," Jane was saying, handing him a tissue. "Wipe your face, love." As Harris did as he was told, blowing his nose loudly, Jane turned to Pascal and held out a hand. "Hello. I'm Jane, Harris's sister. I've just arrived from London."

Pascal shook her firm grip. "I'm glad you've come." He glanced at Harris who clearly needed support. "We just heard about the arrest. Was it today?"

"Yesterday. In the morning. Rousted them from bed. Isn't that always the way?"

Pascal shrugged. "Madame, I am affiliated with a branch of law enforcement. Not the *Police Nationale,* just the wine fraud division. But I know how things work here in France. If I can be of service to you and your brother, and of course Ernest, please let me know."

"I— we appreciate that," Jane said. She was a delicate thing in looks but had a strong, capable quality that Pascal appreciated in women. It was reassuring that someone was here for Harris. He appeared undone by events.

"Where have they taken Ernest then?" he asked her.

"Bergerac, I believe. I just flew in there. Is it a nice place?"

"It's not horrible, madame. They will take care of him there." Until they ship him to Paris or Bordeaux. "Does he have an attorney?"

She turned to Harris. "Did you find someone?" Harris shook his head hopelessly. "On the list."

"I can send you some names, if you wish. When I get home."

"Do you live nearby?" Jane asked, suddenly chatty.

"In Malcouziac. Not far, in the Dordogne."

Jane picked up her duffle bag and took her brother's arm. "Harris has your number then? Brilliant."

Merle made Pascal recount the entire conversation in the car as they drove home. "His sister? That makes sense. They do look similar. What does she do for a living?"

"I did not get that far, *chérie*. But I think Harris is in good hands."

"Poor man." Merle watched Pascal for a few minutes, trying to figure out what he was thinking. "You have a plan, don't you?"

"Just a few scribbles on the blank slate of my mind." He smiled. "Make a list for me?"

Merle grinned. "I thought you'd never ask."

Twenty-Eight

DORDOGNE

Returning to Malcouziac, walking through the village in their summer finery, Merle and Pascal were quiet. They held hands, nodded to appreciative passersby, but kept their own counsel. Merle knew that Pascal's dream of owning a vineyard was in jeopardy with the arrest of Ernest Brooks. She also hadn't told him her plans for the two small cottages near his own house. She wondered if she wanted to continue that project. Were two real estate ventures one too many? If the vineyard fell through, she could pursue her own project. It seemed selfish though, since he was so excited about the prospect of being a winemaker. Her little *gîtes* were a whim in comparison.

She frowned as they turned onto Rue de Poitiers. Why was her project less important than his? Maybe it was timing. They would be pulled in different directions, something she didn't like. It was hard enough having Pascal away in Bordeaux for the majority of the time. It was more difficult living in that little apartment. What would happen if he owned a vineyard? He still would work for the wine fraud division, wouldn't he? She couldn't see him quitting his job. Despite the bureaucracy he loved his role in keeping French winemaking pure and free from scams and fraudsters.

As they unlocked the door shutters, waved to Madame Suchet

130

across the street, and stepped back inside the cool old stone cottage, Merle came to a realization. She needed this project, as much as Pascal needed his vineyard. There was such potential there. Even if it would be hard work, it would be fun, exciting. Maybe she could do it bit by bit, as the money was available.

Pascal threw off his faux linen jacket and she draped her shawl over a chair back. "Here's your list." She handed him the piece of notebook paper, small and crammed with handwriting. "I can re-do it if you can't read it."

He stared at the list. "No, no. I can read it. Number one: find Ernest a good lawyer."

"Right." She had found one here for an old boyfriend who got into trouble in the village but that was years ago. "He needs some big city muscle."

Pascal nodded. "I will make some calls." He headed out the kitchen door to the back, to the walled garden. Or as they called it, 'the summer office.'

Merle changed out of her frock and set it to soak in the bathroom sink. She put on her regular clothes— jeans and a t-shirt from Tristan's old school—and sat down at Pascal's desk to read her notes from the week. She had found three possible charities who helped find housing for the poor in the region. She opened her laptop and did some research. The most promising one was in Montauban. She also discovered that landlords can't evict people over the winter, not until April 1. Was that tent person evicted? She dug out the information for the property agent, Thérèse Levett, and dialed her number. Her voice was cheerful and sing-song, like she was having a very good day.

"Ah, Madame Bennett. Have you come to a decision about the cottages?"

"I'd like some information. Do you know who is sleeping in that tent in the back garden?"

Thérèse said she did not but promised to put in a call to the mayor of Pâquiers who knew everything and everybody. Merle asked about the charity, Abri Sud-Ouest, she'd read about online. Thérèse said they were well-regarded.

They agreed to talk later and hung up. What if— Merle had another idea. She jotted down a few thoughts, getting her energy back into the project, as Pascal came back inside from the garden.

"Albert stopped over. He wants us to come to dinner tomorrow."

"You said yes, I hope," Merle said.

"Of course." Pascal sat down on the horsehair settee. "I have found an attorney for Ernest, I believe. I just have to send them the information."

"A criminal attorney?"

"In Bergerac." He worked his phone, sending a text message. "Done. I hope that works out."

"You work quickly, monsieur." She spun the desk chair toward him. "Now. Are we going to have a proper supper?"

"Maybe just some soup. It's not too hot yet for soup, is it?"

"It's never too hot for soup."

THE NEXT DAY Pascal received a reply from Harris, thanking him for the attorney's name. He said they'd found someone on their own. Pascal assumed someone local. Well, he tried. He went back to the list. He would call his contact on the murder squad when he was in the office.

After a sumptuous meal with Albert on Sunday, roast duck with a cherry glaze, Pascal said goodbye to Merle— again— and headed back to Bordeaux. He was sick of this commute. He hated going back to the city even more. He had complained to Albert over dinner about his horrible little flat, making Merle feel bad for picking it out. He was embarrassed about that and apologized later. This whole weekend had been an embarrassment. He felt useless and out of sorts. He'd almost come to blows at a garden party. Just the thought made him cringe. A gypsy had been murdered and a (likely) innocent man arrested.

And worst— at least for him personally? His dream of the vineyard was gone, evaporated.

Twenty-Nine

BORDEAUX

Pascal woke early Monday morning, snug in the airless bedroom in the tiny flat. Everything about this place was small and cramped. He felt like a giant in it, oversized and bumping into walls.

The first thing he did when he reached his office in Cité du Vin was call Carine Barrault. The property agent didn't answer. It was after all before nine on a Monday, probably her slowest day of the week. Carine would return his call sometime. In the meantime, paperwork, meetings, and espresso awaited.

On his lunch break he looked at the list Merle had made for him and sighed. There were too many items, too complicated. Instead he walked around the old town, inside what remained of the ancient defensive walls of Bordeaux. Instead of a feeling of freedom that a good walk gave him, the smallness dogged him, all cramped, shaded, and moldy with impossible alleys and the narrowest of streets. It wasn't much removed from Malcouziac, built in the 15th century. The huge *place*, with its ornate fountains, was nice but was there a middle ground between ancient and decrepit, and tacky and modern? There had to be. But it might be miles into the suburbs.

Carine did not return his call that day, or the next. By Wednesday he had erased her from his mind. She wasn't going to be his housing savior. He would have to figure something out himself, or live with the smelly flat.

On Thursday, he got a call from Harris's mobile. It was Jane, not Harris, surprisingly. Pascal hadn't been expecting to hear from her, or from either of the British owners of the vineyard. He'd been trying with some success to put Château des Corbeaux out of his mind. He hadn't read anything more in the news about Ernest's arrest.

"Excuse me, Monsieur d'Onscon," Jane said. She sounded irritable, or even desperate. "There's a problem. I didn't know who else to ask."

"Anything I can do to help, madame."

"The police—" Her voice broke and she cleared her throat. Pascal frowned. What now? "They have taken Harry in for questioning. What does this mean?"

"What did they say?"

"Nothing. Or maybe it was something but in French. My French is terrible."

Pascal looked at his watch. It was two in the afternoon, too early to ditch the office even if he didn't have a pile of correspondence to handle. "Do you have a name or phone number of someone at the *gendarmerie*?"

"Yes. It's the Police, in Bergerac."

"Have you called?"

"I can't understand them. I studied Italian in school, for god-only-knows what reason. I don't know what I should do. The lawyer Harris called for Ernest isn't answering either."

"I can send my companion, Merle, to your house. She is in Malcouziac while I am here in Bordeaux so she is closer. Will that be helpful?"

"Does she speak French?"

"She does." Not the best but she would manage. "I'll call her right now. Sit tight, madame. Help is on the way."

MERLE WAS in the middle of a video call with her four sisters when her phone rang. Pascal's handsome face popped up. But she couldn't talk right then.

"Who is it?" Elise asked. It was morning in New York. She was putting on her makeup while she chatted. Stasia was still in her pajamas. Annie had already been to yoga and looked refreshed. Francie was in Paris with Dylan and was screwing up her courage to deliver her sisters the news. This was not a time to break away for a romantic convo with her boyfriend, as much as she would prefer talking to Pascal. Francie was taking forever to get around to her subject.

"Pascal. I'll call him back." She smiled at her sisters. It was actually fairly rare to get them all on one call, usually it took threats or bribes. Today all was serene. Each of them sat smiling in their little box on the laptop monitor.

Except Francie.

She looked blotchy and her eyes were puffy. Her hair looked bad, like she needed a haircut. She glanced around nervously as if someone— Dylan?— were lurking behind her. But he wasn't. He was at the office, as he always was these days. Francie had admitted he was very busy and worked very late, making her time in Paris not so much fun.

"When are you coming home, Francie?" Annie asked. "We miss you. Jack and Bernie keep asking. I'm sure you don't miss us, with all of Paris at your feet. But we miss you."

Francie's eyes darted again and she swallowed hard. "I don't know. I've asked for some time and the partners have been great." She took a deep breath and stared at the camera. "Something's come up. Actually — I'm pregnant."

Gasps ensued, then smiles, then squeals of congratulations from the three sisters previously in the dark. From her non-reaction, the three figured out that Merle was privy to this secret. "How long have you known?" Stasia asked.

"Me?" Merle said, clutching her throat.

"Not you. Francie," Stasia said. "How far along are you? All the details. Come on, spill."

"About four months." She clamped her mouth shut. No smiles from Francie.

"And Dylan? How's he taking it?" Annie asked.

Francie wagged her head. "He's okay. Not over the moon though, I have to say."

"Freaked out?" Stasia asked.

Francie winced. "We just never talked about marriage or kids or moving in together or basically anything about the future. So it's a shock."

"Well, it's a shock here too," Elise said, pulling her hair out with both hands. "I mean, you're forty-five, right? Is it safe to get pregnant that late?"

"It's not uncommon," Merle said. "Happens all the time."

Elise made a surprised face. "Oh. I guess I better be more careful."

"Or not," Stasia said, grinning. "Depends on what you want out of life." She was the sister with the most kids. Only two, Oliver and Willow, but still she had the most experience. She always touted the joys of family life and none of them had the nerve to disagree with her.

"It'll be fine, Francie. Most men are scared at first. You should have seen Rick when I told him about Willow. He almost fainted. Even though Dylan has a kid, he's probably petrified, Francie. To men children mean the future, a commitment not only to the kid but to you, the mother, that is goes on for his the rest of his life. That's responsibility. Also vulnerability, knowing that they have that sensitive, loving part. That gnaws at them when they want to be carefree and tough. Then they see that little baby and melt. You'll see. Dylan's a good guy. He'll come around."

Francie, listening carefully, nodded. "Thanks for that, Stace."

"But when are you coming home?" Annie asked again. "You need to get started on all that prenatal stuff, get a doctor. And where will you live? At Dylan's or some new place?"

Merle held up her palms. "Okay, dial it down, ladies. Francie and Dylan have to figure all that out for themselves."

"You've been holding out on us, Merdle!" Annie cried, laughing.

"It wasn't my news, was it?" Merle cringed inwardly, as if her sisters were ganging up on her and Francie. "Maybe give the girl some space to work things out with her man, huh."

Elise bit her lip, as did Francie. Annie pushed back her hair and sighed. Stasia tipped her head sideways and squinted. None of them were fans of advice from another sister. Each had requested it in the past and dished it out regularly. Merle was aware her tone was harsh. This was not the time to tread on toes and yet she couldn't seem to stop. She felt so protective of Francie suddenly.

"You may not have talked to Francie much before she left, I don't know." She glanced at the three sisters; no one disputed that. "She had a rough first trimester. She was dead tired and thought she had some weird medical condition. Turned out she did—pregnancy— and also anemia." Merle glanced at Francie. "I hope this is okay to tell, Francie."

"Better you than me apparently," Francie muttered, rubbing an ear.

"She's already seen a doctor in Paris and things are improving. Right?"

"Got iron pills and vitamins and all that." Francie said, still not smiling. She pulled out her waistband on her trousers. "I feel so gassy all the time. Jesus, I am going to be fat."

"Temporarily," Stasia reminded her. "I'm thrilled for you, honey. I am."

Merle could almost hear Francie saying: *that makes one of us.*

"Me too," Annie said. "To bits." Elise sounded in the Dylan range of thrilled, but said she was so happy for them both.

"I'm sorry I didn't tell you earlier but honestly I didn't find out until a few weeks ago," Francie said, sighing. "After I got to Paris, if you can believe it. My due date is in October. I had to have some extra tests. Apparently I am what they call a geriatric pregnancy." She made a face and rolled her eyes.

More advice flowed from the sisters, unsolicited and devoid of much actual medical information. They forgave Merle for keeping the secret, and wished Francie all the best care in the world. Then Elise and Stasia had to go to work and the call was over.

Merle closed her laptop with a click. Her sisters' voices faded to silence. She could hear their laughter and chatter in her head, then quiet. She walked out into the garden and watered the pear trees espaliered against the house. She sat down on the low wall and sighed. Sometimes her sisters wore her out.

It would all work out for Francie, she hoped. No, it would. When she put her mind to something, Francie could not be stopped. But was Dylan really one of her projects? Could he be 'managed'? A baby certainly couldn't be.

A weird buzz from the video call stayed with her. Overstimulation, she supposed, after being alone here all week with only the occasional *petit loir*—the resident dormouse—as company. Then she remembered Pascal's call and went back inside for her mobile phone. She clicked on his voice message. All it said was 'Call me now.'

He picked up after one ring. "Ah, blackbird, there you are."

"Sorry. I was having a video call with the sisters."

"Uh-huh." He seemed distracted. Usually he asked about her sisters but not this time. "Can you go over to the vineyard? To Château des Corbeaux?"

"Right now?"

He explained that Harris had been taken in by the police and that Jane was alone and confused. "She has no French, *chérie*. You know how that is."

"I do. I can go, of course. Should I take an overnight bag or will I be coming back?"

"Take a bag just in case. If you are still there tomorrow I can meet you."

"What should I do for her— for Jane?"

"Just be a friend, I suppose. She's alone in a foreign country, and her brother may be arrested as well."

"What?"

"Only a guess, blackbird. But where questioning goes, arrests usually follow."

Thirty

NEAR SAINTE-COLETTE

The gates to Château des Corbeaux were wide open this time, unlike when Merle and Pascal had visited after the Ambassador's soirée. The stone mansion didn't look any cheerier, with empty planting urns gracing the front steps, still waiting for a gardener to grace them with flowers. Harris's Mini sat under the olive tree, looking dusty. Merle knocked on the big wooden door and heard footsteps inside.

Jane pulled the door wide, a grimace of a smile on her face. Her hair was piled in a messy topknot and she wore thick, red glasses that slid down her nose.

"Oh, hello. Merle, right? Come in."

The cavernous front hall reached three stories high with wooden rafters way up there. The walls were draped with old banners and tapestries, mostly moth-eaten and faded, their design no longer decipherable. The foyer had a military feel, with a knight's shield and crossed swords on the walls. Arranged up the stone walls of the staircase dour paintings of men and ladies of centuries past looked down their noses at the present occupants. Shadows cast the entire space in darkness. The only window was high on a landing. The dank smell of ancient dust and mildew permeated the air.

"Gloomy old manse, eh?" Jane said, walking into a mostly-empty parlor on the right. An old roll-top desk and a leather stool were the only furnishings. "Come this way, to the back. That's where the guys mostly live."

Merle followed the slender woman through the wood-paneled parlor and a warren of hallways to an open, sunny kitchen, their steps echoing. A rough hewn table and ancient ladder-back chairs with ratty reed seats sat next to a bank of windows facing the vineyard. On one side of the large room were two upholstered chairs in a faded flower chintz on either side of a wooden cocktail table littered with papers and drinking glasses. Jane swept the surface clean, picking up the dishes and depositing them in the soapstone sink. She stacked the papers and set them on the dining table before offering Merle a cup of tea.

"I'd love tea. Thanks." Merle sat in one of the armchairs while Jane busied herself with the kettle and cups. "Have you heard anything from Harris?"

"Not today," Jane said, frowning. She nudged her glasses up her nose. "They called last night. I've been reading up on French law, mostly to distract myself from worry."

"I'm sorry. It must be nerve-wracking." Merle wondered why they'd kept Harris overnight. It didn't sound promising.

Jane brought the teacups over and handed one to Merle. She settled uneasily in the other chintz chair. "I hope you can talk to the police for me. Is he under arrest or something? He's been gone almost twenty-four hours. I am clueless. I feel underwater, trying to get information from them."

"Have you thought of going to the police station?" Merle asked gently.

"It's in Bergerac."

It wasn't that far. Maybe she didn't drive? Jane sipped tea. She wore a thin white cardigan and tan slacks with red tennis shoes. She was very thin. Her neck appeared too long and her shoulders too bony. Very British though, confident and understated.

Merle replied: "On your own, I can see that would be a little difficult."

Jane grimaced and drank her tea carefully, one tiny sip at a time.

"Should I call them now?" Merle glanced at her watch. It was nearly five o'clock. How late would the Police phones be open? "No time like the present."

Jane popped up. "I'll get the number."

With the slip of paper in hand, Merle dialed the number on her mobile phone, steeling herself to speak and understand rapid, colloquial, legalese French. A low grunt accompanied the click of connection.

"*Allo,*" Merle began. In French she spoke haltingly, she knew, but it was as good as she could do. "My name is Madame Bennett. I would like to speak to Inspector Ducré."

A clunk as the receiver hit the desk. Some shouting could be heard, and a door slammed. Merle raised her eyebrows at Jane who sat back in the armchair, her legs tucked up under her, cradling her teacup. Finally some clicks and a man with a gruff, low voice came on the line.

"*Allo*, Inspector. I am calling for the family of Harris Austin, an Englishman." She glanced at Jane who nodded. "I understand he is in the *gendarmerie* for questioning in the case of the death of a vagrant on his property."

"*Quoi?*" The Inspector covered the mouthpiece then returned. "Monsieur Harris is here on his own. He was requested to attend the identification of the prisoner who died."

Merle startled. "A prisoner who died? Who was that?"

"Monsieur Brooks. *Il est mort.*"

"Oh, no," Merle whispered in English. Then she returned to French: "*Que s'est-il passé?* What happened?"

"*La crise cardiaque.* The doctor thinks. We wait for the autopsy for final judgment." The policeman cleared his throat as if he'd said too much. "*Pardon.* Who is calling again?"

"*Une amie*—a friend of Harris Austin's sister. She's right here but she doesn't speak French."

"Please put her on the phone. I have someone to translate." Again voices in the background as Merle handed the phone to Jane.

"They have a translator." She grimaced. "I'm afraid it's bad news about Ernest."

Jane took the cell phone carefully and raised it to her ear, stoic in the face of whatever came next. "Yes, I'm here. Jane Austin, that's right. His sister."

Merle blinked at her name. Of course she was 'Jane Austin.' But how bizarre really, to be named for a famous author. But there were more pressing concerns. Jane's face crumpled. Somehow she contained her tears.

"I see. Yes, heart attack. How does that happen in a jail? Was no one watching him?" She pressed her fingertips into her forehead. "Stress, okay. I guess. Right. If you say so." She listened some more. "Can I speak to Harris?"

While she waited for them to locate her brother, Jane said to Merle, "I can't believe this. Ernest was so— so alive. So strong. There must be some dereliction of—"

She broke off and listened again. "Well, where is he? All right. Can you give him a message? He doesn't have his mobile. Yes. Write this down please. Jane and Merle will come this evening."

Merle whispered. "Before seven o'clock."

"By seven o'clock. Oh, ah, crikey. Nineteen hours. Can you have him at the front desk? *Réception?* At *Police Nationale?* Right. Thank you."

Jane jabbed the disconnect button on Merle's phone and cursed loudly. "What the bloody hell."

Merle set her phone on the table. "Is Harris all right?"

"They didn't really say. Just that he was somewhere in the constabulary— the police station." Jane put her face down into her hands. "What a nightmare. Poor Harry."

Merle supposed it was inappropriate to say what she was thinking, that at least Harris hadn't been arrested. "How sad." She sighed. "How long were they together?"

"Twenty-four years." Jane glanced at Merle with a strange look. "Did you know they had a civil union? A PACS?"

"Here in France?"

Jane nodded. "Three years ago or so. Right before they bought the vineyard. Harris especially wanted it that way, all legal and equal so they would inherit each other's portion."

Merle nodded. "That was good thinking." She glanced at Jane. "Are you an attorney?"

"Solicitor. Mostly civil. I did their wills."

"Me too. I was a lawyer back in the US. The family tradition."

Jane nodded, distracted. "I was going to go home in three days. I have—" She bit her lip, mentally going over her schedule, Merle supposed.

"He may need you even more now."

Jane stood up. "We should go."

Merle waited under the spreading branches of the olive tree as Jane got herself ready. Merle told her not to change her clothes, that she looked fine, so Jane just went to brush her hair. While she was doing that, Merle called Pascal.

"Bad news, I'm afraid."

"Arrested?"

"It's Ernest. He's had a heart attack in jail. He's dead, Pascal." She could hardly believe it.

Pascal swore loudly. "Those *connards*. They couldn't keep a person safe anywhere."

"I suppose they can't watch every prisoner every minute."

"They can, blackbird. They have cameras everywhere. It is their duty to watch them." He sighed. "This is horrible. Tragic."

Jane emerged from the front door of the mansion and walked quickly toward Merle. "I have to go. I guess I'll stay with her, or them, tonight."

Jane's hair didn't look much better and the slash of red lipstick on her thin lips was awkward. But she had a determined look on her face, one Merle had seen many times in the practice of law. Jane was ready for whatever came next: a battle, an argument, a reconciliation. Grief, sadness, tears. She had her armor on. She buckled herself into the passenger seat of Merle's Peugeot, having assumed correctly that Merle would be driving.

Merle gave her a brave smile. "Okay?"

"No," Jane said flatly.

"Crack on then?" This was one of Merle's new expressions after her holiday in Wales. But probably the wrong time to use it.

Jane frowned at her. "Go."

Thirty-One

BERGERAC

Inside the modern *Commisariat de Police* that smelled of feet and garlic and disinfectant, Merle made her request at *réception*. 'Please bring Harris Austin to the front.' The clerk, a middle-aged woman with a bad complexion and greasy hair, squinted at her. Merle repeated her request, slower this time, with as much of a nasal accent as she could manage. Then she wrote down Harris's name on a slip of paper, followed by Jane's name, and the Inspector's name. The clerk squinted again and disappeared behind a door in the scuffed wall in the back.

Jane sat primly on a hard chair, her purse in her lap. They said nothing, as they had been silent on the drive in. Merle had almost asked her about being named for the author of *Pride and Prejudice* but decided against idle chit-chat. There seemed to be nothing more to say about Ernest. It was, as Pascal said, a tragedy. What could be done? They would just have to figure it out as it went along.

It didn't go swiftly. They waited a half hour. Jane sighed and checked her watch. Another hour passed, not pleasantly. Merle got up and paced the small waiting area, hoping the clerk would notice her and take pity on them. It didn't happen. In fact, the clerk was replaced soon after by a young man who never looked up from his monitor or phone or whatever he was doing. Seven o'clock came and went.

Merle leaned against the wall by the doors and practiced patience. What the hell were they doing in there? She wanted to yell at the new clerk but decided against it. Jane was not so sanguine. She stood up, her face red with anger and fists balled. First she confronted Merle.

"What the hell is going on? Why aren't they bringing him out?" she hissed.

"I don't know. Do you want me to ask?" Merle didn't think it would help. But maybe it would help Jane.

"Of course I do," Jane almost yelled.

The clerk, whose name tag read 'Jérome Lortie,' startled when Merle began to speak to him through the scratched plexiglass shield. He blinked up at her, turning his phone face down on the sticky gray counter.

"*Bonsoir, monsieur*," Merle said, going for friendliness to start. "We have been waiting for almost two hours for my friend's brother to be released. Harris Austin. I spoke to Inspector Ducré? Can you find out what's happening for us?" She smiled brightly.

Jérome stood up and smoothed his shirt. Crumbs fell to the floor. "Inspector Ducré? I am sure I saw him leave the building. But I can check?"

"Do check. Thank you."

Merle walked back to her chair and sat down next to Jane. "Well?" Jane asked impatiently. Merle shrugged.

In ten minutes the clerk returned. He called out to Merle. "Madame? The Inspector has gone for his dinner and does not return until tomorrow."

Merle stood up slowly, composing her reply in her head. At the counter she knocked to get Jérome's attention again. "We are still waiting for Monsieur Austin. He is not a prisoner. He was here only to identify a prisoner who died in the jail. Do you understand?"

The clerk blinked uncertainly then nodded. "Name?"

"Harris Austin." Merle spelled it.

Jérome typed on the keyboard to his side and squinted, hitting a few more buttons. "I am sorry. We have no one by that name in the jail."

Merle clenched her jaw. "He's not in jail." She glanced back at Jane. "Is the translator here? For English?"

"Ah, she is English?" Jérome asked brightly as if this was a quiz show. He glanced at Jane.

"Yes, she is English. Monsieur Austin is also English. Is the translator here?" She had a bad feeling the translator was enjoying dinner.

"*Je parle*— I speak English, madame," Jérome said with a smile, in heavily-accented English. "How can I help?"

"You can find Harris Austin, Jérome. He is somewhere in this building."

The clerk squinted and looked askance. He typed something else on his keyboard. "I am sorry. He is not in this building. But I see his name now. I did a very grand search for you and now I see him."

"Where is he?"

"At the hospital, madame."

"Oh. What hospital?"

"*Centre Hôpital.* I write the address for you." Jérome took his time copying the address in terrible handwriting and pushed it over to Merle. She glanced at the scribbles and frowned at the clerk.

"Where in this so-called hospital would one look for Monsieur Austin?"

"I do not know, madame. Is he ill? Maybe he is in a treatment room?"

"He is not—" And Merle lost her patience, pocketed the piece of paper, and waved Jane up from her chair. "Let's go."

THE DETECTIVE in the Murder Squad called Pascal back about four that afternoon, four days after the initial call. It was the usual time for unofficial conversations, while a policeman was taking a cigarette break outside whatever building where he was working. Two years ago Pascal had helped Barto solve a murder case in Champagne and they had kept in touch off and on. Pascal knew one day he would need to call in the favor.

"D'Onscon." Barto took a drag on his cigarette. "Who have you killed now?"

"Only the deserving, I assure you. Have a minute? I need some information."

"I suppose."

From past dealings with the unconventional and gruff detective, Pascal knew to simply keep moving forward. "There is a homicide investigation ongoing, out of Bergerac, I believe? A transient name of Roméo, found dead in a vineyard near Sainte-Colette."

Barto grunted. "Arrest made."

"Yes. Now the man arrested has died while a guest of the *Police Nationale.*"

"*Dommage.* You think we beat him to death?"

"No, no." Well, maybe but it was not the time. "I was hoping you could tell me some of the particulars, now that the guilty party has died. For instance, what evidence do— did— you have against Ernest Brooks? And the like."

"Does it matter? Case closed."

"It matters to me. And the relatives of Monsieur Brooks."

Barto sniffed. "*D'accord.* Shouldn't be difficult. Probably in the closed cases already."

"Can you send me a copy of the file? If you have time this week?" Always need deadlines with public servants, he'd found.

Barto promised to do his best and hung up. Pascal put on his jacket. He couldn't work any more today. He told Josef he would be available by phone or email. It was after all only Thursday, but he didn't care. He was out.

He was passing Saint-Émilion on the toll road when his phone pinged. A text from Barto. Pascal pulled off the highway into a petrol station and threw his car into park. He couldn't believe Barto had completed his task so quickly, but *zut*, he had.

Attached to a brief text, '*Voilá,*' were four photos of documents. They were difficult to read on his phone. He zoomed in to the first one, a charging document for the arrest of Ernest Brooks. It took some time to read but eventually the key piece of evidence came forward. A bloody pick axe had been found in the ditch by the road. The victim's blood was on the tip of one sharp end, and Brooks's fingerprints were all over it.

Pascal sat back in the car seat. He knew that was enough for an arrest. The blood was the victim's. The fingerprints, the perpetrator. Or that's how it would line up. The *policiers* had it all laid out for them and were glad to oblige. Case closed.

He clicked off his mobile and got back on the highway. There was something up, he was sure of it. No one really cared about Roméo. And now that Ernest was dead, the case would simply vanish.

He put on his blinker and merged into traffic before putting his foot down hard on the pedal. He had read how the vintners and other neighbors had reacted to the arrest of Ernest, with satisfaction, even a sort of sneering glee. At the ambassador's soirée, no one seemed anything but surprised by Ernest's arrest. No one defended his honor in that moment. Was it homophobia? Pascal didn't know. But the reaction was uncaring.

And what would happen to Harris now? Would he too be tainted by the local hatred? Whether it was wealthy Brits buying vineyards or two gay men doing the same, did the reason for the hatred matter? Whoever killed Roméo— and Pascal was sure it wasn't Ernest—was still out there. Would they target Harris next?

As he drove faster, swerving around cars and trucks, he thought of Luc Naudé. Was he desperate enough for the vineyard to ruin the two men who owned it? By killing a gypsy? It seemed far-fetched, even for Naudé.

But also, incredibly possible.

Thirty-Two

BERGERAC

A memory of visiting Albert in *Centre Hôpital* a few years ago came back to Merle as she stepped into the main lobby. Not a pleasant reminder. French hospitals are every bit as jumbled and confusing as American ones. You can get lost in the blink of an eye, and wander for weeks if not nabbed by security.

Institutional kitchen smells wafted through the halls and into the lobby. It was now after eight o'clock. Merle was tired. She was ridiculously annoyed with this mission. She decided the only thing she could do at this point was throw herself on the mercy of the first kind soul she encountered.

It took three, in the end. Two who couldn't understand her French, and one who could. *Formidable.* Merle asked the last woman, a young supervisor with spiky blond hair and dark circles under her eyes, to please announce Monsieur Austin's name over the loudspeakers and ask for him to come to the lobby. She was efficient, did as asked, but her French was difficult to understand.

"May I?" Merle asked, pointing to herself. *"Parlez en anglais pour le monsieur?"*

A large group of tourists entered about that time, half-carrying an injured person, snagging the attention of all. The supervisor handed Merle the phone receiver and pushed a button. *"Allez."*

"Monsieur Harris Austin. Mister Harris Austin," Merle intoned as if she was at an airline departure gate. "Please come to the front lobby off Avenue Professeur Albert Calmette to meet your sister. Mister Austin, please proceed immediately to the front lobby of the hospital."

Merle handed back the receiver to the supervisor who gave her a thin, annoyed smile. Jane had found another hard chair. "Now we wait," Merle said.

"Of course we do," Jane said with more than a touch of acid.

Fifteen minutes later Pascal called. Merle put the phone to her ear. "We're at the hospital. The clerk at the police station told us Harris was here. But who knows, really?"

"I am in Bergerac," Pascal said, "Well, almost. I will meet you there."

It took another forty minutes for Pascal to arrive. The traffic at this time in the evening was heavy. No sign of Harris Austin in the meantime. Merle hesitated to ask to page him again as the women behind the counter looked harried. Jane had taken to angry pacing and grinding her teeth. Merle felt a surge of relief when Pascal nearly fell through the doors into the lobby. She told him that they'd waited two hours over at the police station and now almost an hour here.

"I think Jane needs to eat something," Merle whispered. "She's running on fumes."

"Where is Harris?"

She shrugged. "The Inspector said he was here to identify the— Ernest. Maybe the morgue?"

Pascal snapped his fingers and went to a large directory posted on the wall. He read it quickly, turned back to Merle, and snapped his fingers again as he trotted off down a hallway.

PASCAL GOT LOST TWICE but eventually reached the basement of the hospital where the morgue was located. The directions on the signage left something to be desired. How awful, he thought, that Harris had to come here and see poor Ernest. He had hoped Harris would make it to a patient room at least, even if it was too late to say goodbye.

He turned a corner at a trot and there he was. Harris sat slumped on a wooden bench in the hall. Pascal slowed so as to not startle the man. But his eyes were closed, his arms tucked up against his torso, his head on the bench.

Pascal stopped, cleared his throat. Harris's eyes flickered open and he sat up. He blinked up at Pascal, sighed, and struggled to his feet. "Finally. My rescue," he muttered as he shuffled down the hall past Pascal.

The bistro around the corner from the hospital complex was simple and not terribly sanitary to Merle's eye. But they were beyond caring at that point. The four of them dropped into the last chairs at the last table, squeezed against the wall by the kitchen door.

The reunion between Jane and Harris had been oddly perfunctory. A short hug, nods, and an "I'm so sorry" from Jane. Harris looked numb. Perhaps, Pascal thought, that was the body, the mind's, way of protecting itself, just shutting down until it could deal with the storm of emotion. He glanced at Merle who gave him a sad face and side glance at Harris. Jane sat very upright and read the menu with a scowl.

"What would you like, Harry?" Jane asked. Harris stared blankly at the wall. He hadn't looked at his menu. "An omelet? They can't mess that up, can they."

The service was thankfully swift. They got their three omelets and steak frites for Pascal, and ate quickly. Merle ordered a glass of wine. They were out of rosé, very odd. She settled for whatever was in the pitcher. Jane shared the red with her.

The evening air was cool as they walked back to the parking lot. Pascal had qualms about Merle driving. She was tired and out of sorts and didn't really like to drive country roads at night. He didn't have to ask her twice. Everyone piled into his BMW and Pascal promised they could come back for her car in the morning.

Out of Bergerac the cars thinned. They passed through the small village of Sainte-Colette, nearest to the vineyard. Everyone seemed to have gone to bed. Not a soul on the streets but one gendarme in front of the staid town hall, the *'mairie.'* Back out the other side of the village, the darkness enveloped them. The gravel clattered under the tires as they turned off the main road.

The château was a dark hulk. The light was nearly gone from the sky, bathing the old stone in a pale violet glow. The leaded windows on the front of the manse winked briefly with the reflection then went black. Pascal pulled in next to the Mini. Jane helped Harris into the house, leading him to his bedroom in the back. Merle and Pascal lingered in the front hall.

"Will they be all right?" he wondered aloud.

"She seems very capable." Merle rubbed her eyes and checked her watch. "Ten-thirty already. What a day."

Before they could figure out a plan, Jane returned, her forehead lined with worry and fatigue. Her voice was brisk though, and sure. "There are at least four bedrooms up the stairs, on the first level. Turn right at the top of the stairs. I am in the first on the left, with the blue coverlet. The others look suitable, if a little dusty. Pick one."

She turned to go then stopped, her tennis shoes squeaking on the tile. She looked over her shoulder. "And thank you."

PASCAL STARED at the weak English tea in the white mug placed before him the next morning. It had the smell of old socks. He sat opposite Merle at the rough farmer's table in the château's kitchen. He didn't like tea and was fairly certain this particular brew would not be palatable. Merle raised her eyebrows and took a sip of hers. She murmured appreciation to Jane, sitting at the end of the table. The fourth at the table was Harris, still in blue and white pajamas. He looked terrible.

The night had been hard on them all but hardest on Harris. He rested his chin in his hand and closed his eyes, only to have them pop open as if remembering something awful.

"Eat something, Harry darling," Jane said. "Toast for instance."

Pascal and Merle had tucked themselves into the third bedroom on the left, facing the front of the house. The room was very plain, painted gray with no curtains, and, as Jane promised, very dusty. The coverlet had to be gently folded and removed. Merle found a faded quilt in a wardrobe and threw it over them. The sheets were cool and smelled of mildew.

"Maybe we should try the second bedroom," Pascal suggested as they settled in.

"Like Goldilocks? Find the one that's just right?"

He looked at her. "Is that something I should know?"

So she told him the story of Goldilocks and the Three Bears as she remembered it from a book of fairy tales when she was very young. Her voice lulled them both to sleep.

Now Pascal took a piece of cold toast and attempted to chew it. He gave up and dunked it in the lukewarm tea. When Harris woke up enough to eat a little, Pascal couldn't wait any longer. He had to speak and then get out of here.

"Quite a shock, I'm sure, Harris," he said gently. "I'm so sorry."

"Me too," Merle said. "Very sorry."

"Thank you. Both," Harris said. "It's such a blow. Poor Ernest." He took a deep breath and looked at his sister. "We have some planning to do."

She nodded. "The funeral. We need to call his family."

"Bloody hell," Harris groaned.

"I'll do it," Jane reassured him. She looked at Pascal. "Is it true that the funeral must be within six days?"

"Yes. From the time of death. Unless there are reasons."

"What day did he die?" Merle asked.

They looked at Harris. "Two days ago, about 11 o'clock, they said." He rubbed his bloodshot eyes and cursed under his breath.

Jane straightened. "So we have four days. Do you have the numbers?"

Harris shuffled over to the sideboard where his ledgers and other papers were haphazardly piled. He pulled a small black address book from a drawer. "Somewhere in there," he said sadly, handing it to Jane.

This seemed like the time to leave. Pascal nodded to Merle and they rose from the table. They made their goodbyes to Jane and told her to call when the arrangements had been made. Pascal pulled Jane aside for a moment in the hallway.

"Can you ask him some questions? About the dead man they found?"

She frowned. "Why? It's over."

"I am— I am not satisfied. Can you ask him some things?" He handed her a small piece of paper with his questions listed. Merle had written it out for him again. Jane took it reluctantly.

"There are more pressing concerns," she said, squinting at the list. "But I'll try."

Thirty-Three

DORDOGNE

As Pascal drove Merle back to Bergerac to pick up her Peugeot the next morning, she pondered the list he'd had her write up, questions for Harris, and what they meant. Her conclusion was — a: He didn't think Ernest killed the vagrant, and —b: he intended to find out who did. How he planned to do this was unclear. A transient dumped in a field wouldn't have witnesses. Would he?

If he had been killed somewhere else, and then left in the château's vineyard, then maybe there were witnesses wherever he was attacked. But how to backtrack to the initial scene of crime? Two years ago when Merle helped Pascal— only a little— solve the crime of the dead vintner it had taken many twists and turns to get the focus back to the scene. How had that happened, she tried to remember. The relationships between the players had been a big part of figuring that out. Here, Roméo appeared to have no one. He was a vagrant and homeless, a beggar. In a way, an easy target because who would press for justice?

Pascal was quiet, as he usually was to concentrate on his driving. He peeled into the hospital parking lot and stopped abruptly. "Where are you?" She pointed him to a distant slot where she climbed out of his car.

"See you at home?" He'd never said if he had to go back to Bordeaux. She hoped not.

"Very soon, *chérie*." He blew her a kiss and she waved as he backed out and turned onto the street.

Halfway back to Malcouziac, she got a text from him. He was already in the cottage, at work presumably, as he asked how to set up the computer printer she'd installed in the bedroom closet. She called him and talked him through it. It would have been easier to wait the twenty minutes until she arrived at home but something in his voice was impatient and serious. Before he hung up he asked her if she was still in Bergerac.

"Almost home," she replied.

"Ah. Okay, never mind." He hung up.

As she walked up Rue de Poitiers, the summer sun highlighting the colorful shutters and pink roses vining up house fronts, Jane called.

"I hate to bother you, Merle," she began with a sigh. "But I need help again. If I knew someone else here, besides Harry of course, I wouldn't be such a helpless toad."

"No problem, Jane. How can I help?"

"I have to pick out the casket— or maybe an urn. The flowers, everything. Harry seemed okay this morning, didn't he? Well, he's back in bed, under the covers. He refuses to do anything."

Merle looked at her watch. It was barely noon. She'd be back on the road soon, she predicted. It was a bit annoying but what could be done? Obviously Jane was unable to cope in French and Ernest must get buried.

"Of course I can help. Have you set a time for the funeral?"

"Monday, late afternoon. Nothing happens over the weekend. The funeral home is helpful but their English is about like my French. Just as well. His family wants to come so the extra days are needed."

"How did that go?"

"There was wailing, I can tell you that," Jane said.

Today was Friday, and as she said, little commerce happened on Saturday or Sunday. "So it must be today then?"

Jane sighed. "I am bloody useless. Are you even home yet? I'm so sorry. I rarely drive— I don't even own a car anymore—but maybe I can manage Harry's and meet you?"

Merle was able to put Jane off for a couple hours and agreed to a two p.m. date in Sainte-Colette. The simple country funeral home there was handling the details. Merle found Pascal standing in front of his laptop, pulling his hair.

"*Merde.* I cannot figure this out." He rolled his eyes.

Merle sighed. It was nice to be needed, she supposed.

TEN MINUTES later Merle came down the stairs from the bedroom with a sheaf of papers in her hands. It had taken her only minutes to discover there was no printer paper in the tray and get things rolling. Pascal ground his teeth. He hated office work and this was one good reason. But he liked working at home, he supposed, so he had to do without Josef here. Merle was a good sport about his lack of technical skills. She was reading the pages now.

"What's this? I can't read it in French but I see Ernest Brooks here."

He held out his hand. "Charging documents. In the death."

"Of Roméo?" She stepped back and kept reading. "His last name was Auguste?"

"Yes." Pascal dropped his hand impatiently.

"Do they know anything about him?"

"I don't think so. Can I read it now?"

"You haven't read it already? Where did you get this?"

"Your old friend, Barto. Very obliging of him."

Merle smiled. "You and he are two peas in a pod. Is he working on the case?"

"No one is working on it now. That is why I need to go over it carefully, make sure nothing was overlooked."

Merle squared up the pages and gave them to him. "Is that your job?"

He leaned in and gave her two kisses and a third on the lips. "When did that make a difference?"

She held his face in her hands for a moment. "What are you getting yourself into." It wasn't a question, or if it was, they both knew the answer. He smiled into her eyes and wiggled his eyebrows. She pinched his cheek. "Jane needs me again this afternoon, to help her with the arrangements. Apparently Harris is down for the count."

"The count?"

"He's hiding under the covers, trying to keep reality at bay." She shrugged.

"Ah. That is sensible, under the circumstances. But you said Jane was capable."

"Except when dealing with the French." She smiled. "Lunch?"

"If you have time."

She went into the kitchen to put together some cold sausages and cheese for him. She said goodbye and left again. Pascal sat down to read the documents.

The charging document had little new information in it. He read through it quickly. The evidence was mainly the pick axe with blood, identified as that of the deceased, and fingerprints of Ernest. There was a small scrap of paper in Roméo's pocket that read 'Corbeaux' in very poor handwriting. It seemed strange that they hadn't found anything else, in the house or outbuildings. No blood spatters, no bloody clothes, no incriminating anything. The axe itself wasn't far from their house, in a ditch opposite the derelict vineyard. Not terribly far from the body.

The tiny note was curious. Only Roméo's fingerprints were on it. Had he been seeking out Château des Corbeaux? Looking for directions? Had Ernest or Harris offered him shelter? Or had someone intentionally given him that note to lure him out there?

The autopsy was the next document. Roméo Auguste suffered from various ailments— heart disease, liver disease, malnutrition, an eye condition, and some sort of foot fungus. But none of that was fatal. Only the blow to the head. Blunt force trauma, the pathologist wrote. An object three inches long, possibly an inch wide.

What could that be? The pick axe, Pascal supposed, if he was hit with the middle section, next to the handle. Roméo had been dead for at least ten hours before he was found, possibly fifteen. That put the time of death when? He shuffled through the paperwork to find the report of first officer on the scene. The call had come in to the Sainte-Colette *gendarmerie* at 8 o'clock on Tuesday evening. So the man would have been killed that morning, perhaps very early. But where? No conjecture was made.

The final document was a *Brigade criminelle* report of the initial investigation of the death. Statements witnesses made of sightings of Roméo in the village and on farm roads beyond. The woman who owned the boulangerie had seen him going through her garbage bin the day before, in the afternoon. That would be Monday. Another woman called in to say she thought she saw him walking out of town that evening but she wasn't close enough to be sure it was Roméo. No one knew where he slept. He moved around, witnesses stated, from shed to barn to ancient *borie*, the old sheepherder's stone huts. The closest *borie* had been searched. There were signs of an old campfire but no more.

A wealthy man, a vineyard owner, offered tidbits to the Police. He had let Roméo sleep in a shed on his property a few times in the winter, when it was very cold. But the man stole vegetables and chickens from his wife's kitchen garden and scared her badly so the vintner had run him off. He regretted the interaction, he said, but did nothing to help Roméo find a place to shelter from the harsh weather. He had no idea where the man ended up.

A man identified as an art dealer said he had spoken to Roméo once or twice but had little to add. The local priest had sometimes helped the man, giving him soup and a blanket, the report said. The priest claimed Roméo wasn't interested in having a home to maintain. He liked the outdoor life. He was happy and free. "We must respect the wishes of every soul," the priest contended.

Pascal stared out the window at the tiny vine Merle had planted. It was pathetic. The green leaves were barely visible but she had been diligently watering it. Those backpackers he'd thrown out of his house—had he been too harsh? Why hadn't he let them sleep in the backyard? Or at least give them something to eat? Maybe they weren't Norwegian. Maybe they were from some awful, autocratic country they had to flee from, afraid for their lives.

He rubbed his forehead. He had jumped to conclusions. They were no different from the Chicken Man, tramping from place to place, hoping for handouts. They were a bit arrogant and entitled, at least the man, but that was no excuse for callous disregard.

Pascal picked up the autopsy report again. Roméo was only forty-two years old and he had the ailments of an old man. Rough living had taken its toll. He was missing the tips of two fingers on his left hand, an old injury. One ankle was bruised in the recent past. More bruises behind his knees. He had nothing in his stomach.

Was he from the area? How and when had he arrived in Sainte-Colette? Had he walked in from somewhere? No answers in the investigation. They hadn't found out anything about him besides his name and the fact that he talked about his military service. (The detectives hadn't bothered to check if that was true.) He had not been wearing shoes, boots, or socks when his body was found. Where were they? Did he not have shoes? Did he walk everywhere barefoot? His blood alcohol was high, nearly 0.10 percent.

Where was he going? And what the hell was he doing?

Thirty-Four

SAINTE-COLETTE

Merle stood silently next to Jane, staring at the vast display of memorial plaques, urns, chubby cherubs, and vases covering the walls and tables in the large 'hospitality' room at the funeral home. Jane had been a half hour late, driving carefully from the château into the village then onto the side road to find the funeral home. By the looks of the business, death was a big money-maker in France. They'd already taken a look at the caskets, dramatically lit with spotlights and lined with silk, with equally dramatic pricing.

Harris, Jane had explained, had balked at cremation in the end. Ernest had made a plan for it but Harris said no. The fiery end absolutely mortified him. So they had picked the cheapest casket they could find in the room. "It's going underground," Jane said loudly. And you couldn't argue with that, especially if, like the director, you didn't speak English.

He was a short, round, jolly sort of man with a white Santa Claus beard, not the gloomy, scrawny funeral director you might expect. His soft voice and quiet manner were well-suited to his task of helping the bereaved. Merle had never met Ernest and Jane admitted she didn't know him well. So they did their best for Harris without, obviously, breaking the bank.

The director assumed Jane was the grieving wife and Merle didn't correct him. It was too complicated. Now they were expected to pick out a memorial plaque or gravestone or statuary. "Where the bloody hell are we going to bury him?" Jane whispered to Merle.

"Has Harris worked that out?"

"Not that I can tell. Maybe the family will take him back to England."

"Expensive though," Merle noted. "Like all of this. Is there a budget?"

"He had funeral insurance, thank the gods. But really. This is all eye-watering." Jane ran her finger over a marble plaque, the sort that sat flush with the ground. "Should we wait on cemetery stuff? In case the family wants to do something?"

It was agreed they could wait. The rule was burial in six days, not finished gravesite. Jane signed the paperwork for the service and casket, handed over the insurance information, and they were on their way. Back to the village to find flowers. Jane led the way in Harris's little green car that looked like a throat lozenge on wheels. Merle followed at a ridiculously slow speed. Parking was accomplished, at length. But the florist, the only one in the village, was closed.

"Now what?" Jane said, cupping her eyes to peer through the windows at the displays of lilies and roses inside. "Do we call them?"

Merle read the number on a weathered sign on the door. She punched it into her phone. It rang inside; no one answered.

"Let's find a café. Have you had lunch?"

Jane agreed to be led to food although not without grumbling about the cost of it. She reminded Merle of descendants of Puritans she'd met in New England. Maybe Jane was one too, fundamentally opposed to spending money. Merle had long since accepted the prices in bistros all over France because the service and the food itself was almost always impeccable. The French seemed incapable of ruining a meal and prided themselves on serving patrons respectfully.

The café they spotted sat on the market *place* with a red awning, in Merle's experience always a good sign. Jane let her order for them both. With two country salads and two glasses of rosé on the way, Merle sat back in her chair. The sunshine was warm on their legs. Jane was frowning at the children playing in the fountain nearby.

"For the flowers," Merle announced, "I see a few possibilities. One, we do it. We pick roses and whatever and make a couple big bouquets for the front of the room. Two, I can try to order something with a florist in Malcouziac. Or, three, wait until Monday morning and swing by the florist here and grab whatever is already arranged and ready."

"What if there isn't anything ready and/or appropriate?" Jane asked.

"There's that."

"Or they aren't open on Mondays."

The wine arrived, with a baguette and good butter. Merle pushed the bread toward Jane. The woman had sunken cheeks and the pale complexion of someone who didn't take care of themselves. Merle hoped that was just because of circumstances. Jane wore a sack-like brown dress today with her red tennis shoes. Her collar bone protruded at the neckline.

"I'll see what I can do back in my village," Merle said. If worse came to worse she would meander around and clip roses off hedges. Jane hadn't offered to do any flower arranging. Maybe she just didn't care. "Flowers aren't a high priority," Merle said.

Jane didn't disagree. She crossed her arms and sipped her wine. Her frown extended to her hairline. It was a difficult time for her brother, and by extension her.

"Are you having people come to the house after the service?" Merle asked. It was customary, especially for neighbors who wanted to bring baked goods. And they would.

Jane's expression deepened. "Must I?"

Merle shrugged. "No, but I have a feeling people will come anyway. You might as well be prepared."

Jane rolled her eyes and downed her rosé. She signaled the waiter for another glass.

"Is anyone else in your family coming?" Merle asked.

Jane shook her head. "He wouldn't let me call anyone."

"Is he estranged from them?"

Jane shot her a look. "What do you mean?"

"Sorry. Nothing."

The waiter slipped a fresh glass of wine in front of her and whisked away the empty one. Jane took a breath. "We have a brother, Rupert. He's a— a wanker, to be honest. Very upwardly mobile. He wouldn't come anyway. He doesn't *approve* of Harris's *lifestyle,* by which he means, his *life.* They don't speak."

Merle thought they should at least give Rupert, intolerant wanker that he was, the chance to redeem himself. "I'm sorry. What about Ernest's family?"

"Oh, they don't approve either. Is it any wonder they left the UK? But now that he's gone they are suddenly ready to reconcile. It's a joke. Too little and considerably too late. His mother and sister and a couple cousins are coming, I think. I guess I have to play hostess. And I hate to play hostess— to anyone."

Merle didn't have any advice for that. She thought about her own sisters, how warm and accepting they were most of the time. How they loved to play hostess and go to parties and support each others' dreams. She was lucky. Jane looked very unhappy. Merle hoped she had a significant other somewhere. The salads thankfully arrived.

Merle reconsidered Pascal's digging into the death of the homeless man as she watched the schoolchildren run around the *place.* Who knew him, who might have some information about who he was? Wasn't that the first step in figuring out what happened? Did he have relatives to be informed? But she knew no one in this village and, if it was anything like Malcouziac, the citizens were unlikely to open up to an outsider.

The waiter appeared again as they put down their forks, sated with lettuce, olives, ham, eggs, and all good things. Merle had an idea. "*Merci.*" She smiled at him and spoke in French. "I once saw that nice homeless man, *le sans-abri,* around here. I have some bread and fresh cherries for him. Do you know where I can find him?"

The waiter, a nice-looking twenty-something probably on his college break, raised his dark eyebrows. "You mean Roméo?"

"Yes, that's his name."

"I'm sorry, madame. He has died. It was in the news."

Merle feigned shock. "Oh, dear. That's terrible. Was it from living rough?"

The waiter looked uncomfortable, juggling the empty plates. "It was

—un acte criminel—foul play." He turned to go and Merle leaned forward to thwart his escape.

"Is there a fund set up for him, for a funeral or his relatives? I would like to help."

As he walked away the waiter looked over his shoulder. "Ask the priest."

"What was that about?" Jane asked as they walked out into the sunshine on the cobblestones. "With the waiter."

Merle smiled. "A small fiction. I told him I was looking for the homeless man."

Jane winced. "Why?"

"I wondered if anyone knew more about him, where he was from. I asked if there was a fund set up for his funeral. That occurred to me after I saw how much they cost."

"And is there?"

"Maybe." Merle paused and looked at Jane. "Do you want to visit the priest with me? The church looks quite well preserved." She gestured at the tall spire that dominated the other end of the *place.* The church was small but neat, its yellow stone cleaned and the brass doors polished. "But maybe you need to get back to Harris."

Jane paused and for the first time all day the wrinkles on her forehead eased and a smile tugged at her lips. She blinked. "I love a moldy old church."

Thirty-Five

MALCOUZIAC

There was one thing Pascal could do from home in the hunt for information about Roméo Auguste: dig around on the internet. Military records were often found there, mostly by people researching their dead relatives. But nothing came up under that name. So Pascal did the next best thing, call in a favor.

He started with a tech he knew at the *Police Nationale*, one of those data geeks that can find anything if it's linked to the archives of the state. Everybody was linked to the state these days. He checked the time. He still had a couple hours before everything shut down for the weekend.

Denis-Antoine answered immediately. He wore his headset for a reason, after all. He was glad to hear from Pascal who had sent him six bottles of good French wine the last time he'd been of service.

"Criminal record, military service, any government assistance, that sort of thing," Pascal said.

"What's the name," Denis-Antoine asked, already clacking away on his various computers. His set-up was like the cockpit of a spaceship, multiple screens and keyboards.

"Roméo Auguste. Age, possibly forty-two. No known address."

After a few minutes of typing, Denis-Antoine came back with the bad news. "Nothing. Are you sure of the name?"

"Try it the other way 'round."

"Auguste Roméo. Okay." Another pause. "Nothing."

"Hmmm. Can you try variations? Rémy Augustine, things like that?"

"I'll just put the first letters in and see what happens. R and A. Male. Oh, and the age. Location?"

"Gironde and Dordogne."

After a wait the tech said, "Well, there's a long list. It didn't filter by age for some reason. Do you want to go through it? Maybe a thousand names."

Pascal sighed. "Sure." He gave the tech his email address and thanked him.

"Some *Bourgogne* this time, Pascal. My mother thanks you."

The email arrived quickly. Pascal looked at the attached file with the list of names and groaned. Forty pages of names. Well, he would see if he could make the printer behave.

When he returned downstairs from the bedroom closet, victory over the printer in hand, he had another email from Denis-Antoine.

And so the printer must obey again.

A frustrating hour later Pascal sat in the garden, his reading glasses perched on his nose. He hated the glasses but since he was nearly fifty and every 50-year-old in France either used or needed reading glasses, he was resigned. Only his vanity was hurt.

A heavy black pen in hand, he crossed out obvious non-starters on the list. This took some scrutiny, and guesswork. He didn't want to cross out someone who might actually be Roméo. Working his way down the list, through the Raymund's and René's, he began to wonder. How was he to tell if one of these men used 'Roméo' as a nickname? And Auguste could be a middle name. Maybe start with the location first, those living closest to Sainte-Colette. He went into the house for a map of Nouvelle-Aquitaine and began again.

By dinnertime Pascal had narrowed his focus to six possible names. All the men lived near Bergerac or Saint-Émilion. None were officially in Sainte-Colette but he couldn't find a single one in that village. He wrote their names and addresses on a separate sheet of paper.

Each was around 40 years old. Maybe he should have asked Denis-Antoine for middle or hyphenated names. He had a feeling Auguste was not the man's actual last name. He did a quick search on his phone for last name 'Auguste' in France. Well, there were plenty but still he wondered.

It was after six. Where was Merle? He stared at the shadows on the garden wall. This was getting him nowhere. He gathered his papers and went inside. His reading glasses had given him a headache. It was time for a glass of wine.

MERLE ARRIVED a half hour later with dinner in hand. She'd made an exception to her rule to cook at home except when celebrating or guests were in residence. She'd stopped at a restaurant they both liked, situated between Sainte-Colette and Malcouziac. It was a country inn with delicious stews and soups, some of Pascal's favorite meals. She brought in a small tub of *boeuf bourguignon* and a baguette. She warmed the stew on the range, poured herself a glass of wine, and set the bowls outside in the warm evening air.

"How is Jane then?" Pascal asked as he tore off some bread and dipped it into the stew.

"Managing. Barely." Merle ate a spoonful and took a deep breath. "So good."

"What kept you so long?"

"Oh. We got the funeral business done, more or less— the florist was closed and we might have to scavenge for roses— so we ate lunch in Sainte-Colette. What a sweet village. I asked the waiter at the café if he knew what happened to the homeless man. That I had some food to give him. I pretended to be someone who helped him before."

He smiled. "So charming."

"Well. After hearing the tragic news, I asked if there was a fund set up for his burial. He told me to ask the priest. So Jane and I went to the church."

"And did you find the priest?"

"We did."

Merle and Jane discovered the young priest, busy in his office at the parish rectory next door to the church. He was a plain, pleasant man with an earnest demeanor, pale complexion, and dusty brown hair, just the sort of person you would imagine going into the priesthood. Merle asked him if there was a fund set up to pay for the burial expenses of Roméo. "I called him by his first name, as if we were acquainted."

"And is there?"

The priest told Merle there wasn't but he'd be happy to make that happen. He looked surprised he hadn't thought of it himself. The women blessed his effort with enthusiasm. He opened a ledger to a fresh page and wrote in the title, 'Burial Fund for Roméo Auguste.'

"I said, 'oh, is that his last name?' Like I'd never heard it before."

Pascal blinked. "What did he say?"

"He said that was what everyone called him. But that Roméo left a bundle behind once. And the priest looked through it. He said he wanted to find out how to contact Roméo to retrieve his things."

"And?"

"There was no address or phone number. Just an old government identification card. For health services maybe."

Pascal waited impatiently, arms crossed.

Merle smiled. "His name is— was— Roland *hyphen* Auguste Sardou. Not Roméo at all."

Pascal slapped the table. "I knew it!"

"You did? Which part?"

"I suspected that Auguste was part of his given name, that's all. And I have spent hours searching through lists of names of men with the initials R and A. What a waste of time."

Merle squeezed his hand. "You should have just asked me to help."

"And did you contribute to the fund, *chérie*?"

"Jane and I each gave twenty euros. I would have given more but that's all I had on me."

Pascal took her hand in both of his. "It's a start." He jumped to his feet. "Now I must re-start my search."

LATE THAT NIGHT, long after Merle had gone to bed, as the moon shone on the sheets and lit the room with a blue glow, Pascal crawled into bed. There was no satisfaction, no elation for all his work, and Merle's, in discovering the identity of Roméo. None of his story was uplifting or hopeful. Pascal stared at the ceiling's cracks, wondering how this information was at all relevant to the mystery of who had killed him.

Merle rolled over and brushed his shoulder. He looked down and saw her eyes were open. "Still awake?" He stroked her hair.

"I was wondering," she said softly. "What's happening. Why you are doing this? Trying to find Roméo's murderer. Are you trying to impress Harris or something?"

"What do you mean?"

She propped her elbow on her pillow. "Do you think absolving Ernest of guilt will somehow make Harris want to sell you the vineyard? That he'll be so grateful and, I don't know, want to be partners?"

Pascal frowned at her then looked at the moon, half full but so bright. She was wrong. He closed his eyes for a moment. Was she? He looked into his heart, trying to be honest with himself. He had desired the vineyard in a primal, needy way, like it was a seductive woman, as if it would save him from stagnation and slow bureaucratic death. But would it? He would still have the job. He wouldn't quit. And a lot more headaches with a vineyard to run. No, the vineyard was a dream he clutched like a life preserver. But it would not save him. It would not make him whole. His problems would still be his problems. He would still turn fifty and grow old.

This was not about the vineyard. Not when Ernest was dead and presumed a murderer. Not when a homeless man died a violent death.

He sighed. "No, blackbird. I have given up on that dream. It was hard but I am over it. It won't happen, I accept that. I was obsessed. I had this buzz in my head, stars in my eyes. But this— quest or whatever — is just for Ernest. To clear his name. And for Roméo. To find out what happened. Who killed him. Who left him dying in an abandoned vineyard like a dog. It seems no one cares."

She touched his cheek with the back of her hand. "No one but you, my handsome crusader. And that is enough."

Thirty-Six

Merle rose late the next morning. The birds had sung and flown off. In the kitchen the espresso was cold so she made a new pot. When it was done she carried her demitasse cup into the garden to bathe in the sun. Pascal had set up the umbrella by the laundry house and moved the green table and chairs under it. It looked like an outdoor office, papers, laptop, pens, everywhere.

He was on his mobile. "Yes, I understand." He raised his empty cup to her. She took it back to the kitchen and poured him another espresso, wondering how many he'd had already.

"*D'accord. Merci.*" He dropped his phone on a stack of papers. "Thank you, *chérie.*" He sipped his coffee and sighed.

"Have you discovered anything about Roméo, er, Roland-Auguste?"

"Indeed, blackbird." He grabbed a sheet on the table and stepped over to where she sat on the chaise under the spindly apple tree. "Look at this."

She glanced at the paper, covered with dates and entries like a spreadsheet. "You've been busy." She read the sheet.

Roland-Auguste Sardou, also known as Roméo Auguste, was born in a small village in the Limousin department. He left school at 14, enlisted in the military at 17, was discharged at 19. After his service he floundered, getting arrested multiple times for petty crimes. He tried to re-enlist at 22 but was turned down. He was arrested at 27 for auto theft and a few other things and put in jail for three years.

"Not a great tale," Merle said, wincing.

"Keep going."

His address at discharge from prison was his parents' house in the same village where he was born. But the next year he was registered at a shelter in Bordeaux for the homeless. The social services agencies signed him up for various things: social protection, food aid, health assistance, and so on. He seemed to use the services for a few months then ran into some trouble and the shelter lost track of him.

There was nothing between age 32 and 40.

"Where was he for those years?" Merle asked.

"I haven't discovered. Off the grid, I guess. Not using services, also not arrested."

"So maybe employed?"

"No taxes paid but he could have been paid in cash. That is common at vineyards and farms."

The first sign of him in Sainte-Colette was two years ago when he was arrested for stealing chickens. The arrest records had him living in a tent in a public park, illegally. Merle mused again about whoever was camping in the backyard of the little twin cottages. Was it someone like Roméo, or the squatter in Malcouziac who was a little off in the head? Where were the mental health services?

"Do you think he needed a psychiatric check?"

Pascal said, pointing: "Right there. He had one after the arrest in Sainte-Colette. He passed it and spent a month in jail for the chickens."

"I wonder why he didn't leave the area."

"Too many chickens."

Roméo had more skirmishes with law enforcement over the next two years, until around Easter this year, when he was asked to leave town. Brief notes in the file said some citizens paid his bus fare to Bordeaux and sent him on his way.

Merle handed the sheet back to Pascal. "Colorful." She frowned. "I guess people slip through the cracks in every society. Does that help you figure out what happened to him?"

Pascal shrugged. "Not yet."

"I wonder who these nice citizens were who sent him packing. And how he got back to the village."

"I am working on that," Pascal said. "Just barely one step ahead of you."

AN HOUR later Pascal announced his intention to drive back to Sainte-Colette and do some digging. He promised to stop in on Harris and Jane and see if they were all right.

At the door Merle called after him. "Ask the priest. He knows everybody."

Back inside she sat down at his desk and opened her laptop. What were her sisters doing on this first Saturday in June? What was her son doing? She tried to call Tristan over FaceTime but he didn't answer. She sighed and closed her computer.

The lists she'd made, ideas about the little houses in Pâquiers, lay under the laptop. She tugged on them, sliding them out. So many possibilities, so much work. But maybe just try to make the one on the right inhabitable, as she'd considered before. What would that cost?

She put her chin in her hand and daydreamed about refurbishing the cottages, what color she might paint them, what flowers to plant, the porch chairs, the yard, the bathrooms, the kitchens: all of them swirled in her mind as if dreaming could make it so.

Francie's list of suggestions was detailed and bullet-pointed, just the way Merle liked. First on it was kitchen cabinets and appliances. What would they cost? It had been a few years since she'd outfitted her own kitchen. She opened her laptop again to search for local prices. As she navigated to a store in Bordeaux that sold ranges and refrigerators, the email notification popped up in the corner.

It was from Thérèse Levett, the property agent. Interesting coincidence. All you had to do was think about a property and your agent contacted you.

 Bonjour, Merle. How are you this fine summer day? I just wanted to inform you that the price on those two little houses is going down tomorrow. If you are still interested, let me know. I think there is much interest in the town. À bientôt, Thérèse L.

Merle stared at the email. It was written two days ago. The price would already have been reduced. By how much? It was already ridiculously low at €20,000. A little more in US dollars: $23,000 or $24,000. She contemplated writing back to ask the new price, or searching on the web. Instead she picked up her mobile and called Thérèse.

It rang so many times Merle almost hung up. She began to leave a voicemail when Thérèse came on the line. "*Allo! Pardon.* I am showing some very fine people a property." She lowered her voice. "Not *your* property, madame." She giggled.

"Not yet, madame."

"But soon? You are still interested?"

Merle paused. "Is there a new price?"

"There is. The tragedy is that the mayor's widow, remember— the owner? She has died and the estate is eager to get rid of the property."

"Oh? Why?" Merle frowned. There must be something very wrong, besides what she could see— rot, mold, and squatters.

"It is the grandsons. There are five of them. They want to split things up and move on. They are not interested in the property."

"If I was to make an offer— *if* I did, what is the process of inspection? In the US we do home inspections and the deal can be canceled if issues are found."

Thérèse excused herself for a moment, saying goodbye to her other clients. "I am sorry. They are sold in the condition you see. *Telles quelles.* What do you call it? 'As-is'?"

"So what is the new price?"

"Fifteen-thousand. But I must tell you someone else has made an offer."

"Oh, okay. That's fine."

"Do not sound of resignation, my friend. It is a low offer. Ten-thousand."

"Did they take it?"

"No. It is just sitting there, for about a week. I think they do not want to take it."

"So if I offer something above ten-thousand they might take it?"

Thérèse agreed it was possible. Merle said she'd think about it and rang off. Her hands were shaking. Her heartbeat thudded in her ears. She took a deep breath and blew it out. She wasn't a risk-taker, a gambler. She was the person who made a hundred lists of pros and cons before making a decision.

What the hell was she doing?

Thirty-Seven

SAINTE-COLETTE

The priest's name was Père Thaddée Auclair. "Call me Thaddée, please," he said, shaking Pascal's hand in his small, cluttered office in the rectory. A smell of cooking permeated the place, bacon and oil. It was a sparsely furnished, austere sort of place, more monastery than gilded temple. None of that Vatican glamour.

"How can I help?" The priest asked, a cordial smile on his face. He turned over a notebook he'd been writing in, his sermon for the next day perhaps.

"I'm told you knew the homeless man who was killed recently. Roméo." Pascal waited for his nervous nod. "I am trying to find more information about the man. To try to place him on the night he was killed. Had you seen him that day?"

"Are you with the Police? I spoke to them already."

"Just a concerned friend. I am with the wine fraud division so I work around here." Pascal waited to see how that went over then repeated: "Did you see him around the time he was killed?"

The priest blinked rapidly. "I— I saw him two, maybe three days before. He sometimes stopped in to get a bite to eat and I was happy to oblige."

"Was that visit remarkable in any way?"

"Remarkable? No. But—" He frowned and looked at the side wall. Pascal waited him out. "He mentioned something about being harassed by some local boys. I didn't think much of it. I imagine it happened to him often."

"What sort of harassment?"

"Name-calling, I believe. He didn't say exactly. I noticed some bruising on his hands and feet. He rarely wore shoes, at least in the summer."

"He wasn't wearing shoes when he was found."

Thaddée shrugged. "He said Jesus was shoeless."

"Did he think of himself that way, as a prophet?"

"I don't know. I'd say more like a martyr, although to what I was never sure."

Pascal thought about that. If he was getting harassed constantly, he probably would consider himself a martyr, or at least a glutton for punishment. "Did he accept the *intimidation*? Was it part of who he was?"

The priest stared at him for a long moment. "Suffering was a part of him. He felt it deeply."

"Did he accept it as his lot in life?"

"Perhaps. He had done things he wanted to atone for. I heard his confession a time or two. He wanted to be happy. He told me that several times. Stories of happy days he had, living in orchards, surrounded by flowers and bees, stretched out in the sunshine, washing in a stream. He said the bees never stung him. That they knew he was just like them, trying to live a good life. Trying to make honey, he said." The priest smiled sadly.

"Can you tell me what he confessed to? Was it an *acte criminel*?"

The priest shook his head. "*Privé, monsieur.*"

"Maybe not to those he victimized. He stole quite often, didn't he?"

"Well, when you're desperate and hungry, of course you do. Like Jean Valjean in the story, stealing a loaf of bread because his family was starving."

Pascal nodded. "I understand. The *gendarmes?* Not so much. Perhaps a month in jail wasn't so bad then? He got his meals." The priest shrugged. "I heard some citizens raised money to buy him a bus ticket? To Bordeaux?"

"Yes, I—" The priest covered his mouth with a hand and shook his head as if telling himself to say no more.

Pascal waited for him to calm down then asked, "Was it controversial? Sending him away?"

Father Thaddée looked at him beseechingly. When Pascal raised his eyebrows, the priest sagged in his chair. "These are my *paroissiens*, my flock, monsieur. I didn't like it," he said softly. "It was cruel."

"What was cruel about it?"

"The way they ganged up on him, all the elites. Families who had helped him in the past but now wanted him gone, out of their lives. He made their town dirty, they said. They hounded him until he left."

"They disliked him."

He nodded. "And so he grew to dislike them, although that wasn't his first instinct. He didn't hate people, in general. He was a simple man with simple needs. He wasn't violent, just confused. They had given him a place to sleep out of the cold, some food from their tables, then they turned their backs on him."

"Then why did he come back?"

The priest scrunched his face in thought. "He didn't say."

"*When* did he come back? Did he tell you that?"

"The day before I saw him."

Pascal walked out of the gloomy parish house into the morning sunshine. The pretty market *place* was surrounded with bouquets of summer flowers in purple, red, and white. They hung from lampposts and lined the edges of the sidewalks. The fountain trickled merrily. A cheerful sight, he thought, disguising perhaps rot in the village.

The priest's story made him think of Luc Naudé, the man he'd almost come to blows with at the Ambassador's party. He could see Naudé making a spectacle of Roméo, telling him, as he'd told Pascal, that Sainte-Colette was *his* town and to never darken it again. Was he the instigator of the bus ticket to Bordeaux?

But it wasn't illegal, was it, to buy someone a bus ticket out of town? Not very sympathetic but not against the law. Pascal sat on a bench and pulled his notebook from his back pocket. He wrote down what the priest had said then flipped to the history of Roland-Auguste Sardou. The owner of the *boulangerie* was one person the police talked to. And there, across the place, was her establishment, *Boulangerie Marianne.* Complete with a painting of the French icon in her flag-waving, bare-breasted glory on the front window.

Pascal smiled, eyeing Marianne's bosom. He decided to like this bakery. Unfortunately the owner, whose name was also Marianne, had little new to say about Roméo. She didn't allow him into her establishment because he was dirty and barefoot. She'd thrown him out once and he got the message. If he found scraps in her garbage bin though, she didn't run him off. He liked her bread after all.

It was late afternoon by the time Pascal drove east to Malcouziac, having spent the entire day talking to people about Roméo and his demise. He was no closer to knowing what had happened to him, but at least had some kind of timeline now. The hills glowed red as the sun went down behind him. Summer was truly here now. Roses bloomed by abandoned homesteads, vines trailed with white flowers, and tourists were out and about.

Merle was in the garden again— or still. He stuck his head out and asked if she was ready for wine. "Bring it on!" she called in a distinctly American way like she was on a television game show. He poured her some rosé and for himself, a Côte du Rhône. He unwrapped the cheese tray in the refrigerator and took it all out into the warm afternoon sun.

She looked flushed, her cheeks rosy.

"How was your day?" He set the cheese and wineglasses on the green table. She'd pulled it out from under the umbrella. Maybe she was sunburned. "You look a bit pink, *chérie.*"

She sipped Perrier from the bottle. Also American. "I got hot. I went for a brisk walk in the countryside to clear my head."

"Was your head cloudy?"

"It was." She smiled at him. "And you? How was your day of investigating?"

"Your friend the priest was most enlightening. Very sympathetic."

"I had that impression of him too."

Pascal told her the priest's story of his acquaintance with Roméo, the harassment he'd endured, the banishment, the last time the priest had seen him.

"Who are these local boys?" she asked. "And the members of his flock?"

"I am still working on that. I have my suspicions."

"That man at the soirée? He looked cruel enough."

Pascal admitted he had the same thought. "We'll see if we can find any witnesses. It may be difficult. They seem to be very tight-knit. That is the term?"

She smiled. "You always get it right, Pascal. And Harris and Jane?"

"Harris seems a little better. Out of bed at least."

"Good. And Jane is coping?"

Pascal shrugged. "Harris was ready to talk."

"That's a good sign. That takes courage."

"Well. Maybe. He and I took a walk around the south side of the house, beyond the outbuildings. He had to tend his chickens, collect some eggs. You would have enjoyed it, blackbird." He smiled, recalling her childlike excitement at gathering eggs at his sister's house. "Do you know there is a ruined abbey on the property? Just two walls remain, and a lot of rubble. It was knocked down during the Revolution."

Her eyes sparked. "I have to see it. I love old stuff."

Pascal looked away from her eager face. He would love to show her all the things he'd found on the property— but that wasn't going to happen.

"So, what did you ask him?" she said. "I've already forgotten the list."

He reached for his notebook in his back pocket. It was bent and ragged but still served its purpose. He pulled out the list she'd made for him. "You remember. No one has a better memory than you."

"Once upon a time. Now I daydream all day." She glanced at the sky.

"Okay, sure. Number one. What were you and Ernest doing on that Monday before the death? He said they were at home as usual. Neither went out. He rounded up his hens about seven o'clock. Ernest came inside for dinner soon after. Nothing unusual."

"So they are each other's alibi."

Pascal nodded. "Number two. Did you know Roméo or have interactions with him? He said he had met him once, in town. He tried to give Roméo some change but he refused, saying the shopkeepers didn't allow him in their shops. So Harris went to the boulangerie and bought him a baguette. Also he saw Roméo walking the farm roads last year during harvest. He assumed that the man had work somewhere nearby."

"Nearby Corbeaux?" Merle asked.

"Yes. I tried to get him to pin down where he'd seen Roméo walking, and he thought it was close by but he couldn't be sure."

"But he didn't work for Harris and Ernest."

"No. Three. Did Ernest know Roméo or mention him? Apparently Ernest did know him and had also helped him in the past. Harris wasn't sure what Ernest had done. Maybe given him money or food. He didn't know where they met. But he was sure they had spoken."

"I suppose the police knew that too."

The rest of the list was a dud. They sipped their wine and ate a little cheese in silence, each thinking of what new questions might lead to enlightening answers.

"Did you ask if Roméo had ever been to the vineyard before?" Merle asked.

"Harris said he only met him in town."

"But Ernest might have had seen him at the vineyard, spoken to him there?"

Pascal shrugged. "I don't think we'll ever know, *chérie*."

"What about that little piece of paper with the name of the vineyard on it?"

"Harris had no idea where that came from. In fact, he didn't even know about it. I believe it freaked him out, as you say. Such an obvious link between the vineyard and the dead man."

Merle frowned. "Maybe too obvious? Do you think someone planted it on him?"

"It's possible."

"Do you have a photo of it? Maybe we can check handwriting samples?"

Pascal smiled. "With five-thousand locals? Like the glass slipper?"

She sighed. "What we need are leads. Solid ones." She leaned forward, alert. "Oh, and flowers for the funeral. Do you know the florist here in Malcouziac?"

Thirty-Eight

SAINTE-COLETTE

With the always helpful Madame Suchet across the street, Merle was able to locate the local florist. Merle realized she'd met Roseline Lajoie at the weekly market where she sold flowers in the summer, grown in her own extensive garden. Madame Suchet knew where *la fleuriste* lived so on Sunday they walked over and asked her if she could make two memorial bouquets for Ernest.

When the bouquets were ready, about midday on Monday, Merle picked them up from the shop, Verts et Fleurs. She had often walked by the pink storefront, bursting with blooms and ferns and pine boughs in season but had never ventured inside. It smelled heavenly, roses mostly at this time of year, but also lilies and jasmine. Merle stood in the middle of the jungle of blossoms, stunned by the beauty. Roseline had a definite bias toward pink roses. They were everywhere, round and fat. Eventually Merle had to go, paying for the bouquets and gathering them up in her arms.

The service wasn't scheduled until four o'clock. Merle arrived three hours early, carefully transporting the large arrangements into the building from her back seat where she'd strapped them into seat belts. With the blessing of the funeral director she set each one on a fluted black pedestal at the front of the small room and went back to her car, mission accomplished. As she walked through the car park, a florist van with a Saint-Émilion address painted on its side panels pulled up to the door. A man in a gray jumpsuit opened the back. He looked at tags on bouquets then took an enormous wreath carefully out of the truck and carried it into the funeral home.

Merle sat in her Peugeot. She had nowhere to go so waited to see what would happen next. Were these flowers for Ernest? Maybe there was another service today. Her curiosity roused, she got out of the car again and leaned against it, playing with her phone. The delivery man, a teenager with a pretend mustache, reappeared. For a moment she thought he would close the back doors and leave. But he jumped into the back instead. She moved closer.

He climbed down again, turned, and took a massive lily arrangement three feet tall, wrapped in plastic, from the truck and into the funeral home. A small casket spray sat on a shelf in the back corner of the interior of the truck, spring flowers in pink and blue mixing with white lilies. The name on the tag was 'Brooks.' She leaned closer. The sender— also Brooks. These must be from his family members.

Merle drove away, feeling a little better. Ernest's family was scheduled to arrive yesterday from England but the fact that they sent flowers as well was heart-warming. He was loved.

Merle wasn't fond of funerals. But she would be there for Jane and Harris, as would Pascal. The service was for the living. Plus Jane had practically begged.

In the city parking lot outside Sainte-Colette Merle texted Pascal: "Meet me in S-C at that sweet café on the *place*? I'm ordering wine ASAP." He replied that he'd be there in thirty minutes. She walked through the town, looking in windows, admiring flowers growing in window boxes and planters. She called Francie as she strolled.

"Hey there," Francie said. She sounded energetic but slightly wary.

"Where are you, world traveler?"

"Home. We flew back yesterday. Pretty sluggish today but I guess that's just jet lag."

"Dylan flew with you, I hope," Merle said. Francie did not like flying much, since her ex-husband the pilot was revealed to be an alcoholic.

"He did. He's being very sweet, Merle, just as the sisters predicted. I think he's actually a little excited about it."

"'It?' Are you going to find out boy or girl?"

"I already did. They insisted on genetic tests in Paris. That 'geriatric' thing. But I haven't told Dylan. I pretend I don't know." She laughed. "It's more fun that way."

"Are you at his house now?"

"No, my apartment. I have to go to work tomorrow so I'm just going to sleep all day. I mean, why not? It's quiet, it's dark."

"How is the fatigue then?"

"It's better. My latest blood work was fine. I'm not anemic any more."

Francie talked about finding a doctor and a midwife and a doula and a nanny and a birthing support group. Having a child was a team sport these days. But she sounded ready to tackle all the decisions. This would be her ultimate task.

"But right now, back to law." Francie sighed. "And I suppose I have to tell them now that I'm fat."

"What will you tell them, besides the obvious?"

"Due date. Maternity leave. Health insurance, that sort of thing. Scheduling of depositions and all that in the fall. Luckily I am intimate with the managing partner." Francie *was* the managing partner at her firm. "One thing though. Are you going to be in the US this fall?"

"I can be. Do you need me?"

"I was going to ask Elise to be my backup, in case Dylan flakes out or has a business trip, but I'd rather have you."

"Then I'll be there. Whether Dylan flakes out or not. I'll buy my ticket tomorrow."

By the time the call was finished, Pascal rounded the corner at the far end of the market place. It was funny how they'd sort of adopted this town by now. Not wonderful, under the sad circumstances but still, a small bonus. She would like to return on another day, browse through the market or those small shops on the *place*: a *brocante*, a gourmet food shop, and, nearest to where she sat, an art gallery. The window of the gallery displayed a jumble of appealing things: small oil paintings, old books, two large ceramic vases with flowers spilling out of them.

Pascal waved and they met at the red awning of the café. After their *bisous* a waiter waved them to a table.

"*Vin rose, monsieur, s'il vous plaît. Un pichet.*" A pitcher of rosé. Pascal winked at Merle. "We need fortification to get through this afternoon."

With wine poured Pascal looked thoughtful. "You never told me about your cloudy mind, blackbird. Why you needed to go on a walk to clear it."

Merle had been avoiding the subject since Saturday. She still didn't know what to think about the derelict little cottages.

"Oh, that." She waved a hand carelessly, almost knocking over her wineglass. "It was nothing." He squinted at her, waiting. He deserved an answer. "Well, it was a little something that I blew up in my mind."

Pascal looked confused. "Your mind blew up?"

She sighed. "I spoke with the property agent in Pâquiers. Thérèse Levett, she showed me the two cottages." She waited for him to get a picture in his mind. When he frowned she knew he had it. "Those, yes. Overgrown and derelict. But roofs intact, that's something."

"No pigeons?"

"None. A squatter though, just like Malcouziac. Only in the back garden."

"That's why she called? To tell you about a squatter?"

Merle took a sip of wine and carefully set down her glass. "She called to tell me the price had been reduced by five-thousand Euros."

"What was it before?"

"Twenty. So the price is now fifteen. She said someone made a low-ball offer of ten but it has not been accepted." Her heart thumped in her chest. She took a deep breath and surreptitiously blew it out behind her wineglass.

Pascal sat back in his chair. "Do you seriously want to buy those junk houses?"

"Why do you call them that? You haven't been inside. One was recently lived in by an old lady. How bad could it be?" Merle frowned at him. "Are you saying you don't want me to buy them?"

He raised his hands, palms out. "I'm sorry. It is your project."

She reached out for his hand. "But we are a team, aren't we? Partners. I am involved in everything Pascal and you are involved in everything Merle. If you are dead set against this project, as you call it, then say so. It shouldn't come between us."

He blinked, squeezing her hand back. He took a sip of wine. She couldn't tell what he was thinking. That she was an idiot for wanting to remodel those shacks? What was *she* thinking?

This one she knew the answer to. She was thinking that the purchase of the twin cottages would be stressful— on both of them.

But somehow she wanted to buy them anyway.

Thirty-Nine

SAINTE-COLETTE

Pascal and Merle slipped into the room, finding seats behind a family group of four, midway down the rows of chairs. The funeral chapel, or whatever you called it, was draped with black fabric, top to bottom on the walls and windows, with spotlights on the casket and flowers at the front. A small lectern stood at one side of the flowers.

And there were a lot of bouquets. Two large funereal wreaths hung on stands, plus vases of lilies and roses. Another bouquet lay prone against the casket. It was more colorful, as if somehow the inventory of white blooms had been exhausted.

He and Merle had barely spoken after he made that gaffe at the café. Why did he have to be so dismissive of her dreams? She had supported his dream of a vineyard, hadn't she? He was an idiot. Just thinking about his fantasy of being a vigneron made a hard knot form in his chest. He still wanted it, he knew. But Château des Corbeaux was not the answer.

He turned his attention to the people in the room. Who knew Ernest well enough to come to his funeral? Well, you didn't have to be more than a neighbor or acquaintance to attend. Would the killer of Roméo show up? Unlikely. Père Thaddée walked up the aisle with Jane

Austin on his arm. They both wore black slacks. Jane wore a simple white blouse with a black satin tie, the priest his white collar. Was the priest going to deliver the eulogy?

Pascal tipped his head to look around the woman sitting in front of him and startled, realizing too late that they had chosen seats right behind the Naudé family. He hadn't expected them to attend, since they disliked Ernest and Harris so much. Naudé's wife was blonde and fashionable in her black silk dress. The teenagers sat next to her, two boys maybe thirteen and sixteen, he guessed. Strapping boys, especially the older one. They were playing games on their phones.

Luc Naudé turned to whisper in his wife's ear and spotted Pascal. His head jerked back and he scowled. Pascal smiled. The skin on Naudé's neck reddened as he looked back toward the front of the room. He glanced to the other side, perhaps thinking of moving. Just then a parade of women came down the aisle, all dressed in black. Merle had only worn a black skirt today, with a red blouse that stood out in the sea of *noir*.

One elderly lady and four middle-aged ones made up the new party. They sat in the front row on the left. Ernest's family from England, he guessed. They looked English, that is to say, they didn't look French. They also appeared chatty, especially three of the women who looked like sisters, their hair all dyed the same shade of rust. Pascal heard a high-pitched giggle from them and saw Mama give them a hard stare.

"His cousins," Merle whispered, glancing at them. "And sister and mother. We'll meet them later, at the house."

Mon dieu, we must go to the house. Pascal nodded. *Try to behave,* he could hear her thinking. Merle nudged him and pointed with a hand in her lap at the back of Luc Naudé. She mouthed his name. Pascal nodded and rolled his eyes.

Harris arrived and the service began. The funeral director was in charge. There was no music. Pascal tried not to listen. He let his mind wander. The old abbey, lying in ruins these two-hundred years, swam into his mind. The tended vines and the untended vines, the growing grapes, the sun on the hillside as it set. The chickens scurrying through the rows, eating grasshoppers. It was so French and so appealing. He sighed loudly.

Harris didn't perform particularly well. He tried though, you had to give him that. Ernest's sister named Polly had a powerful voice and shoulders like Ernest. Then his mother took the lectern unexpectedly. She apologized to Harris for all the years of censure and neglect. This caused a fresh round of weeping.

Finally the priest gave a benediction. It was bland, ecumenical. He appeared to be reading something unknown to him as he stumbled over words.

Then it was over. Pascal wanted to run from the room but made himself slow down, walk to the side aisle, and duck his head to make his getaway. Without looking back he swung the front door wide and nearly jogged to the BMW. The sun had warmed the tarmac. He jumped inside, sweat popping out on his forehead.

Death and Luc Naudé dogged him. A narrow escape.

He stuck the key in the ignition, ready to peel out when Merle arrived. No sign of her among the mourners he spied in his rear view mirror, filing down the sidewalk. There was the Naudé clan, thankfully on the other side of the lot. He slumped in his seat. He didn't want to speak to the man, or punch him in front of his wife and kids.

Finally Merle appeared at the back door, placing a large wreath on the seat. She tucked the stand in and got in the front. "What's that?"

"I told Jane I'd help bring flowers back to the house. The cousins got the vases so I got this one." She glanced back at it. "Those lilies make me nauseous." She rolled down her window.

"We must go over? I mean, of course. To drop off the flowers."

"And give our regards. We don't have to stay longer than your rules for a cocktail party. That's what—one hour?"

He sighed, pulling around cars and onto the road. "One hour. I can do it."

———

HALF AN HOUR later Pascal lurked in the corner of the sunny kitchen at the château. Even a funeral wasn't an excuse to open the formal parlor. Probably the lack of furniture. They had set up the wreath in there with all the other funeral decor. At least the dining room table served as a place for random dishes and baked goods. There was quite a pile. He grabbed a macaron and a glass of champagne.

He had already spoken briefly to Harris and Jane. Then he'd done his best to avoid the others. Merle was talking to the English women who seemed fascinated by whatever she was saying. They were tipping champagne down their throats and staring at the grapevines, eyes wide. He looked at his watch. Forty minutes to go.

He caught Merle's eye and pointed to the door, miming smoking a cigarette. She smiled and waved him on. He no longer smoked, or at least she thought he didn't. Truth was he'd lost his taste for it but it was good excuse sometimes.

Outside he rifled through his car, trying to find a cigarette. No joy. Well, he would walk around, that was healthier anyway. He walked down the farm lane that led to the outbuildings, past the dusty old barrel room, then the barn where once the grapes were crushed and mixed, and the large shed he imagined as a bottling facility. He made himself keep going, away from those dreams.

A red chicken followed him but he had nothing to feed the old hen. She ran at him, pecked at his shoes angrily. *"Allez!"* he cried, pushing her away with his foot. She squawked and ran back to her flock. He glanced back at the house guiltily.

He reached the ruins of the abbey at the far end of the lane. It sat on the edge of the manicured vineyard, near a wild patch of woods and shrubs. From there the forest began and ran up the hillside, trees and rocks and the occasional goat.

All that remained of the abbey was two standing walls of weathered stone, perpendicular and joined in a corner. How big must it have been? He scuffed the earth, looking for foundations. An odd rock protruded from the weeds. He walked toward it, a straight line from one of the standing walls. The stone was square, hand-hewn by ancient masons. This must be a foundation stone, a cornerstone. He marveled at the length of the abbey, now visible in his mind's eye, at least thirty meters. Was it the Benedictines? They were always planting vines and making wine.

He walked back to the pile of stones near the standing walls. This appeared to be the only remaining debris from the demolition of the abbey. Why were these stones still here when the others presumably had been carted away for another building? That was the usual result of destroying an old building. Only this pile, about four feet high and six feet long, remained. Someone must have made this pile, he thought, as the demolition would not have made such a compact arrangement.

He pulled a few stones off the top of the pile and threw them into the grass. They were heavy and grainy with age, blackened by weather. Was this pile concealing something? He tossed stone after stone off one end of the pile until he got to ground level. A flat slab lay indented into the soil at the edges, with weeds and lichens growing on it. He threw more stones to one side. The end of the slab was nearly four feet wide. It looked like the top of a stone tomb. Dignitaries were often buried in churches, especially in the Middle Ages. He could see ivy leaves trailing the edges. He threw off more stones.

Sweating, half the stones removed from the top of the object, he paused, feeling the ache in his back. What was he doing? But now he noticed something inscribed in the top of the tomb. He rubbed the area, cleaning off mold and lichens. He leaned back, squinting at it, but couldn't make it out. Latin perhaps? The name of some saint? He took out his phone and snapped a photo of the inscription, then backed up for another of the entire scene.

He felt dirty, like he was a voyeur, a grave robber. Did he really want to see the bones of some old papist? He reassembled the pile, replacing half the stones so the tomb was covered with rock. He kicked a few of those he'd thrown back toward the pile. Satisfied with his attempt to disguise the burial site, he walked back to the house, wiping his face with his shirt sleeve.

In front of the château he stopped to collect himself. He was still perspiring and didn't want questions about what the hell he'd been doing. His hands were dirty and sweat ran down his neck. Could he make a quick stop in the bathroom before rejoining the group inside? He leaned against the olive tree, in the shade, trying to cool off.

Footsteps crunched on the gravel drive. He remained in the shadow of the tree, waiting to see who was arriving. A woman, the blonde from the service, the spouse of Luc Naudé, was carrying a cake on a large platter. Behind her trailed the two teenagers, shuffling along, heads down.

She barked an order over her shoulder. One boy skipped ahead and knocked on the door as she waited to the side. He knocked a second time then tried the handle. He pushed the door open and called inside: "*Allo?*"

"*Coucou,*" the woman called. They filed inside, calling once or twice more. Standard procedure for a funeral party. Pascal decided to follow them, curious how this would go. At least the deplorable patriarch hadn't shown his face.

He found them standing in the front hall, looking this way and that. "Back this way," Pascal said, pointing them through the parlor and side hall.

He introduced himself as they walked. "*Enchanté.* Harmonie Naudé," madame said curtly. She was in her forties, coiffed and impeccably dressed, but there was a hardness to her brown eyes. She paused, trying to be polite but making sure he knew it was a trial. "This is Jean-Luc." The older one, big enough to be dangerous at rugby. "And Rémy. My sons. We are neighbors to Ernest and—"

"Harris," Jean-Luc muttered. She repeated it, with a half-smile.

"He's back here," Pascal said, continuing to the kitchen on the back of the house. Lights had been turned on as the evening sun faded. The doors to the back patio were wide now and several guests lounged on chairs outside. He left the Naudé family to fend for themselves as he went to the kitchen sink to wash his hands. As he dried them and dabbed his neck with the towel, he watched as they stood awkwardly in the middle of the room. Apparently they knew no one here. The guests didn't even look their way.

Harmonie Naudé finally set her cake on the kitchen table. She straightened, a crooked smile pasted on her face. She glanced back at her sons for guidance. At that moment Jane Austin stepped over from the windows and stuck out her hand.

"*Bienvenue, madame.*" The other woman shook her hand, looking relieved. She rattled off something in French. Jane replied, "I'm sorry, I don't speak French. But whatever you said, thank you. And also for the lovely cake."

Harmonie looked at Jean-Luc for help. He was a tall lad with his father's looks. He told his mother in French what Jane had said. "My mother wants to say that we are very sorry for the loss of Ernest, for his death. It is tragic."

Jane nodded. "Thank you. I am Harris's sister. You should tell him that." She glanced toward the patio. Harris sat at the garden table, an empty flute of champagne in front of him. "But have a glass of wine. Over there." She gestured to a group of open bottles on the kitchen counter.

Jean-Luc motioned to his mother and the three of them went to get drinks. The boys poured themselves champagne plus one for Mama. The teenagers moved away from her, swilling their bubbles. Pascal stepped over to Harmonie.

"You are neighbors then? Where is your house?" He smiled at her, keeping his tone friendly.

"Across the road. The vineyard there." She pointed in that direction. "You are friends with Ernest?"

"Yes. Very sad what happened. I blame the police."

She frowned. "For a heart attack?"

"Brought on by a false arrest, yes."

"False?" She tried to soften her expression. "*Peut-être.* I suppose we will never know now."

"And you are friends with Ernest and Harris? As neighbors are?"

"Oh, yes. We adored them both. Such kind people. Ernest would help us at harvest, just like the French do, eat supper with the workers. He was most welcome in our home. It is a tragedy, what happened."

Pascal bit his lip and looked around the airy kitchen. "So you don't mind that they are homosexual? I wondered about this part of France."

"Mind? Why should I mind?" She sipped champagne. "Some people can be cruel. But not I, I assure you. I am here to mourn for him, am I not?"

Pascal gave her a sympathetic nod. "Myself, I am against the marriage of two men. But, as you say..." Would she take the bait? She seemed a bit too self-contained to reveal her true feelings but he had to try.

"Not for my boys, surely." She glanced at him. "Do you live nearby?"

"No, madame. In Bordeaux."

"Ah, many degenerates there, the homeless and drug addicts. The country is much healthier for young men. Hard work, fresh air." She set down her glass. "*Enchanté, monsieur.*"

And she walked off to find her sons. They stepped onto the patio to speak to Harris. They spoke to the wrong man first, a friend of Harris's who had come from England for the service. He pointed out Harris and they all turned toward him, embarrassed. The younger son, Rémy, hung back. He looked like he wanted to sink into the earth. Pascal watched from the kitchen sink, smiling.

Merle appeared at his side. "What have you been doing?" She sniffed his shirt. "Hard labor? Arrested again?"

He smiled. "I will show you. But not today."

Forty

MALCOUZIAC

They sat in the garden that evening, as the light in the sky turned violet. Merle had made them country salads for supper and heated up soup. They had both eaten too many cakes and other treats at the party for Ernest. Merle called it a wake then questioned herself.

"What is a wake then?" Pascal asked.

"A party for someone who has died. Often with drinking and song, if you're Irish."

"No singing, was there? Ah, well."

She leaned over her coffee and asked, "So what were you doing during the wake? Running a marathon?"

He smiled. "You were right. It was like prison labor. Throwing rocks."

"What?"

"In that ruined abbey. It may be nothing. But there is a large, ancient tomb under the pile of stones and I'd like to know why it was hidden." He wiggled his eyebrows. "A mystery. I wonder about the previous owner. He must have something to do with it, *oui*?"

He pulled up the photo of the tomb from his phone. "Look at this."

Merle squinted at it. "What does it say?"

"Latin possibly. The name of a saint? I will do a little sleuthing. If only to find out who owned the vineyard before Ernest and Harris."

"You mean Oscar?" Merle smiled, enjoying surprising him.

"Is that his name?"

"Don't you remember Madame Hugo saying she knew him? Her old friend, Oscar, who owned the vineyard for many years."

Pascal sat back. "How did you—"

"I listen, *chéri*."

Now that he remembered the conversation between Madame Hugo and Luc Naudé, a glimmer came back. That 'dear man.' But he'd forgotten the name. He was too wrapped up in his anger.

"Do you know his last name?" he asked Merle.

"No. Do you?"

He shook his head. "I need to find out about him."

"Call the Ambassador."

It seemed so simple, just ring up the French Ambassador to Great Britain. But where was she? In France, in England, in Paris or at her château? How to reach through the many layers of diplomatic protection wrapped around her? It wasn't as if he had a direct line. He thought about it all night. There had to be an easier way than bothering the Ambassador with his irrational quests. She still scared him a little.

THE NEXT MORNING Pascal returned to his office job in Bordeaux. He drove straight to the Cité du Vin where he clicked on his computer and dug around on the internet. First up, Oscar of Château des Corbeaux. He put in the name of the vineyard and a map appeared, telling him where it was located. Not helpful. Nothing else in the search about an Oscar. But who better to ask then the current owners.

Harris didn't answer his mobile. He may have turned it off, tired of the parade of mourners. Pascal didn't blame him. Instead he asked Josef to get property records for the vineyard from wherever such things were stored.

The clerk stared at him from under his dark eyebrows. "That is a monumental task. Some of those vineyards go back centuries. None of it will be computerized."

"This one must be ancient. It has an old abbey on it, or the ruins of one. Check church records while you're at it."

Josef glared harder and turned on his heel. "Wait," Pascal called. "First just find one owner before the current one. Oscar somebody. Then see if someone in Paris can do the rest of the research for you."

Two hours later Josef sent Pascal a short email with the results of his search.

Oscar Boissieu. Born 1929, Died 2016. One daughter, Marcelle. She sold the Corbeaux vineyard in 2018 to current owners, Ernest Brooks and Harris Austin.

Is that enough? I have work to do.

Pascal wondered if he could find out what Ernest and Harris paid for the vineyard. Then he shook himself. Of course he could. But— *don't go there.* He thanked Josef and told him again to send the rest of his request to Paris. "Tell them it is deep background but urgent at the five level."

Oscar Boissieu. Pascal put the name into a search engine and found an obituary from 2016 in the Bergerac newspaper. Oscar's wife had died many years before and Marcelle was the sole heir to the château. Should he contact Marcelle? See what she knows about the ruin and the tomb? He searched for her online.

Marcelle Boissieu never married, it appeared, and had no offspring. She now resided in a care home in Angoulême for Alzheimer's patients or those who had otherwise lost their wits. He dialed the number for the home. In a matter of minutes it was confirmed that Marcelle had advanced dementia despite being only sixty-six years old. A sad story.

Pascal took a deep breath. He had work to do like Josef. Maybe this was a crazy goose chase, a ridiculous thread to unravel. It was just an old tomb in an ancient abbey, probably full of nothing, plundered centuries past. There must be scads of them, all over France. What did he hope to prove by running down the history behind it?

And yet. He looked up the website of the French embassy in

London. In the upper corner— Madame Hugo's lovely face. Would an email get through to her? Probably not.

Instead he sent the photo of the top of the tomb, showing the inscription, to Albert, his old friend and retired priest in Malcouziac. He would know his Latin. It was something.

IN MID-AFTERNOON MERLE ran into Albert at the tiny market off the *place*. She had considered going into Bergerac for groceries but in the end she would make do with what she had, a very French way to eat. They rarely threw anything out. She was always learning some new dish made from potato peels or carrot tops or random bits of gristle and bone. She was inspecting tomatoes when he appeared in the produce section.

"*Bonjour*, Merle," the priest said in his gentle voice. They kissed cheeks. "I hear Pascal is looking into church relics."

Merle rolled her eyes. "I'm not sure why." She eyed Albert with his bright yet rheumy eyes. "What do you know about tombs in abbeys?"

"Very little, I'm afraid." He pulled out his mobile phone, a recent purchase he was still struggling to understand. "He sent me something but I cannot see it. Is it there?"

Merle took the phone from him and opened the photograph. "It's an inscription he's trying to interpret. Can you read it?"

Albert squinted at it. "So small." Merle showed him how to move it with a finger. "Ah. You are brilliant, my child. Here—" He pointed at a section of the inscription. "This part— *Deo Optimo Maximo*. It means 'to God, most good, most great.'"

"Ah. No name of whoever was buried there?"

"It is difficult to see. Oh, here." He pointed again. "Make it bigger." She obliged him. "That says '*Le Comte*,' I think. The Count. But of what? I can't see beyond."

"Would the local church nearby have information about what was in the Abbey before it was destroyed?"

"It's possible. Most abbeys were monasterial though. Just for the monks, not for worship by civilians."

"So could this Count have been a monk?"

Albert shrugged. "What are you having for dinner?"

"Chicken. Can you join me?"

He smiled. "*Bien sûr.*"

They walked home together, parting at the bottom of Rue de Poitiers. Merle carried her sack up the street, thinking of hauling groceries up the five flights of stairs to the smelly flat in Bordeaux. Had Pascal dropped the ball on finding a new place? She hadn't been back to the city in weeks. Summer had arrived *à la campagne.* Why would anyone leave the countryside in June?

Of course she missed him. He was obsessed with that vineyard, despite saying he had given up on his dream there. He hadn't, this abbey business was a sign of that. Anything to stay a little closer to Château des Corbeaux. She had seen his wistful expression as he gazed at the vines.

As she was putting her groceries away her phone rang. It was Irene Fayette, Pascal's neighbor. "Have you seen it?" she growled without explanation.

"What?" Merle froze, frightened.

"At Pascal's. Jacques went by as you requested. No one is renting this week, correct? So he walks around to the back and he sees it. Someone has broken a window."

"Oh, no. Did they go inside?"

"He doesn't check. He scoots along back here. Too dangerous for an old man."

"Right. That's good. I'll check the cameras. Thank you, Irene."

In the parlor she opened her laptop and the application that ran the security cameras. When had this break-in, if that's what it was, occurred? She had never tried to go back and see the video feed from days before. She hadn't really been thinking about Pascal's house beyond checking in renters. Everything had been going smoothly.

An hour later, and a call to the company, and she finally was looking at a fast-motion-in-reverse feed from the backyard camera. It soon went dark, only outlines of trees against a moonless sky. Day again, a sunset, shadows stretched then shortened. She watched, chin in hand, getting weary of this task already. It was so boring, not like it is in the movies. It grew dark again. She was ready to ditch the project and make dinner when something moved in the grass. There—a tail. She slowed the speed of the playback.

No, not a tail— a short brown ear. Two ears, then two more with a large humped back. Then, suddenly, a snout lifted up out of the tall grass. A wild boar. And not just one. She watched as three of them walked backwards on the video. She turned on the speed to high and zoomed ahead. Switching the feed to forward, she watched the three boar wander through the tall grass and reach the steps to the kitchen, snuffing at various things around the back door. Big, hairy hogs, but not too scary. One dark brown boar, the largest of the three, nudged another one to the side and put his nose against a pane of glass in the dining room window as if peering inside the cottage. He raised a hoof to the low sill. Whether intentionally or not, the glass broke, shattering, shards flying. It surprised the *sanglier*. The three wild boar fell back, scrambling to their feet and running back into the woods.

Merle smiled, relieved that the intruder was just a four-legged porker. She would call Irene later and reassure Jacques. She poured herself a glass of wine. Dinner awaited. Albert would be here soon.

Forty-One

BORDEAUX

Pascal's afternoon dragged on. He was buried in forms in triplicate, in endless email chains, in those blasted faxes from the 1980s. He had just had a brief conversation with his boss in Paris, Étienne, when his phone rang again.

"Call for you from US," Josef said. "Line four."

Curious, Pascal pushed his paperwork aside and punched his phone.

"Hey, Pascal, it's Dylan Hardy. How are ya, man?"

Pascal blinked. A call on his office line from the boyfriend of one of Merle's sisters was not impossible, just improbable. "I'm good, Dylan, and you?"

"Not bad. Got this baby thing going so that's something." Pascal chuckled then frowned. Where was this going? Dylan continued: "I've been thinking about our conversation—in the car? You know, about the vineyard? The financing and all? My possible investment? Do you still want me to help? I have the money. It's still that shiny object in my imagination. And I know Francie would love to be close to Merle."

Close to Merle? Would they be moving into the château? Pascal frowned. What had he said those weeks ago? "Um, well, sorry, the deal has gone soft. Did you hear about one of the owners? Ernest Brooks.

Arrested on suspicion of bashing in the skull of a vagrant on his property. Then he has a heart attack in jail."

"Cripes. Is he okay?"

"We just attended his funeral."

"How awful. What about the other guy? Is he going to run it alone?"

"No idea," Pascal said. "It's a bit too soon to be re-negotiating. Honestly, I consider it done. Over."

"I'm sorry. I thought that back acreage looked very grape-y."

Pascal smiled. "It still does. But, well, timing is everything and the timing is crap. I am looking into what really happened to the transient who was killed, but it is difficult." He hesitated then said, "This also popped up. A tomb embedded in the floor of the ruined abbey. It's intriguing. Someone covered it on purpose with a huge pile of rocks."

"No kidding? What's in the tomb?"

"I don't know. I'm trying to figure out a legal avenue to open it. Not my property, you know."

"Right. Ask the other guy then. I bet he'll be interested in finding out what's in there."

"I may just do that."

They chatted about their girlfriends, Francie's expanding waistline, plans for her possibly to move in with him, and rang off.

Pascal stared at the phone. He couldn't let his mind wander back to buying the vineyard. It would just wreck him again. He still wondered what happened to Roland-Auguste. He needed to find out who was so angry with him that they demanded that he disappear.

Also he had to find out more about Oscar. Somehow the Oscar mystery seemed more realistic, a bit easier. But Harris was unlikely to know anything as the old man died a couple years before they purchased the vineyard. Luc Naudé probably knew him but Pascal never wanted to speak to that *connard* again. He only knew one person who had definitely known Oscar and was pleasant. But would she be at home?

He left the office at five, slipping out without anyone stopping him for more paperwork, always a victory. Instead of going to the apartment he pointed his car east and was on the highway in minutes. He was taking a chance, dropping in at Madame Hugo's château without an invitation. But his options were running out. He had to act on his curiosity before it fizzled out.

He called Merle from the road. "I am heading your way soon, blackbird. Late dinner?"

"Oh, how spontaneous you are! Albert is invited here for chicken."

"Is there enough for a man with an appetite like *moi*?"

"We'll manage. What time do you think?"

"About eight. If I am not there, start dinner with Albert. I have some business along the way."

ÉLOISE HUGO'S vast Château Vianden with its pretentious turrets, triangular flags, and walled gardens sat on the top of a small rise, easily seen as he pulled off the highway. Pascal drove past Sainte-Colette and around the bend toward the manse. He pulled up by the front this time, ignoring the large gravel area for parking. Where was the Ambassador's black car? He craned his neck. Ah, there was a garage converted from a barn off to one side, behind some trees.

He knocked with an enormous brass lion head. No sounds from within. He glanced around the property. The main gate was open; he'd driven right in. Someone must be home. He knocked a second time then saw a button for a bell off to the left, embedded in the stone. He pushed it and heard the tolling of chimes inside.

The door cracked open finally, revealing a young woman in a black uniform. She raised her eyebrows silently. "Bonjour," Pascal said. "Is the Madame at home? I was just passing." He dug out his card from his wallet. "We are acquainted."

The woman took his card and squinted suspiciously at it. She shut the door without a word, leaving him on the stone steps. So she must be home. Good news.

The wait however was long. He checked his watch and watched twenty minutes tick by. Finally, at 25 minutes, the maid returned. Her expression had smoothed. She nodded at him and muttered, *"Entrez, monsieur."* He followed her up the stairs and down a hallway that was carpeted with thick wool and painted a robin's egg blue. Crystal chandeliers split the darkness with sparkles.

The young woman stopped at a door, knocked lightly, and turned the knob. She examined Pascal, as if skeptical. Perhaps her mistress was making a mistake.

"*Madame est ici,*" she muttered, waving him in and shutting the door behind him.

The room was bright with evening sun, streaming through tall mullioned doors that faced the front of the château and led to small balconies. It was large, both bedroom and sitting room. The bed was high and antique, a four-poster. He blinked. His eyes focused on Madame Hugo, reclining on a chaise. Her head was back, eyes closed. Her hair was down, lying on her shoulders in spirals. She looked like a queen of yore. He cleared his throat.

"Ah, there you are," she said, eyes opening. "Monsieur d'Onscon. To what do I owe this pleasure?" She sat forward, straightening. "Come sit. I have been resting but it is past time that I get to business."

Pascal perched on a small dining chair near the creamy velvet chaise. Madame plumped pillows at her back. She looked pale. Was she ill?

"Pardon, madame, for the intrusion. I hope you are well?"

She fluttered her eyelashes. "Oh, do I look so terrible? After the soirée I always take some time off. Even an ambassador needs to relax, take time to smell the roses. This is my favorite time of year in my gardens and vines."

He smiled apologetically. "*Excusez-moi.* You look—fine."

She laughed. "You are a poor liar, Pascal. May I call you that?" She handed his card back to him. "Why are you here? Have you located Louis Bordeaux?"

"No, I'm sorry." He winced. "Is this a bad time to ask for a small favor?"

"Is there ever a good time?" She smiled. "What is it?"

"You mentioned at the soirée that you knew Oscar Boissieu, the owner of Château des Corbeaux until his death."

"He was a friend, a fine gentleman."

"This is a bit strange but did he ever mention anything about the abbey on his property? The ruin?"

"No. Is there one?"

Pascal nodded. "Two walls and some rubble remain. But also there is a tomb embedded in the floor, into the ground. He never said anything about it?"

Éloise gave him a look. "This is why you came to see me? To ask about a tomb?"

Pascal made to stand up. "I'm sorry, madame. I—"

"Sit down. I'm teasing you." She patted his arm. "Let's think about this. A tomb?"

"Hidden under a pile of debris. It appears purposefully hidden."

"Oscar was a cagey bastard. Secretive."

"Was he? What sort of secrets did he have? Did he confess them to you?"

"Oh, no. He was too smart for that. I know everyone." She smiled.

"Would he bury a vintage? Could it be wine in the tomb?"

She thought about that. "Possible. But he needed the income. He did tell me that, that he was having trouble keeping the vineyard going."

"He abandoned the back half, let it die. Did he tell you that?" She nodded. "Is this crazy, this idea I have that he buried something in the tomb and then covered it with stones?"

She chuckled. "Yes, it is crazy. But that doesn't mean it's not possible. I can see Oscar doing something like that. As I said, I got the feeling he held things back."

Pascal blinked. "Tell me about him. Besides wine, what were his interests?"

"I always had the feeling he was much deeper than he appeared. He tried to come across as a simple country vigneron, pleasant but vague, a farmer. But he was educated. He read history, studied at the Sorbonne, I believe. He would regale us with stories at soirées sometimes."

"About what?"

Her eyebrows pinched. "Let me think." She tapped her chin with a finger then shrugged. "It's been too long, Pascal. I can't remember what he talked about. France, I believe. The Republic. French history? I don't know."

"If I leave you my number will you call if anything comes back to you?" He put his card on the side table, scribbling his mobile number on the back.

"Are you leaving?" She looked disappointed. "You could stay for dinner."

He stood up. "Thank you. That's very kind. But Merle, remember her? She waits for me."

"The lovely Merle. How is she?"

"Very well. *Adieu*, madame. Enjoy your respite. Again, please call any time."

Forty-Two

MALCOUZIAC

Merle and Albert were just sitting down to dinner when Pascal came through the front door. They chided him about his perfect timing and poured him a glass of wine. Merle had made *coq au vin*, chicken in wine, one of his grandmother's recipes they never tired of. Albert declared it was his all-time favorite. Merle dished out the pieces of chicken and passed the pappardelle, the wide noodles, around the table.

"Did you get your business finished?" Merle asked.

He nodded. "More about my obsession with the tomb. Madame Hugo."

"You visited her by yourself? How brave." Merle explained to Albert who Madame was. "An ambassador. One of those elites."

"She visited here in the winter," Pascal told him. "Maybe you saw her in her full-length mink coat."

"I wish I had," Albert said, eyes twinkling.

"A vision, but terrifying." Pascal looked at Merle. "You told me she knew Oscar so I had to see what she knew about him."

"And?"

"Not much really. He may have attended the Sorbonne. That is somewhat unusual for a vigneron. Wine studies, sure, but pure academics are not common. But she knew nothing about the tomb or even that a ruin lay on his property."

"Albert could read some of the words on it," Merle said.

"Yes," the old priest said. "*Deo Optimo Maximo.* To God, most good, most great. Also, I remember, one of the mottos of the Benedictines. It was their abbey?"

Pascal nodded. "I found a reference to it online, on one of those history websites that lists all the monasteries knocked down in the Revolution."

"They made wine all over France, didn't they?" Merle asked. "But that doesn't tell us who or what is in the tomb. Albert also could make out 'Le Comte.' But no name attached."

"My thinking has changed. I don't think who was buried in the tomb really matters," Pascal said. "It's my theory—just a theory—that Oscar Boissieu hid something in there. Why else would he have piled all those rocks on top to conceal it?" He shook his head. "I need to find a reason to open it though."

"You can't just ask Harris?" Merle said.

"At this point I look like a crazy conspiracy guy. Plus he is in mourning. I need facts."

"Have you searched for Oscar online?"

"I found his obituary, and where his daughter is living. A place for those who have lost their memories."

"I see a project for after dinner," Merle said, smiling. "I will help."

After Albert went home, sated from chicken and wine and fine company, Merle and Pascal sat down at their respective laptops and began a deep dive into the life of Oscar Boissieu. Any mention of him in any document or news article or book was examined. The usual things came up: obituary, wine festivals, a tennis tournament he refereed, honorees for this or that war, Marcelle's birth announcement in a Catholic newspaper, *Le Croix*. On hour three, nearly a hundred pages back on the search engine, Merle finally found a different type of reference to the right person—she hoped.

"Look at this," she called from her position at the dining table. Pascal got up from his desk chair and looked over her shoulder. "An article in an old newspaper— from 1939. They must be scanning old issues. *The New York Times* is doing that."

"What newspaper?"

"*L'Indépendant des Pyrénées-Orientales.* Not sure where they published. Wait." Her fingers flew across the keys. "Perpignan. Since 1846, still in business. Distributed in that department and also the Aude." The article was in French but she could understand most of it. "Shall I read it? The headline is '*Le garçon trouve un trésor.*'"

BOY FINDS TREASURE

Excitement reigned yesterday when a schoolboy named Oscar Boissieu made a shocking discovery while digging for fossils in the hills near Béziers. Oscar was on a summer holiday, visiting his grandparents in the nearby village of Mailhac. He was known to hunt for fossils and pottery shards, bringing his grandparents sacks full of them to display on their shelves. But on this day he found something truly unusual.

This area in southwest France, near the Mediterranean coast, has long been known for its Roman artifacts. Romans began trading and settling in the region centuries before the time of Jesus Christ. But what young Oscar found was thought to be something from before the Roman period, when the Gauls and other tribes lived here.

His maternal grandparents, Estelle and Valéry Gardet, describe Oscar, age 10, as a curious boy, an excellent student who enjoys reading and history. So his wanderings on the outskirts of the village gave them no worry. They knew he was digging for something. But what he found amazed them.

One day two weeks ago Oscar brought home what appeared to be an antique coin. Neither the Gardet's nor Oscar had ever seen anything like it: crude, tarnished, and not quite round, with raised engravings. The boy spent days in the tiny village library, trying to identify it. Finally he concluded it was possibly a coin of the realm of Marseille because of markings on one face. Intrigued, he went back to the area every day for the remainder of his visit, coming home each night covered in dirt, according to his grandmother.

His diligence was rewarded. Yesterday Oscar found a small ceramic pot filled with similar coins. The pot itself was buried and broken in pieces but he was able to carefully dig it out. He hasn't examined all the coins, or identified them, but the look of wonder and astonishment on his boyish face says it all: He has found his prize.

A local schoolmaster, a learned man who dabbles in rare coins, a person called a 'numismatist,' has looked at Oscar's find and singled out several pieces as quite special. "Some are from Gaul, some from northern tribes like the Sos, some Greek coins. Marseille was established by the Greeks six centuries before Christ and on many trade routes. This was someone's *tirelire*," he explained.

Monsieur Gardet said the boy's find will be taken to a museum for examination and safe-keeping. The exact site of the find is not being publicly disclosed to keep the integrity of the spot intact for professional archeologists.

Merle sat back in her chair. "Did I read it correctly?" she whispered. "I don't know that word, *tirelire*."

Pascal sat next to her and turned her laptop toward him. He read silently. "It means piggy bank." In a moment he pushed the computer away. "We're sure this is the right person?"

"Right name, right age."

He nodded. "You read it perfectly, *chérie*. Madame Hugo told me he was interested in history. Since he was a boy apparently."

"Would he have stopped treasure hunting after finding that amazing trove of coins?"

Pascal raised his eyebrows. "I wouldn't. I'd be hooked for life."

Merle grabbed his arm and squeezed. "We must open that tomb."

Forty-Three

Pascal sat in the garden the next morning, drinking espresso. He had lain awake again last night, wondering what might be in the tomb, what Oscar had hidden away. He knew why the vigneron would not want anyone to see his stash, if it really was a stash of ancient coins and medieval objects. Looting archeological sites was illegal in France whether they are protected or not. Anything you kept for yourself, that you didn't report and offer up to the authorities, could get you into legal trouble. All such items were considered the treasure and property of the state. There was a museum in Paris that displayed ancient coins, the *Cabinet des Médailles*, which Pascal had never bothered to browse. Now he wished he'd paid more attention to history.

Merle had found articles about looters with large collections hidden in their homes. When they are raided the authorities are always shocked: thousands of Gallo-Roman coins, medieval jewelry, Iron Age weaponry. But the looting continued, often with the consent of landowners. Did Oscar use a metal detector? Probably, although they are banned in France for personal use for precisely this reason.

But how did Oscar's possible loot fit into the story of the death of Roméo and the subsequent death of Ernest? It was a puzzle. He closed his eyes and tried to think. Did someone know of the loot? Did Roméo know? He was a bit of a simpleton, according to the priest. But someone may have told him. Harris and Ernest seemed unaware but possibly they were hiding their knowledge.

The crunching of gravel foretold the arrival of Merle with her own demitasse of espresso. She sat down across the green table from him. "What if— what if we visit Harris and Jane again?"

Pascal nodded. "But first perhaps the priest again? What's his name?"

"Père Thaddée." She squinted at him in the morning sunshine. "He knows more than he's saying?"

"Sans doute."

IN SAINTE-COLETTE they found the priest in his small garden, hoeing weeds around pathetic little tomato plants. The entire sunny plot in the back of the rectory needed tending, that was obvious from the profusion of weeds and overgrown shrubs. But the young man stuck to his tiny vegetable plot, digging hard in the soil.

He looked up as they came out the back door of the parish house, directed by the housekeeper. He shaded his eyes and smiled his courteous smile. "Bonjour, madame, monsieur," he called, dropping his hoe and brushing off his hands.

Pascal didn't think he remembered them so introduced them again. He said he wanted to contribute to the burial fund for Roméo, delighting the priest.

"Let's go inside, out of the hot sun." He led them into his cluttered office where they sat in the chairs facing his desk. "Now where is that record?" he muttered.

They waited until he discovered his ledger book and sat down. Pascal retrieved a € 20 note from his wallet and slid it across the blotter. "How is the fund progressing?" Merle asked sweetly. The page looked untouched since her earlier visit.

"Very well, thank you for your suggestion," the priest said, smiling at her. "And you, monsieur, for your donation."

"Have any of the local families donated?" she asked.

"Early days, madame."

"Are they likely to help with his burial when they are the ones who ran him out of town?" Pascal asked.

The priest blinked rapidly. "Well."

"Who did that? I'm curious," Merle asked blithely, keeping up her innocent act. "A bus ticket to Bordeaux was given him, I understand. With a threat to stay away?"

The priest lowered his hands against the ledger. "That is in the past, madame. Please do not distress yourself with such matters."

"Oh, I am not distressed. And it is not really in the past if the investigation into his murder continues."

The father shook his head. "That is finished."

"Is it?" Merle glanced at Pascal.

"If it is finished," Pascal said in as gentle a voice as he could conjure, "then why not tell us who bought the ticket? It is over and no one else can be prosecuted for the murder."

"I am sorry. I cannot help you." He closed the ledger with a slap of paper and stood up. "Thank you for your donations."

Pascal and Merle didn't rise immediately, trying to figure out how to get the information from the priest. But he stared angrily at them then stalked out of the room. Merle rolled her eyes. "Let's go."

Outside in the *place* the weekly market was in full swing with flowers, produce, cheese, and meats on display, bought and sold under umbrellas in the morning sunshine. Pascal glared at all the commerce, such a commonplace thing in France but very annoying today. Why would the priest keep the village's secrets? Was he part of the conspiracy to get rid of Roméo?

They skirted the edge of the market, heading around the right side. Merle paused to look into a gourmet foods shop that was selling peaches and plums in a huge sidewalk stand. She bought three white peaches and tucked them into her purse.

Pascal waited for her down the sidewalk, in front of the art gallery. He watched the frenzy of shoppers, haggling over leeks and greenhouse tomatoes, his hands deep in his pockets. He had no answers, no ideas. Now they must go to Harris with little more than a hunch and an old newspaper article.

Merle stepped up next to him. "Ready? Let's go see Harris," he said.

She didn't move. He glanced back and she was looking into the display window of the gallery. She pointed at something and said, "Look, Pascal. Come here."

He stood beside her, staring through the glass where Galerie Colette was written in gold lettering. Inside were four or five red coin holders, the type collectors used. The small sign in front of them read '*Monnaies médiévales et antiques.*' Merle looked at him, eyebrows up.

"Yes?" Pascal said with a shrug. "There are thousands of coin dealers."

"In this town?" Merle tugged his arm. "Come on."

The gallery was not the typical sort with solitary paintings hung on the walls. There were paintings but also a jumble of ceramics, old books, *objets d'art*, porcelain plates— and rare coins. It was full to the brim with old things. "Browse around," Merle whispered before she went the opposite direction, toward the coins.

At the sound of the bell on the door the proprietor appeared from the back room. He was about fifty, with wild yet thinning hair, a large dark mustache, and spectacles. He was quite short and round with dandruff on his navy blue sweater. He nodded at Pascal. "Bonjour, monsieur. How may I help you today?"

"Just admiring your collection, monsieur," Pascal replied.

They both turned as Merle gasped across the gallery. "Look at this, honey," she called out in American English. Pascal tried not to smile.

"What have you found, my darling?"

"Come see." Pascal, followed by the proprietor, wove around the tables laden with books and vases to find Merle standing in front of the coin display. Small shelves lined a section of wall, each with a cardboard holder for some fifty coins. Not every slot was full, but most. "So many delicious finds," she cooed.

When the men arrived, Merle began to interrogate the proprietor on the ages of various coins. "Oh, Roman. Don't you have anything older? Like Greek maybe? I love the really old stuff."

The proprietor, who introduced himself as Monsieur Donnet, pointed out a card near their knee level. He picked it up and spoke in heavily-accented English. "These, madame, are from old Marseille, when the Greeks called it Massala."

She took the card and held it up to the light then flipping it to see the reverse sides. "Ah, I have seen some of these before. Not that rare, are they?" Donnet shrugged. "Where do you get these, may I ask?"

"From collectors mostly. I have a wide range of acquaintance." He smiled.

"In France?" she asked.

"Of course, madame." He glanced at Pascal. Would he mark him as a cop? That often happened. But rarely with an American spouse.

"Is that legal?" She asked. "To dig up coins in France?"

"I wouldn't know, madame. I only buy and sell. I do not dig."

Pascal blinked. Of course he knew it was illegal. Everyone knew.

Merle smiled. "So basically, no questions asked? I like that. I may have to do some digging myself."

Donnet tugged on his mustache and chuckled. Pascal let the moment ride then changed the subject. "I heard that a vagrant, some sort of gypsy, was selling coins here. Is that true?"

"A vagrant?"

"Yes, what was his name, *chérie*? The one the priest told us about."

She set the card back on its shelf. "Um. Romeo? Like Romeo and Juliet?"

"Roméo. That was it," Pascal said. "Someone told us to get in touch with him. Did you know him?"

Donnet took off his glasses and wiped them on a handkerchief. "I knew him, yes. But sadly he is dead."

"Oh, no," Merle cried, really playing the part.

"The priest told us, remember, darling?" Pascal said. To the dealer he said, "We were told about him in Bordeaux. Was he run out of town for selling illegal coins?"

The dealer bristled. "He did not sell illegal coins to me. Or any coins at all."

"Then why was he run out of town? Do you know?"

Donnet looked them over and said, "You are not from here?" Pascal said *'non.'* "There was a group of men who didn't like him. He stole chickens. And lived in a tent or someone's barn. So they bought him a ticket to Bordeaux and off he went."

"Oh," Merle cried again. "How cruel. Why didn't they help him?"

"That was my feeling, madame," Donnet said, his color rising. "It was a callous ploy. There was something else behind it but I could never discover what it was."

"Some other reason besides he was a vagrant?" Pascal asked.

"I always thought so. But I couldn't prove it. That winemaker, he had it in for Roméo."

"Which winemaker is that?" Merle asked. "I want to avoid the wines of the cruel and callous."

"Then do not drink Domaine Champs-du-Puy, madame. They paid for the bus ticket, at least that was the rumor."

"How did he return to town? Did someone pay for his ticket back? Was that you?" Pascal guessed.

Donnet slumped against the table then. "I was trying to help him. I wish I hadn't. He—he was—"

Pascal patted his arm. "We heard, monsieur. Do not distress yourself. That other winemaker did it, correct? The Englishman?"

The dealer nodded. "That's what they say."

A pause then as Pascal and Merle looked at each other. Then Merle said, "Could you write down the name of that winery you said to avoid? I can't understand your accent and I despise wicked people, don't you?"

Forty-Four

SAINTE-COLETTE

Pascal and Merle sat in the BMW, staring at the slip of paper the dealer had given them. He'd written 'DOMAINE CHAMPS-DU-PUYS' in small, neat block letters. Merle had clutched it all the way back to the parking lot.

"Where is the photo of the note found on Roméo?" she said impatiently.

He was swiping through his phone. "One moment, *chérie*." He stopped, enlarging the photograph to see the handwriting more clearly. "Hold the note here," he instructed.

They peered at the photograph and the note. Both were written in capitals, a simple, blocky text without flourishes. Both were written in blue ink on white paper. "Identical," Merle declared.

Pascal zoomed in further, looking for any special flourishes that would indicate that they matched. He wasn't convinced. "Could be." He clicked off his phone. "But what does it mean?"

"That Monsieur Donnet sent Roméo on a mission that night, to go to Château des Corbeaux."

"But why? To dig up the tomb? By himself?"

Merle sighed. "Maybe he was meeting someone there."

"Someone who killed him?" He sounded incredulous.

Merle glanced at him. "We're not getting much closer, are we?"

Pascal started the engine. "Time to visit Harris."

———

JANE AUSTIN OPENED THE DOOR, an open book in her arms and a distracted look on her face. She seemed annoyed then surprised to see them.

"Hello, Jane," Merle said. "We just dropped by to see if there was anything you needed. But if you're busy we can come back another time." She looked past Jane into the dark mansion. Nothing was moving but dust motes in the stream of sunshine from the high window on the landing.

Jane blinked. "Oh, come in. I'm just doing some research for my job. I'm still here and not there," she muttered as she led them back to the kitchen again.

The bright room at the back of the house was equally quiet. No Harris, no sister or mother. "Have the relatives gone home?" Merle asked.

"Yes. And they took Ernest with them." Jane frowned. "Not a happy decision," she whispered.

"How is Harris?" Pascal asked. "Is he here?"

"He's better. He's outside with his chickens. Come on. We'll find him." Jane set down her book and led the way out the kitchen door, across the bluestone patio, and into the yard. The hens were pecking in the vineyard rows, searching for insects. The vines, Pascal noticed, were untended, growing long tendrils that should be sheared off or wrapped around wires. No one was taking care of the grapes. It saddened him.

"Harry! Someone to see you," Jane called near the hen house.

A head popped up in the vines. Harris wore his straw hat and carried a pair of *secateurs,* shears for manicuring the vines. So he was trying.

"Who is it?" he called.

"Merle and Pascal," Merle replied. "Come to check up on you."

He needed no further nudge to stop working in the vineyard. In a few minutes he had removed his gloves, hat, and kerchief, and set down his shears. He sighed as they sat down together at the patio table, shaded by a large olive tree. A pot of straggly lavender sat on the corner. Jane said she would get water. "Unless you want wine?" She asked, glancing at her wristwatch. "It's past noon."

They said water was fine. Soon she returned with a pitcher and four glasses, looking both satisfied and disgruntled to play hostess again. Pascal asked Harris how he was coping and was rewarded with a one word answer: 'Fine.'

"And the vines? They are looking healthy." Pascal glanced at the nearby rows of grapes.

"Are they?" Harris asked. "Right. Yes."

Merle frowned at Pascal. He plunged ahead. "Have you found any old artifacts on the property, Harris? Just curious about that ruined abbey."

Harris gathered his eyebrows together and wiped his forehead. "Artifacts?"

"Old Roman coins, that sort of thing? We heard that the previous owner was an avid collector of such things."

"Was he?" Harris shrugged.

Jane sipped her water. "What about that thing you found?"

Merle and Pascal said together: "What thing?"

"Should I get it?" Jane said, disappearing into the house.

"What is it?"

"A strange little *objet d'art*."

"Where did you find it? Out by the ruin?" Pascal asked.

"No. In the house." Harris looked warily at Pascal. "If I told you there was a false wall in the main bedroom, would you be surprised?"

"A priest hole?" Merle asked. "Did they do that in France?"

"Could be," Harris agreed. "That was my thought. It's like a closet behind the closet. Airy, pretty big, no windows but vents let in fresh air."

"What was in there?" Pascal asked. "Bibles?"

Harris smiled and shook his head. "Only this one small thing." He looked up as Jane returned, skipping through the kitchen door. She carried a round object in one hand. She sat down and set the object in the center of the table.

Merle leaned in to look at it. It was only superficially round. The surface was made of a series of flat five-sided plates, each with a round hole leading to the hollow center. Knobs stuck out all around. It was small, about three inches across, including the knobby protrusions.

"What is it?" Pascal said.

"I did some research," Harris said. "I'm not sure but I think it's rather rare. It's called dodecahedron, for its twelve sides."

"How bizarre," Merle said. "What was it for?"

"That's not been properly decided," Harris said.

"Maybe knitting," Jane said. "Isn't it wild? I love it."

Pascal bent in for a closer look. "Bronze, is it? How rare is it?"

Harris sat back. "From the Roman period, or earlier. Only about a hundred have ever been found."

"And it was in this secret closet?" Merle asked. She glanced up and caught Pascal's eye.

"Do you want to see it?" Harris said, standing up. "Come on. Bring the dodec, Jane."

In the first floor hallway they turned left, away from the bedroom they'd slept in that night. At the end of the hall a single door opened into an expansive bedroom that stretched the width of the house, front to back, across one end. It was cheery and bright, with windows on three sides and a riot of pink flowers on the wallpaper.

"We thought this must have been the daughter's room at one time," Harris said. "Or the wife's. We never got around to taking down the wallpaper."

"It's gaudy," Jane said, frowning.

Merle smiled. "I can see it might be overpowering."

"Slightly," Jane groused.

"Where is this secret room?" Pascal asked.

Harris led them to the left side of the room, through a dressing area and into a walk-in closet, mostly empty. There were few clothes hanging on the rods. He pushed the coats and trousers aside and knocked on the back. "Hollow, right. See this seam?" He put his fingernails into a slender crack and carefully pulled out the wallpapered section. "Not a wall at all. Hinges on the inside. Mind the edge here."

Harris bent down and stepped into the dark room, pulling a cord. A bare bulb lit up the space. The others filed inside. It wasn't a large space and with four people inside it seemed cramped. Narrow wooden shelves banked three walls, floor to ceiling. They were bare.

"What was on the shelves?" Merle asked.

"Just that one thing, the dodec, as we've named it. The rest were empty." Harris turned in a circle. "Up there is a vent for fresh air. It connects to the stairwell wall. Pull the cord for the light."

Pascal found the string on his shoulder. The room went dark but for a glimmer of light from the vent. He pulled it again then backed out the small door, into the actual closet and dressing room with its mirrored vanity and marble sink. Merle followed, pulling spider webs out of her hair.

Jane and Harris carefully replaced the false wall and rearranged the clothes, as if preserving the hidden place against marauders.

"How did you find it?" Pascal asked.

"It was Ernest," Harris said. "He loved to poke around in odd corners. He heard the hollow sound and figured it out. He said he was sure there was some famous art in there, hidden from the Nazis. But no. Just that one weird *objet*."

"Did you show the object to anyone, Harris?" Pascal asked.

"We took it into town once. Right after we found it, about a year ago, when we didn't know what it was." Harris looked at him. "That art dealer in town identified it for us. Then we found more information on the internet."

"Monsieur Donnet?" Merle asked. "With Galerie Colette?"

"Nice chap. Told us it wasn't worth much but he did tell us it was from the Roman era. So quite old."

"Did he want to take it off your hands?" Pascal asked.

Harris smiled. "Absolutely. But Ernest wouldn't part with it."

Merle walked to the window in the bedroom, overlooking the front court and driveway. The sunlight shone through the delicate leaves of the twisted olive tree, making patterns on the gravel. She looked over her shoulder.

"We visited with Donnet today. Time to show him the notes, Pascal."

Forty-Five

CHÂTEAU DES CORBEAUX

The four sat at the rough kitchen table, Merle and Pascal on one side, Jane and Harris on the other. Harris had poured them wine and Jane had put out a variety of cheeses. They stared at the notes, on Pascal's phone and the other one, passing both around the table. Jane and Harris put their heads together and concentrated on the writing.

After a long pause, Merle exhaled. Enough. Action was needed. *We can't stare at the notes forever, hoping they will reveal their secrets.* She sipped a little sauvignon blanc. "What do you think?"

Jane nearly jumped at her voice, startled from her reverie. She pulled back from her brother. "They look by the same hand to me," she said. "What do you think?"

Harris looked up at them all and lay the phone and note carefully in the center of the table. "What does it mean? I mean, if Donnet wrote both the notes. If he wrote the note found on Roméo, it means he sent the man out here. He sent the man to his death."

"But it doesn't tell us who killed him," Pascal said.

"Does it tell us *why* he was killed?" Merle asked.

Pascal shrugged. "I don't think so. Unless someone else wanted whatever Roméo was sent to find."

223

"The dodec, apparently," Harris said.

Pascal gave him a level look. "Have you considered there may be more plunder hidden on the property? That Donnet knew about it and sent Roméo here to scout the grounds?"

Jane made a face. "That's a lot of assumptions."

Merle said, "What do you know about Oscar Boissieu, the previous owner?"

Harris shrugged. "Very little. We never met him. He died a couple years before we bought the vineyard."

"Did you meet his daughter, Marcelle?" Pascal asked.

"Just the lawyers. We bought it from his estate, not the daughter, as I recall."

"Did they tell you how he died?"

"A stroke, I think. Very sudden. But he was quite old so maybe not unexpected. That was why the house was never really cleared. We inherited all the linens and beds and silverware."

Jane leaned in. "One of the guests at the wake for Ernest was from around here. A French woman but she spoke excellent English. She said she knew him. That no one discovered his body for nearly a week. That made me sad."

"Plenty of heartbreak at this old château," Harris said gently, patting his sister's hand.

"He had no employees?" Pascal asked.

"I don't think so," Jane said. "The woman indicated he was a bit of a hermit unless he needed help at harvest."

Pascal drummed his fingers on the table. "There has been some vandalism here, is that true?"

Harris nodded. "The first year it was pretty bad. You've seen the back wall of the barn? We'll probably never get that cleaned off."

"Who do you think was responsible?"

"The *gendarmes* told us it was local kids. They were known but— you know, the shrug?" Harris demonstrated. "Nothing happened."

"Roméo was also harassed by someone," Merle said. "Maybe the same kids?"

Jane sipped her wine. Pascal popped a piece of brie in his mouth. "What now?" Harris asked.

Merle looked at Pascal. "Can we go for a walk?"

Harris and Jane frowned, confused. Pascal added: "I have something to show you."

They walked in silence, down the lane by the outbuildings, the barns, into the vineyards. The abbey ruins stood as they had for centuries, slowly crumbling into the earth. Pascal and Merle arrived first and stood staring at the jumble of stones in the pile. Merle kicked one with her foot and looked at Pascal.

"One moment, blackbird," he whispered.

The Austin siblings stood back, staring at the standing remains and the sky beyond. Pascal turned to them. "Here. Under these stones. Have you ever wondered why the pile sits here?" He bent and threw off two heavy stones. "Help me, please."

Reluctantly Jane and Harris picked up stones, grunting, and deposited them to one side. Merle did the same but Pascal was the fastest. He had uncovered half the top of the tomb within minutes, knowing what he was looking for this time.

"Okay, stop." He said to the others, breathing hard.

"What is it?" Harris asked, moving next to him.

"Oscar Boissieu was, we assume, a lifelong collector of objects like your dodec. When he was a boy he found a cache of antique coins. He scoured the hills around his grandparents' village. We believe," he glanced at Merle, "that he did not stop hunting through ancient sites, digging up objects."

Jane put her hands on her hips. "And this? You think he hid his loot in here?"

"This is someone's burial place," Harris said. "I don't think we should disturb them."

Pascal rubbed a spot on the tomb's surface. "See this? He died in 1544."

"Why would all the stones be piled over the tomb?" Merle asked. "Something must be in there besides bones."

"I don't like it," Harris said, a shiver passing through him. "Leave him at rest."

There was no talking Harris into opening the tomb. He paled at the thought and shook his head. He said it was bad luck and disrespectful.

Jane led her brother back to the château, leaving Pascal and Merle with the task of disguising the tomb again.

Merle sighed, getting back into the BMW and brushing her dirty hands on her slacks. "Well, we tried."

Pascal slapped the steering wheel. "What is he afraid of? Ghosts?"

"He just lost the love of his life. Give him some time." Merle looked at the mansion. "Maybe we should go apologize." She opened the car door. "Come on."

Reluctantly Pascal got out of the car and ran dusty fingers through his hair. He was hot and sweaty from throwing stones again but he followed Merle to the front door. She knocked gently. In a moment Jane appeared.

"We just want to apologize, Jane," Merle said. She glanced at Pascal. "To Harris, and to you."

"I am sorry. I got carried away," Pascal said. "Of course it is Harris's decision. It is his property."

Jane opened the door wider. Harris stood behind her in the dark foyer. He stepped forward into the doorway. "Do you think Donnet—or whoever—will come back for the dodec? Is it safe here?"

"I don't know," Pascal admitted. "But I would hide it again."

Harris nodded. "I thought the same. What will you do about the notes, the handwriting match?"

"Share it with the *policiers*. I know some officers who will make sure it gets a look."

Jane crossed her arms. "And will you tell them your theory about the tomb?"

Pascal smiled. "Perhaps not. Still just a theory."

Jane stepped outside and took Merle's arm as they walked back to the car. She whispered to Merle: "I'm taking Harris back to London in a few days. Just so you know."

"What about the vineyard?"

"I've found a crew of Moroccans to trim the vines. I hope they can do it without supervision but maybe Pascal could stop in next week to check on things?"

Merle looked her pleading eyes. "Of course. I'm glad you're taking him home. He shouldn't be here alone."

Jane sighed. "This big old rambling place? Much too big for one man."

THAT NIGHT PASCAL WAS MOODY, talking to himself in the garden, waving hands around and pacing. They had discussed the murder of Roméo Auguste at length in the car on the drive back to Malcouziac but nothing had clicked. There was something they were missing, some clue that eluded them.

Merle did what she could, cooking a fancy dinner of sautéed lamb chops with garlic confit, after she took a long shower. While Pascal was doing his thinking outside, she sat at her laptop and looked up information about that weird little *objet*, the dodecahedron. In the search of news articles she found one dodecahedron had been found in the police raid of a different house, along with thousands of looted antique metal objects, coins, jewelry, and more. The homeowner, a man who had plundered ancient sites for years, got into quite a bit of trouble— a big fine, confiscation of all his objects, and some sort of jail sentence.

The date on the news article was July, six years ago. Oscar was still alive. He died three months later. Was this story the trigger for him to hide his loot?

She read all the news articles on Roméo again. Pascal had squeezed most of this information from his *Police Nationale* source. Nothing new. They went to bed and tossed and turned, restless in their inability to connect the dots.

Forty-Six

SAINTE-COLETTE

The village slept peacefully in the morning sun. The boulangerie was already busy with customers but the rest of the shops around the place were still shuttered and dark. Pascal peered into the art gallery, looking through the metal security chains at the coins in the cardboard sleeves in the window, and the metal urns next to them. One had scenes engraved into it, and Greek decorations. Where had old Donnet acquired that one?

Pascal shook himself. His obsession with plundered antiquities was a new one, and being fresh it held tight to him. Later, he told himself. He walked down a side street to the *mairie* in a beautiful old mansion, and the *gendarmerie* next to it. He knocked and was let inside by a young woman in uniform.

"*Bonjour, monsieur,*" she said, eyeing him. "How can I help you?"

He introduced himself and showed her his warrant card. She warmed slightly and let him inside the small offices. She moved past the reception desk and sat behind a metal desk, gesturing at a chair beside it where she took statements from victims, he presumed.

Her name was Lieutenant Rouzet. No first name given. She was young, maybe 25, pretty and blonde, the new *gendarmerie*, he supposed. "Now, what business do we have?" she asked, keeping her voice very professional as she'd been taught.

"I am a friend of Ernest Brooks, madame. The man charged with the murder of Roméo Auguste." He waited for her nod. "Roméo's real name was Roland-Auguste Sardou."

Her eyes widened in surprise. She hadn't known that. She waved him on.

"You know that he was found with a small note in his possession with the name of the vineyard on it, Brooks's vineyard, Château des Corbeaux?" Another nod. Pascal removed the small plastic bag containing the second note. "This is written in very similar fashion. For comparison purposes."

She peered at the note. "This case is closed, monsieur."

"Is it? Are you sure?"

"I am not handling it. The *Brigade criminelle* is in charge."

"I understand. I am just passing on this information." He pushed the bag toward her. "It was written by Monsieur Donnet of the art gallery, Galerie Colette. On the *place*. You are acquainted?"

"*Non.*"

"Think about this. A scenario. Donnet sends Roméo on a mission to the vineyard that night. He may have been interested in antique coins or other *objets d'art* in the château. Things rumored to be there for many years. Has anyone asked him about that?" She pursed her lips. "Donnet brought Roméo back to Sainte-Colette. He told me this yesterday."

She blinked. "How did he do that?"

"Found him in Bordeaux. Bought him a bus ticket. Just like the one that the citizens of Sainte-Colette did in April to get him to leave. You know about that?" She nodded.

"What was the reasoning behind that?"

"I have no idea."

"No idea why anyone would dislike Roméo? You knew him, you saw him around the village?" Another nod. "He was a vagrant. He smelled bad. He didn't wash. He slept in barns and stole chickens. I imagine people disliked that. But which people disliked Roméo so much they bought him a ticket to Bordeaux? The rumor is it was Luc Naudé. Correct?"

She shrugged. "I have no information, monsieur."

"Have you asked Naudé how he felt about Roméo returning to the area?"

"Monsieur—"

Pascal held up a hand. "Of course. You did not conduct the investigation. But do you find it curious that Naudé was so concerned about the integrity of his town that he would buy bus tickets for people to leave? Banish people? Is that normal? Is that sort of ill will common in Sainte-Colette?"

She had the decency to look embarrassed. "This is a good village."

"I thought so. Such a lovely *place,* those flowers. And the priest seems kind. He wouldn't tell me who had been harassing poor Roméo though."

"He was being harassed?" More new information.

"So Père Thaddée said. Some kind of intimidation, bullying, maybe even beatings. He would have been an easy target, *non*? He was often seen walking alone on the farm roads."

"That is not an excuse for intimidation."

"*Absolument.* Are there some local youths you've had your eye on? Reports of vandalism perhaps?"

Her eyes dashed to the left and she shrugged.

"Ernest told you about multiple instances of vandalism at their vineyard and nothing was done."

"Without witnesses, monsieur, it is difficult. We have higher priorities."

"Like murder?" Pascal asked gently.

"That is *La Crim'*, not the *gendarmerie*."

"Roméo had recent bruises on his legs, hands, and feet. The priest said he began being harassed as soon as he returned to town. Isn't that something *La Crim'* should look into? Even if they already have fixated on another scenario?"

"I don't have any influence with the murder squad, monsieur."

"Madame Rouzet. Lieutenant. You sell yourself short. If you came up with new witnesses, new avenues of investigation, and it led to the real killer, wouldn't the *Police Nationale* look highly on that? I believe they would." Pascal held her gaze. "You know these youths, you know who they are. It wouldn't take a leap of faith to question them, or search their homes for evidence of vandalism and bullying. Paint cans, paint guns, billy clubs—whatever they use these days."

She bit her lip then straightened her shoulders. "Perhaps, monsieur." She stood. "Now, I have work to do. Please excuse me."

PASCAL SAT under the red awning at the café. The *place* was quiet, only the gurgle of the fountain. He sipped his espresso. He should go back to work. He would go back as soon as his coffee was done. He let out a frustrated breath. Would that young gendarme do anything with that information? He had no idea of her level of empathy for the dead, or the strength of her connection to the villagers. Maybe she knew the vandals, knew the priest, knew the local winemakers. Maybe she was too busy. Maybe she just didn't care.

Perhaps she didn't believe him.

She was clearly out of the loop on the investigation. Not unusual, of course, but it is rather unusual that the murder squad did such a sloppy job of investigating. Anyone could have stolen that pick axe from Ernest's yard, dipped it in Roméo's blood, and thrown it in the ditch. In fact, just the circumstances of finding it in that ditch make it suspect. It wasn't dropped by the body in horror. It was left purposefully for the detectives to find by the road, to lead them to the body.

Or so he thought. There were no detectives now. No one was investigating. As he'd been repeatedly told, the case was closed. The culprit expired. Two dead men and it was over. Why would anyone care about new evidence?

He had one final play, a bit of a hail mary, as the Americans would say. His obsession with Château des Corbeaux had run its course and it was time to come down to earth. To let things happen without his intervention, as much as it pained him. He knew this conclusion in his own work in fraud. Sometimes the evil is never revealed. Sometimes it sits, buried for years, never to be discovered. Like a cache of treasure in an ancient tomb.

He downed his espresso, threw down some change, and stalked through the town square to his car. The weakened remains of his anger clung to him, and he to them.

One last call. Then he would let it go.

"Barto? Is this a good time to talk?"

Forty-Seven

BORDEAUX

The offices at Cité du Vin was bustling, full of delayed meetings, private chats, personnel issues, and the general business of bureaucracy. Pascal set his mobile in his desk drawer and went to work, vaguely chagrined that he'd blown off almost an entire week of his job. The piles of paperwork on his desk were enormous. No one made any comments about his absence however as he largely supervised himself. Josef seemed relieved he had returned. Michel Évrard was friendly by the espresso machine. Other colleagues inquired about his health and invited him to lunch. It was not a bad day.

His conversation with Barto that morning had been cut short by a meeting the detective had to attend. He promised to pass on Pascal's information to the correct *Brigade* team but made no other guarantees. "It is closed, Pascal. It takes a minor earthquake to re-open a murder case."

But he had done what he could, Pascal thought. He was not on a murder squad. He was a bureaucrat in a regional office of the wine fraud division, nothing more. His lip curled at the thought. He wanted more than that. He might have to look for something else in the division if this malaise continued.

He unlocked the fifth floor apartment that evening with some trepidation. Once there had been an invasion of spiders after a long absence. What sort of vermin would it be this time? He'd been gone for a week. Anything could have happened.

But the apartment only smelled like mildew and onions. The sheets smelled of body odor except on Merle's pillow where the scent of lavender lingered. He showered in the tiny stall, ignoring the mold and water stains on the walls. He hadn't slept well all week, thinking of Roméo and Ernest and the tomb and Oscar and Harris and all of them at Sainte-Colette. Now he fell onto the bed, closed his eyes, and was asleep before nine p.m.

He couldn't find his mobile phone the next morning. He searched the BMW, trying to remember where he'd used it last. When he got to his office the sound of the ringing came from his desk drawer. He yanked it open.

"*Chérie*, good morning," he said, sitting behind his desk. The piles were only marginally smaller than yesterday.

"Where have you been? You didn't answer last night or this morning," Merle said angrily.

"I left my phone in my desk. I've never done that before." He began to tell her of his solid night's sleep and how perhaps he should lose his phone every so often for that purpose but she cut him off.

"Stop. It's okay." She took a breath. "Jane called last night. Some police officers came by the château to question Harris again. He told her it was nothing, just a formality, but she was confused and a little scared. She wanted to talk to you."

Pascal scrolled his phone log and saw six calls from Jane Austin and twelve from Merle, with a number of voicemails. "What did they ask Harris?"

"We don't know. He went with them, the officers, but he told Jane it was something routine. Not like the last time. Not about Ernest. Then this morning all hell broke loose."

Pascal walked to the coffee room for espresso. Then he realized he was fully awake already and turned back. "What is it? What's happened?"

"Harris came back after midnight. He told Jane the reason the police took him into the *gendarmerie* was about the vandalism on the property. But that's not recent, is it? Anyway, this morning the sirens were all over the valley. Apparently three homes were raided, looking for evidence of the vandalism. The homes of three local boys. Just like the priest said. Maybe he's the one who finally confessed to the cops."

He stopped in the doorway to his office and looked at the ceiling. The young *gendarme* had taken him seriously. She had found—or already knew— those boys' names and followed through with search warrants on their properties. He paused to send her a silent 'thanks.'

"Who were they, these boys?"

"High school students. One is the son of Luc Naudé, Pascal. The older boy, the big one."

"Yes. I see that. Jean-Luc, I think." He suppressed an urge to crow, to say 'I knew it' like he always seemed to do when he only had a hunch. "Who else?"

"Two of his friends. I don't know their names. Jane and Harris walked down the road to see what was happening at the Naudé house. Call Harris, will you? I want all the details. Are you coming home tonight? It's Friday again."

"Yes, but later. I have to get some work done or they will cashier me."

Merle took a breath. "Of course. I'm sorry, I was worried about you and for nothing. I get worked up sometimes. And Jane was absolutely frantic until Harris came back. They're supposed to leave for England soon."

"Harris is not in any trouble, is he?"

"It doesn't sound like it. But call him then call me back."

Pascal changed his mind on espresso. He waited for it to hiss and drip and took a moment to imagine the look on Jean-Luc's father's face when the house was raided and his son was charged with vandalism. But the emotion was as bitter as the coffee so he stopped. He wouldn't let Naudé make him into a version of himself.

Sitting at his desk again he tapped Harris's number. Jane answered right away. "There you are. Oh lord, Pascal, it was those boys across the vineyard, the Naudé boys."

"Both of them?"

"No, no, just the older one. And two other boys who had apparently been terrorizing people around here. Especially people of color and gays, the police just told us. Many instances. Can you believe it?" Pascal began to answer but she rushed on. "Do you think their parents knew? They came to Ernest's funeral, and the mother was here with them after."

"I met them. I doubt they knew. Or if they did they pretended not to know."

"Some parenting."

"So that's it? Three boys arrested for vandalism?"

Jane paused. "Isn't that enough? Those so-called boys are criminals."

"Yes, it is good news. Is Harris there? May I speak to him?"

After a long pause Harris came to the phone. "Pascal, did you hear? Arrests made in the vandalism here. It's about time."

"I just heard. That will give you some closure, I'm sure." Although the family would still live across the road and would now dial up the hatred.

"I am so relieved." Harris sighed. "Ernest helped those people at harvest. Can you believe it? He helped them on two different *vendanges*. And they never came to help us. I always wondered about that. Isn't it supposed to be reciprocal, if you volunteer to help your neighbors?"

"It is certainly courteous to do so, if you're able." Pascal hesitated. "Listen, Harris, I think the boys' identities were an open secret in the village. The priest knew, I think even the *gendarmes* knew. You told me that, correct?"

"An old guy at the constabulary in the village told me that. He was not very sympathetic. Maybe he didn't like Brits." The other prejudice went unsaid.

"There's a new lieutenant. Maybe it just took new eyes on the problem."

"I met her. Whatever it takes, I say. Bravo."

"So you're going to London, Jane says," Pascal said gently. He changed the subject. He didn't want to warn Harris of the fall-out of these arrests. No one knew the outcome but the boys were unlikely to get more than a slap on the wrist for vandalism, and then their bullying tendencies would simply blossom and grow. Soon they would be off to university to terrorize someone else. Pascal grimaced at the thought.

"She thinks it's for the best. A bit sad, to tell you the truth. Like the end of a sunny dream and you wake up and you're back in dreary old England again."

"But you'll be back, won't you?"

Harris sighed. "It'll never be the same here without Ernest." His voice broke and Pascal feared he was crying again.

"Shall we come by to see you off?"

"We're off to Paris in the morning, early. Jane needs a museum day, she says."

They said goodbye. The poor man sounded so sad. Pascal had grown fond of Harris and Jane. His wild adventure with Château des Corbeaux had come to its inevitable conclusion. He had known it, almost from the start. He would miss it, and the owners. But they would probably return to France and the château when the death of Ernest was no longer so raw.

Pascal took a moment to browse through dull email correspondence before calling Merle. When he did call, she was in a rush, walking to the bank. He promised to fill her in on the Austin travels and travails when he returned to Malcouziac.

"See you tonight, blackbird," he said, and pulled a giant pile of triplicate forms toward him. Perhaps mundane office work would take his mind off feeling like a crushing failure.

Forty-Eight

NEAR SAINTE-COLETTE

That night Rémy Naudé crept down the curving stairs of the manse at Domaine Champs-du-Puy. It was nearly midnight. Moonlight shone through the front windows, making squares of blue on the wood foyer and lighting the rows of grapevines beyond. He took no notice of the beauty. His eyes stung with tears. He grabbed the bannister as he tripped and almost fell near the bottom of the staircase.

He had seen his mother from his bedroom window. The smoke from her cigarette rose through the open casement. A smoke signal, he thought, and he climbed out of bed. Now, at the door facing the flag-stone patio off the parlor, his mother was in silhouette, a shadow immersed in the manicured grounds beyond, her lavender, her roses. He paused, watching her smoke. She ground out one cigarette under her shoe and lit another.

Backtracking through the parlor Rémy looked out the front. His father's Mercedes was still absent. That meant he and Jean-Luc were still at the *gendarmerie*, trying to explain the things the police had found hidden in the barn: dozens of empty spray paint canisters, at least ten paint guns and their colorful ammunition, stencils for graffiti, fascist magazines, pornography, cigarettes, marijuana, vodka bottles, plus gloves and clothes and boots, splattered with paint.

His brother had been defiant. It horrified Rémy. He would never have the nerve to stand up to *policiers* like that. But their father did the same, including dropping a few choice curses. They looked so similar, tall and proud, their lips curled in contempt. Rémy hardly recognized them.

Harmonie, his mother, hadn't watched the search. Did she know what they would find? She didn't seem surprised. Now Rémy returned to the glass doors leading to the patio. She still sat smoking. The thin trail rose into the night from the tip of her glowing cigarette. For a moment it mesmerized him, that twist of white smoke.

Then he opened the door, wincing as it creaked on its hinges. His mother turned her head at the sound. She relaxed when she saw it was him. 'Only Rémy,' as the family always said, as if he was an unimportant afterthought.

"Come," his mother said quietly, waving him outside. "Sit by me."

At twelve Rémy no longer sat in his mother's lap. He was far too big for that. But tonight the thought crossed his mind, that he could crawl into her arms and be comforted like a small child. He straightened, tears in his throat again. He must be brave like Jean-Luc.

She kicked out a metal chair and he settled on its cold seat. "Can't sleep?" she asked. He shook his head. "Same with me." She eyed his face. "Are you okay?"

He shrugged. Admitting he wasn't would do nothing.

"Want a cigarette? You're old enough now— a man, almost thirteen." She pulled one out of the pack. He cringed. "No? That's good. A filthy habit."

"What is going to happen, *maman*? To Jean-Luc?"

She took a long drag on her cigarette and blew smoke upwards. "Probably nothing, *mon petit*. Maybe your father pays a fine. Jean-Luc learns a lesson. Probably not. Life continues."

Rémy pondered this. Nothing would happen? No punishment? Even for marijuana and the vandalism? "And here at home as well? Nothing?"

"We'll see. Maybe he loses his car privileges for a time."

"His car?" Jean-Luc had received the vehicle for his seventeenth birthday, a few months before. He didn't have a license to drive yet but it didn't stop him from racing around every night with his friends. "Did the police take it?"

"I don't think so. Do you want to give it a spin?" She smiled at him.

He didn't smile back. He wanted nothing to do with that car, a very conspicuous American Ford Mustang. "Is it in the garage?"

Harmonie stubbed out her cigarette and squinted at him. "What about the car?" He clamped his lips tight. "Rémy, talk to me."

Rémy calculated his conscience. Why had he come down here? He should have stayed in bed. He adored his brother. Jean-Luc was strong and smart and tough. All the girls talked about how handsome he was. He was a star in rugby and football. He had amazing friends like Félix and Nathan, even though they too had been raided and taken in tonight, according to his mother. The three musketeers, they called themselves, rooting out evil. What they really did was of course much worse. But Rémy loved Jean-Luc.

He began to cry. Tears streamed down his cheeks and racked his chest. The decision was excruciating, tearing him apart. What would happen? But he couldn't keep this inside. He had tried.

His mother touched his hand. "What is it, *mon p'tit bout*? I am here. Nothing is so bad we cannot talk about it."

He gulped, choking down his tears. He wiped his nose. "*Maman*, if I tell you something, you must promise not to bury it. You must promise me—to do something about it, to tell someone. So it won't stay hidden. If you can't do that, if you can't promise, then I won't tell you. It will kill me instead, this secret. It *is* killing me."

She rose to her feet and pulled him up, into her arms. "I promise, my darling boy," she whispered. "Secrets are done. You have my word."

Forty-Nine

MALCOUZIAC

The phone rang early on Sunday morning. Pascal heard it downstairs from where he slept in the peach-colored bedroom in Merle's house— he would always think of it as hers although he'd lived here for years. The room was dark. Just a sliver of sunlight pierced the shutters.

They had been up late again last night, discussing the situation with Harris and Jane, and the vandalism charges against the Naudé boy and his friends. Merle was rightly incensed that they likely would likely get little punishment. She shouted a bit in the garden after drinking more wine than usual. She had a very rigid sense of justice. Pascal had one too but it had been battered enough by the system that he was no longer surprised by outcomes.

The phone— his mobile— stopped ringing. Probably just Harris and Jane saying goodbye as they drove away in his old mint green car. Merle had spoken to Jane. They planned to drive the car back to England on the ferry after their Paris weekend. Pascal rolled over and put the pillow over his head. He would try to sleep some more.

Ten minutes later he threw the pillow on the floor and got out of bed. Merle remained asleep, he was relieved to see. He would make some espresso and check his messages. He took his time in the kitchen, doing the coffee preparation carefully, measuring the Italian coffee into the pot. As he set it on the burner, his mobile rang again.

"Monsieur d'Onscon?" a female asked.

"*Oui.*"

"Hold for the Inspector."

Which inspector would that be, he wondered. He tried to clear his foggy mind. Instead he walked back to the kitchen and poured himself some coffee. He opened the door to the garden and was sitting down when the man came on the line.

"Monsieur d'Onscon? This is Inspector Ducré, *Police Nationale* Bergerac. I am the charge officer in the homicide of Roland-Auguste Sardou, known as Roméo Auguste. I am not sure of your status in this investigation but the *gendarmerie* in Sainte-Colette are telling me to fill you in on details."

"*Merci.*"

"Madame Naudé came into the *gendarmerie* yesterday morning with her younger son. They had released the older boy and the others. Vandalism is so common, as you know. We will take care of that, put the scare into them."

"Okay. Good." Pascal sipped his espresso, wondering how long this man would take to get to the point.

"The younger boy, name of Rémy, had a tale. He says he sees his brother and the two friends cleaning the trunk of a vehicle. Working hard on it, even though it is a fairly new car. Rémy, he is curious so the next day, he checks the trunk himself. He tells us he found a long pole hidden under the carpet, by the spare tire. It had what he thought were blood stains on it."

The Inspector sighed. "We were called in from Bergerac then by the lieutenant, about noon yesterday. We took the boy's full statement. The mother just sat there, mute, frozen. Very strange woman. I suppose the shock made her numb. At least she did the right thing by bringing the boy in.

"We took a team back to the Domaine and searched the car. It belongs to the older boy, Jean-Luc, although registered in the father's name. We find the evidence in question. It turns out to be a vineyard stake with barbed wire twisted around one end. Bits of blood and other matter were stuck to the barbs and a large brown stain on the wood itself."

He sighed again. "I will spare you all the details. We took the juvenile, the older one, back to the *gendarmerie* for more questioning. He quickly points the finger at his friends so they too are picked up again. The stake has gone to forensics for analysis."

"This blood— you think it is Roméo's?"

"Could be a dog at this point. But, yes, we are going on that assumption."

"Thank you, Inspector. I appreciate the call. It has been on my mind."

"We are also trying to reach Monsieur Harris Austin to fill him in. He reported the vandalism at his château. Also there is the matter of the death of Ernest Brooks."

While in your custody. "I will tell him to call this number."

Inspector Ducré rang off. Pascal set the phone on the green table and stared at the miniature pears on the espaliered tree against the house. He remembered seeing the younger boy with his father in Sainte-Colette that day, the first but not the last time Naudé became unglued in his presence. No, the first time was on the road by the abandoned vineyard. But that day in town Naudé had grabbed his arm and nearly swung at him. The boy was probably the reason he hadn't. How easily the man lost his temper.

Had some of the man's temper rubbed off on his older son? Or were they just reckless youths looking for excitement and someone weak to take out their aggression? What exactly had they done with that vineyard stake? Beaten Roméo with it? But he wasn't beaten, just bruised then bashed in the head. Would a wooden stake to the head kill you?

Merle appeared in the kitchen doorway, a demitasse cup in her hand. She wore a thin white nightgown and sandals. Her hair was wild, curling around her head. He smiled at her. She squinted into the morning sun and walked across to the green table, settling herself with hands around the cup.

Pascal waited until she had two sips. Then he smiled at her. "Ready?"

OVER THE NEXT week Pascal got more calls from Sainte-Colette. He made a few himself— to Harris, to Inspector Ducré, to Lieutenant Rouzet. He didn't want anyone to brush this under the carpet. Not again.

On Tuesday Luc Naudé engaged a high-priced lawyer from Paris for his son. The other boys also got representation, although not as fancy. On Wednesday the forensics came back, identifying the blood on the stake as Roméo's. The car was also impounded and blood matching Roméo's was found in the trunk. By Thursday Jean-Luc Naudé, still being held in Bergerac, made a full confession. By Friday, his friends followed.

According to Ducré, Jean-Luc admitted he was the driver of the car that night. It was two or three days after Roméo had returned to Sainte-Colette. His father had been talking about him at dinner the night before, how angry he was that the dirty tramp had returned. But what happened wasn't planned, the boy said. They had the vineyard stake in the back seat. They had used it before, he admitted, although again, he was only driving.

Félix sat in the back with the window rolled down. At nearly six-foot-five he could stretch his long arms out the window while wielding the stake. They would bash signs usually. Once they tossed a cat into the air. It was all just fun. Until they saw Roméo.

Jean-Luc said they had been drinking earlier in the evening and planned to meet up later when their parents were asleep. He climbed out the window of his house after one in the morning. He drove over to pick up Nathan, then Félix, and they finished a bottle of vodka. Jean-Luc admitted he loved to drive fast and crazy in the dark, when no one else was on the roads. But he never meant to hurt anyone.

When they spotted Roméo, Félix draped himself out the window, keeping the stake low. He intended to knock Roméo off his feet, and it worked perfectly. Jean-Luc swerved a little to get the car closer, turned off the headlights, and hit the gas. Roméo took a blow to the back of his knees, flipped into the air, and landed off the road. When Jean-Luc looked back, he saw no one.

Nathan panicked. He told Jean-Luc to turn around, that they needed to check on Roméo. They crawled slowly back along the road, driving on the wrong side. Félix spotted him, in the ditch.

Out of the car the three boys stared at the crumpled body of Roméo. Nathan was crying now, saying they had killed him, wailing how they had messed up. Félix slapped Nathan, told him to shut up. Jean-Luc tried to find a pulse on the man's neck. They rolled him over and saw the wound, a bloody gash on his head. He'd hit a large rock. Roméo was dead.

Nathan took off running in the direction of his house. Félix and Jean-Luc argued but couldn't agree on what to do so they both went home. When Jean-Luc arrived back at his house the sky was brightening in the east.

And his father was waiting.

He told his father the story, straightforward, without anger or tears. His father hated tears and had enough anger for both of them. Luc slapped him, called him a degenerate, a loser. Said he'd never amount to anything. Then they got back in the car and drove to the scene of the crime. They loaded Roméo in the trunk and drove to the abandoned side of the Château des Corbeaux vineyard. There his father searched a shed for a weapon, found the pick axe, wiped it in Roméo's blood, and threw the axe into the ditch. They carried the body into the vineyard and dropped him unceremoniously, face down in the dirt.

"Exactly what he deserves," Luc Naudé declared, according to his older son.

ON SATURDAY, Luc Naudé was charged with accessory to manslaughter, tampering with evidence, obstruction of justice, and many more crimes including lying to the police. Jean-Luc, a minor, was released into his mother's custody but would see his charges in court very soon. Félix Michaux, 18, had wielded the vineyard stake with reckless disregard for life so was charged with assault and battery, involuntary manslaughter, and intentional harm. Nathan Lucroy was told to go home and be better.

Pascal called Harris on Saturday afternoon, after he heard about the charges. He was staying with Jane, sleeping on her sofa. When he heard the news he cried again for Ernest.

***

"I WONDER what things are like at the Domaine Champs-du-Puy these days," Merle asked Pascal.

They were eating dinner in their favorite Malcouziac bistro, Les Saveurs, on Sunday afternoon. Merle had ordered the truffle omelet while Pascal more sensibly got the *moules frites*. He opened a shell and plucked out the meaty mussel.

"Not pretty, I imagine."

"My heart aches for the little boy. Imagine having to turn in your own brother." She shook her head. "I don't know if I could do that to my sisters. Well, I maybe if they were malicious types and I thought they killed someone."

"I think it will turn out well for Jean-Luc. The father? Perhaps not so much."

Merle smiled. "But he's not our favorite dad, is he?"

Pascal chuckled. "By a long shot. That is correct? Long shot?" He mimicked shooting a pistol with his finger.

"Correct. Not by a long shot." Merle chewed the earthy eggs and washed them down with rosé. "I also wonder about Harmonie. Will she divorce Luc, do you think?"

"He is a nasty piece of business. I am sure Jean-Luc is not the only one he has smacked. As you saw at the soirée he is always ready to swing at someone."

Merle shivered. "I hope she's okay." She wondered how she could find out. It didn't seem likely that they would go back to Sainte-Colette now. "And little Rémy. How could he live with Luc again? Wouldn't he take his revenge on the boy who blew this up? Although maybe Luc will go to prison. Do you think he will?"

Pascal wagged his head. "Maybe." He was taking a break from the bucket of mussels when his phone rang in his pocket. He looked at the screen. "I will take it outside, *chérie.*"

Merle waved him off. She put down her fork for a moment to determine if she could eat any more of the enormous six egg omelet. The waitress attempted to take away her plate. Merle shook her head and picked up her fork again.

Outside Pascal paced, his mobile glued to his ear. He glanced at Merle through the window then paced some more. He stopped. Merle held her breath. What had happened now? He looked at his phone again, tapped some buttons and began talking again. Pacing more, he nodded vigorously and hung up.

Back at the table, Merle waited for his explanation for five seconds. "Well?"

"Some news. Good stuff." He smiled broadly. "Harris is selling the vineyard. All of it."

"He is?"

"He has decided." Pascal's eyes sparkled. "I told him, do not sell all of it, you might want to come back. I will work it for you and you get your share."

"What did he say?"

"He will think about it. But he does not want to return to the vineyard. The memories are too strong."

"Wait, can you afford to buy all of it?" Merle asked.

"I will call Dylan. He is rich, yes? He called me to see if the deal was still on. I told him probably not. Will he have invested somewhere else already?"

"I doubt it. Francie says he's hot to be a French landowner." Merle straightened. "Hold on. Does this mean we can live in the château? All of us? Francie, Dylan, you, me— and baby?"

"And Tristan. Sisters too but only for visits." Pascal grinned at her. "It is big enough, yes?"

"It is." Merle rose then and came around the table. Pascal stood to meet her and they hugged tightly, right there in the middle of the bistro. Then they kissed and a smattering of applause rose from the diners. Merle laughed and looked at them, several of whom she recognized.

"We're buying a vineyard," she said, pumping a fist.

"*Nous achetons un vignoble,*" Pascal called to the French citizens. "*Champagne pour tous!*"

Fifty

FRANCE

The following week featured a daily whirl of excitement and judicial pronouncements. Dylan Hardy, as it happened, was waiting in the weeds. He suspected that Harris wouldn't want to stay on, that Ernest's death would put a pall over his enjoyment of the vineyard, the neighborhood, and France in general. Dylan rearranged his investments and cashed out some bonds. Between them, he and Pascal had just enough money to buy the vineyard. Improvements would have to wait but they both agreed to manage the business as fiscally responsibly as possible. Pascal began shopping for vines. They could definitely afford more vines. That sad abandoned half would live and make wine again.

The negotiations with Harris amounted to very little. Dylan handled the legal aspects for both sides. Harris had to wait for Ernest's will to go through the proper channels but Jane said it wouldn't be long. The price Harris wanted was met without protest from Pascal or Dylan. All agreed it was fair.

Fabrice was thrilled for Pascal and agreed to consult on the soils and vines as a favor. It was nice having friends in the right places.

Pascal stopped by the vineyard on his way back to Malcouziac on Friday again, to check on the team of Moroccan vineyard workers Jane had hired. On this second visit he was pleased to see they had taken his suggestions and tied and trimmed tendrils, snipped off some of the smaller clusters, and were keeping the rows clean. He walked a few rows on the manicured side of the property. Ernest's death still darkened the place, and his excitement. It would take some time before he could truly enjoy the vineyard. Pascal decided he would name a vintage after Ernest, with Harris's approval.

How long it would take before the sale finalized? Harris was eager, Dylan was eager, and he was more than eager. But the British inheritance laws and French notaire system said 'not so fast.' It would take at least a month, possibly more, to validate all the forms and registries. In the meantime it was agreed that Pascal would act as caretaker.

The three little terrorists became known as villains in the village, then slowly were transformed into heroes. Jean-Luc enjoyed the notoriety. He held his head high with no sign of shame. Nathan slumped around guiltily. Rémy Naudé was whispered about in school and passed notes by attractive girls. Félix remained in jail in Bergerac, his legend as a badass growing. It wouldn't help him in court but he heard about it from loyal friends.

Luc Naudé on the other hand was virtually shunned by the village. Even—especially— by Père Thaddée who refused to hear his confession on Sunday and turned his back on him in the middle of the *place*. Pascal stopped in to see the priest on his way to Bordeaux on Monday but he also was not welcome. He had brought shame to the village, Pascal supposed, shining light on the rot below the surface.

The rumors about the sale of Château des Corbeaux hadn't yet reached the priest's ears. But soon Pascal would be here every day, or nearly. He'd determined he could commute by train into Bordeaux. It was less than hour and he could work on the way.

Not a peep was heard from Monsieur Donnet at Galerie Colette. He didn't open his gallery for weeks. The police apparently talked to him about sending Roméo out to the vineyard on some errand but he refused to admit it. Had the art dealer wanted Roméo to steal the dodecahedron? It was rare and very collectible. But he wouldn't tell the police that.

Questioning of Luc Naudé contained his admission that he was responsible for buying the bus ticket for Roméo at Easter. He was not at all ashamed by it. He'd heard that his son and his tough guys had volunteered to rough up the vagrant on more than one occasion, calling him all sorts of terrible names that Rémy passed along to the *gendarmes*. That was why Luc wanted Roméo out of the way. To keep his son safe from his own impulses. It simply hadn't worked out.

At the château, Pascal lingered in the back, watching the sky streak with color. The patio, shaded by the old olive tree, was very pleasant. Harris had given his hens away to a neighbor before he left. The coop was quiet. Rising from the patio chair on a whim Pascal tried the kitchen door; it opened, surprisingly. He glanced at the vineyard crew in the distance and slipped inside. The kitchen was clean and bare. The parlor had been stripped of funeral flowers. He climbed the stairs. In the pink-flowered bedroom he stepped into the closet, now no longer filled with hanging clothes. He pried his fingernails into the crack and pulled open the small door.

The empty shelves seemed sadder, and dustier. Why was he drawn to this secret room? Its mysterious purpose intrigued him. What had been hidden here over the centuries? Had Oscar displayed his finds here? Had his parents or grandparents hidden their treasures, or themselves, from the Nazis? Or the revolutionaries? Or the royalists for that matter? Did they store wine in here once? Did they squirrel away food to prevent starvation? He could only guess.

Then he saw it: the small dodecahedron, smaller than a tennis ball, at eye level on the back wall. A sheet of yellow paper lay under the object, a precise black script on it.

> To whom it may concern: Do with this what you will. It doesn't belong to me or Ernest, just as it didn't belong to Oscar. Safe travels through time, dodec. See you in a museum someday. H.

As HE DROVE AWAY Pascal saw them— two black ravens perched on the archway of the gate, talking to each other. He squinted—were they real or a decorative touch? He stopped the car and looked up. One glossy bird cawed loudly and the other joined in. The first tipped his head to eye Pascal below and cawed again before they both flew off.

Raucous devils. He would make friends with them soon.

He parked in the city lot outside the old walls of Malcouziac and walked slowly through the cobblestone streets. The ancient village reveled in its June glory: roses blooming by downspouts, lavender tickling shins, geraniums bursting from window boxes. Two houses on Rue de Poitiers were getting their shutters repainted, one burgundy and one Provence blue. The painters called to each other, urging each other on so they could get home for wine and their wives.

Pascal had left the dodecahedron in the secret closet. When the château belonged to him and Dylan, they would decide what to do with it. A museum, as Harris suggested, seemed appropriate.

Merle had left the front door ajar. He stepped inside and locked it behind him with the protective emotion welling up, the one he always felt when rejoining Merle. *Saine et sauve*: safe and sound. He heard her voice in the garden and followed it outside where he found her pouring a golden Sancerre into two wineglasses.

"Perfect timing, *mon amour*."

He took a sip. The cool sunshine of the wine melted away the day. Wine was a cure, a salvation. He loved Sancerre. And this was quite a good one. He looked at the label.

"Nice choice, blackbird." He looked at her eager face. "Are we celebrating?"

She shrugged, a sly smile on her face. "A good news, bad news thing. First the bad news."

"That's usually best." He sipped more wine. This bottle had to be close to 50 Euros. She was definitely celebrating.

"The bad news is someone else bought the twin cottages in Pâquiers." She gave him a look. "For just twelve-thousand Euros."

"Ah, *tant pis*. You have to say though, someone is a savvy buyer. Two little houses for such a meager sum. Someone is a clever bargain hunter of the highest order," he said, smiling.

"*Someone* put my name on the deed," she added. "That's the good news." She reached her arms around his neck. He could feel the cold wine on the back of his head.

He pulled her close. "*Someone* wants their *someone* to be the happiest woman in France."

She laughed. "Someone is so very happy."

Bonus Epilogue
THE TOMB

Find out what happens when Pascal and Dylan finally open the tomb in the ruined abbey in the vineyard. Secrets revealed in the bonus epilogue of **Château des Corbeaux**.

To read the rest of the story, exclusively for newsletter subscribers, scan this QR code with your reader.

Or go to this link: https://storyoriginapp.com/giveaways/e33a44aa-47f9-11ec-832c-cb018e26072d

Get your own taste of France with this cookbook inspired by the Bennett Sisters Mystery series

Go to BookFunnel for your free download:
https://dl.bookfunnel.com/nwiv9wygjz

Or buy a print copy
on Amazon — they make a great gift!

What is a dodecahedron?

The dodecahedron looks like an alien dropped it to Earth but is a real object from Roman times. No one has figured out exactly what its use was. Only 116 have been found. Some speculate it was for making gloves for different sized fingers. Others think it was handling yarn for knitting. What do you think it was used for?

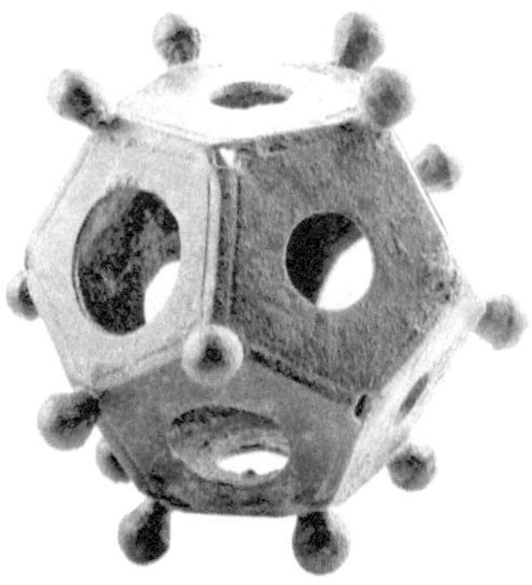

About the Author

LISE MCCLENDON is the author of numerous novels of crime and suspense. Her bestselling Bennett Sisters Mysteries continues to charm readers worldwide. When not writing about foreign lands and dastardly criminals, Lise lives in Montana with her husband and has recently become a fan of sunny winters in the desert. She enjoys fly fishing, hiking, picking raspberries in the summer, and cross-country skiing in the winter. She has served on the national boards of directors of Mystery Writers of America and the International Association of Crime Writers/North America, as well as the faculty of the Jackson Hole Writers Conference. She loves to hear from readers.

For more information visit
www.LiseMcClendon.com

Join the newsletter to keep up with new releases, giveaways, reading recommendations, and bonus material
See the link on her website

Also by Lise McClendon

The Bluejay Shaman

Painted Truth

Nordic Nights

Blue Wolf

One O'clock Jump

Sweet and Lowdown

All Your Pretty Dreams

Jump Cut

PLAN X

Beat Slay Love

Thanks for reading this installment of the Bennett Sisters Mysteries. Your loyalty has made this journey through seventeen books a special one for me. I look forward to hearing what you think. Write a review, drop me a line through my website, or whatever you feel comfortable doing! See you in France again soon.

Many thanks to Emma Cazabonne and Helen Mulroney for checking my French yet again! Merci.

9 781088 022221